# LO

*Timeless tales of t*
*from a bott*
*outsta*

### Gingham and Gold
by national bestselling author Rebecca Paisley

The folks in town said Eulalie Bailey would never find a man. But when it comes to protecting her Texas ranch from a mysterious land baron, she goes right for the heart to win him over . . .

### Heart's Desire
by Lydia Browne

A dashing sea captain would make a fine catch for any eligible lady. But to practical-minded Rebecca Clifton, he's merely a flirtatious heartbreaker—until she starts to see him in a different light . . .

### Music From the Gods
by Elaine Crawford

Was the beauty who emerged from the forest a fanciful wood nymph or a real-life lady? All young Jack Stuart knew was that music played every time he saw her—and he was falling under her spell . . .

### Just Friends, Of Course
by Aileen Humphrey

To win a wager, James Hastings would go to great lengths to meet the lovely Miss Gladwin—but would a love potion help? At least it seemed to soften the heart of her fractious little pug dog!

# Love Potion

Rebecca Paisley
Lydia Browne
Elaine Crawford
Aileen Humphrey

JOVE BOOKS, NEW YORK

LOVE POTION

A Jove Book / published by arrangement with the authors

PRINTING HISTORY
Jove edition / February 1995

ISBN: 0-515-11549-5

A JOVE BOOK®
Jove Books are published by The Berkley Publishing Group, 200 Madison Avenue, New York, New York 10016. JOVE and the "J" design are trademarks belonging to Jove Publications, Inc.

PRINTED IN THE UNITED STATES OF AMERICA

10  9  8  7  6  5  4  3  2  1

# GINGHAM
# AND GOLD

*Rebecca Paisley*

# One

Texas

Eulalie Bailey figured that if not for her, the folks in Flanders Mound would die of boredom. Known as "that wild Bailey girl," Eulalie's rare visits to the small town for provisions set the women to talking about her looks, character, unusual lifestyle, even her special way with animals. As for the men . . . Eulalie had never been quite sure what *they* thought of her. All they ever did was stare. Truth was, she wouldn't have gone into town at all if she didn't need supplies.

Today she cautiously peered out of the dim oak thicket and saw clusters of townspeople scattered all around the main street. Some stood in the road, others sat on the boardwalk steps, and others gathered in front of various establishments. Each group she watched appeared to be in the midst of avid conversation.

Glad that everyone appeared distracted, Eulalie hurried out of the woods and proceeded toward Dawson's Mercantile. Her quick, long-legged stride caused the fringe on her buckskin breeches to sway, and her bare feet stirred up dust that caused her pet raccoon to snort and sneeze.

Once at the general store, she looked down at the fat raccoon. "Set, Rooney." She pointed directly at the ground.

The raccoon sat and blinked up at her.

"You stay put, hear?"

Rooney sniffed audibly, then commenced to nose around

in the mass of bright yellow dandelions that surrounded the wooden hitching post.

Satisfied that her pet would remain where he was, Eulalie smoothed the front of her tattered gingham shirt, propped her rifle on her shoulder, and entered the mercantile. The scents of sour pickles, rose water, camphor, and tobacco drifted around her. As she inhaled the swirl of aromas, a calico kitten swiped at the fringe on her breeches. Bending, she scooped him into her arms and started to cuddle her face into his velvety warm belly.

But she stopped when she saw a bevy of young women rummaging through a stack of colorful fabrics piled upon a long wooden table across the room. Among them was Joyce Flanders.

*The High and Mighty.*

Joyce came from the most well-to-do family in Flanders Mound. Her grandfather had founded the town, and Joyce never let anyone forget her claim to fame.

The girl had such pretty hair, Eulalie mused, and such nice blue eyes. And her figure! Unlike her, Joyce was delicate and small, her breasts sitting high and compact on her chest. Eulalie's were so large she could barely keep them stuffed in her shirt.

Eulalie knew Joyce was a beautiful woman, and when forced to be around her she felt like a fat, ugly weed beside a fragile buttercup.

Quickly she set the kitten on the floor and approached the counter, determined to complete her business swiftly. "How do, Mr. Dawson?" she greeted the shopkeeper as she placed a burlap sack in front of him.

Bent over the newspaper he'd been reading, Mr. Dawson lifted his gaze level with Eulalie's chest. No other woman in Flanders Mound had breasts like hers, and there wasn't a man in town who didn't secretly wish to see them bare.

"I come fer bullets," Eulalie whispered.

He shook his head. "No more trading for supplies, Eulalie."

She laid her hand on the bag. Inside were ten miniature dolls she'd fashioned. Their soft bodies were filled with moss, grass, straw, or crushed leaves, and their long braids were of horse hair she'd collected in the stalls at the town livery. Some of the dolls had acorn heads, some of smooth pebbles, and others of carved wood. All were dressed in buckskin dresses, and all were beautifully crafted.

"But these dolls is even nicer'n the ones I brung last time, Mr. Dawson. I purtied 'em up some, y'see, by givin' 'em red lips. Used beet juice. Then I had to eat them beets so's they wouldn't go to waste, and Lord A'mighty, I hate beets jest about as much as I hate liver. 'Course, sometimes I can eat liver iffen it's got a slew o' onions on it. But there ain't nothin' on God's green earth that can make beets taste—"

"Eulalie, please," Mr. Dawson pleaded. One rarely saw Eulalie, and he figured that that was why she always had such long stories to tell during her few visits to town.

He looked up from his newspaper and stared at her. No matter how often he saw Eulalie Bailey, her hair never failed to shock him for a moment. Those flaming red locks resembled tight springs that bounced all over her head and shoulders whenever she moved. Yes, between her breasts and her hair, Eulalie was a sight to see.

When she noticed him gawking, Eulalie wished she'd worn a big coat and braided her hair. But the spring weather was too hot for a coat, and the trouble with braids was that her hair was so curly, the braids coiled up into two perfect U shapes by her ears. "The dolls, Mr. Dawson," she said, hoping to divert his attention.

He gestured toward the shelf behind him. "You can see for yourself that I haven't sold but one of the dolls you brought the last time you were in town."

Eulalie saw nine of her dolls lined up on the shelf. "Maybe iffen you was to put 'em down lower where they'd be easier to see, folks'd buy—"

He shook his head. "People were interested in the dolls when you first started bringing them in, but they already have as many as they want," he explained, folding and laying his newspaper aside. "If you'll remember, the same thing happened with your grapevine wreaths, the dried wildflower bouquets, the straw baskets, and those wooden knickknacks you whittled."

Eulalie realized she'd have to think of something new to trade for ammunition. The trouble, though, was that after over a year of making things to trade, she was running out of creative ideas.

If only her father had taught her the recipe for his "stagger juice." The liquor had always fetched enough money to buy supplies and a few extras every now and then. But when he'd died the secret died with him, and all he'd left her was his soul-stirring love of the land.

However, that love wouldn't get her any bullets. "I might could carve some jewrie boxes," she offered. "Womans need a place fer their jewries. I could make the boxes right fancy-like by stickin' shiny little crick pebbles on the tops of 'em."

"No."

"How 'bout iffen I make somethin' with bird feathers? I got rimptions o' bird feathers saved—"

"Listen, Eulalie," Mr. Dawson said, leaning over the counter and scowling into her huge green eyes. "My store is cluttered from top to bottom with all the trinkets you've brought in here. If you want bullets you pay for them in cash."

She closed her eyes for a second. Mr. Dawson might as well have told her to bring him a white blackbird. "Y'let other folks trade things," she murmured.

"Yes, but they bring goods I can use."

Eulalie opened her eyes. "I ain't got no cow, so I cain't bring you no milk, cream, or butter neither. I ain't got no—"

"You have all those wild animals running around everywhere," Mr. Dawson interrupted. "Why don't you butcher them for meat?"

She snatched the bag of dolls off the counter. "I'd as soon git a tin beak and peck with chickens than kill my pets!" With that, she whirled away from the counter and started for the door.

"Well, if it isn't Eulalie Bailey," Joyce Flanders called out. She left the fabric table to join Eulalie by the door. "Oh, what a lovely blouse. Faded red and white gingham becomes you. Tell me, was this blouse once a tablecloth?"

Eulalie decided that maybe it was a good thing that she hadn't gotten any bullets. At least now she couldn't shoot Joyce Flanders. "No, it weren't no tablecloth, Joyce. It was curtains."

"Oh, well, forgive me my mistake." Joyce fingered the sleeve of Eulalie's ragged shirt and glanced at the redheaded heathen's large, full breasts. Eulalie Bailey's lush figure caught the eye of every male in town, and had for the past four years. Why, last year Philip Bradshaw, the banker's son and Joyce's then-current beau, had actually fallen off his horse and broken his arm while trying to get a good look at the hoyden!

Joyce thought of all the stuffing *she* was forced to use in order to show some semblance of breasts. And what of Eulalie's eyes? Joyce knew in her jealous heart that nothing in the world was as green as the hellion's eyes. And how they shone! It seemed to Joyce that with each of Eulalie's thoughts, her eyes shimmered with something mesmerizing. Some sort of arresting light that was fairly impossible to look away from.

As for Eulalie's mouth . . . the girl possessed not a single cosmetic, and yet her full, pouting lips always looked as though they'd been painted with a deep pink hue that matched the rosy blush on her cheeks—a rosy tint that only nature could devise.

The whole matter was grossly unfair. Eulalie wasn't even interested in men; all the homespun girl cared for were her wild forest creatures and "her" land. So *why* had she been endowed with the kind of face and figure that turned men's heads?

Joyce shuddered with ire. "But as lovely as your curtain blouse is, Eulalie," she continued, "it is far too small for you. You should give a thought to binding your chest. For heaven's sake, you look like a milk cow."

Livid with humiliation, Eulalie snatched her sleeve away from Joyce's hand and folded her arms across her chest.

"Joyce, yore the onliest hell yore maw ever raised and the worst crop yore paw ever planted."

Having received the reaction she wanted, Joyce smiled. "I don't suppose you've heard the exciting news." She paused to fluff the delicate white lace at her wrists. "Squatting out there on the Del Castillo ranch as you do, you never hear about anything. You're going to have to pack up and move on, Eulalie."

"There ain't no Del Castillos on the ranch," Eulalie snapped. "Last I heared they was all across the ocean in some place called Spain. 'Sides that, the land I'm on—"

"Is not yours. The Del Castillos bought the land from that drunkard father of yours."

"They *stealed* the land, Joyce," Eulalie seethed quietly. "And Paw weren't no drunkard. Scandalize his name one more time, and yore face'll skeer a dog offen a gut wagon when I git through with you."

"Indeed." Joyce raised one finely shaped eyebrow. "And when the new Del Castillo arrives and tosses you off his land, will you ruin his face as well?"

Joyce's question took Eulalie off-guard. "What—*What* new Del Castillo?"

"A few weeks ago, the mayor received word that a member of the Del Castillo family is coming to claim the ranch. According to the packet of information Mayor Perch received from the Del Castillos' solicitors, the new Del Castillo will be arriving from Spain in about a month. The entire town is talking about him, and a great many men and women have already been hired to make ready his house, stables, and lands. They'll begin soon. Everything must be perfect for him, you see. His name is Fernando, and he's Ignacio Del Castillo's nephew. You do remember Ignacio, don't you, Eulalie?"

As if she could ever forget him, Eulalie mused miserably. In her opinion, Ignacio Del Castillo had been the devil's hired hand, and she knew in her heart that when he died a year ago he'd gone straight down to join his boss in hell.

And now another Del Castillo was coming to take Ignacio's place. Eulalie had no doubt that Fernando was every bit as cruel as his uncle. As soon as the man set foot on the ranch, he'd throw her off the land, just as Ignacio had done her and her father countless times.

"Fernando Del Castillo has socialized with real live European blue bloods," Joyce added. "Why, he has actually spent time at Queen Victoria's court. Imagine such a sophisticated man coming to live near Flanders Mound. Some say he's one of the wealthiest men in the entire world! And I'm sure he's quite handsome. Ignacio was certainly handsome, what with his blond hair, blue eyes, and golden skin. Even as he grew older he remained quite good-looking. It stands to reason that Fernando would favor him."

She took a moment to flaunt her well-manicured fingernails. "He's going to throw a huge party for all of Flanders Mound at his ranch house as soon as he arrives. He's not married and is most likely looking for a woman who is familiar with the area and the lifestyle of a rancher. So it makes perfect sense to presume that he's holding the party so he can get a good look at the town's available females. I am making plans to show him around when he arrives. The very least I can do is share with him what I know about a working ranch."

Eulalie frowned. "You don't know nothin' 'bout this land, Joyce. And what the hell do y'know 'bout workin'? Yore s'lazy that you won't never die. Drawin' yore last breath'll take too much energy."

"I will have you know that I have a garden!"

"Yeah? Well, I reckon the only thing y'grow in it is tired."

Joyce gritted her teeth so hard that her jaw ached. "Well, we shall see who Fernando Del Castillo sets his eyes on first, won't we? I've been shopping for fabric for a new gown. Mr. Dawson ordered a shipment of cloth from New York, and it arrived two days ago, just in time for the Del Castillo party. I've decided on a length of emerald green satin. I think emerald green suits a fair complexion and blond hair."

Her gaze traveled down Eulalie's form. "I suppose you'll be invited, too, Eulalie. Tell me, do you perhaps own a buckskin ball gown? Such a dress would be quite breath-taking with a rock necklace and acorn earrings."

"You got a big mouth, Joyce," Eulalie retorted, struggling to keep her anger concealed from the spiteful girl. "So big that I reckon you need nigh on a half a hour to put yore lip rouge on."

Her chin held high, Joyce retrieved the newspaper Mr. Dawson had been reading and handed it to Eulalie. "All the details about Fernando Del Castillo, his arrival, and his plans are in the paper. Oh, but you can't read, can you, Eulalie? How terribly silly of me to have forgotten. Well, suffice it to say that you are going to soon find yourself without a real home. You'll be forced to move from place to place again, just as you and your father did when Ignacio was alive. If I were you I'd go ahead and leave the area for good."

Eulalie stared at all the words on the front page of the newspaper. She couldn't understand any of them, but even if she did she wouldn't have been able to read them.

Too many tears blurred her vision.

Clutching the newspaper, her bag of dolls, and her rifle tightly to her breast, she fled from the store and called for her raccoon to follow.

Clusters of townspeople paused long enough to watch her disappear into the oak thicket before returning to their conversation about Fernando Del Castillo.

It was a good thing he was immortal, Cupid, the god of Love, thought, wincing as he pulled spines out of his tender skin. Jupiter's lightning bolt had struck the most undesirable destination in the area—a dense bed of prickly pear cactus.

Jupiter, Cupid mused. The king of the gods had no sense of humor whatsoever. Imagine the supreme ruler working himself into a fury over such an insignificant and harmless bit of roguery! All Cupid had done was shoot his love arrows at every goddess on Mount Olympus. The heavenly women had fallen desperately in love with him, including Juno, Jupiter's wife. But the love spell would have lasted a mere day, and Cupid had only indulged in the prank out of profound boredom. After all, there was naught to do on Mount Olympus but sit around feasting on nectar and ambrosia.

Jupiter, however, had not been understanding or the least bit amused.

"Cupid, I have had quite enough of the mischief you have caused with your infernal bow and arrows!" the king had bellowed from upon his bejeweled throne. "Did you not give thought to the fact that your antics would surely rouse my temper? Or could it be that you consider yourself mightier than I, and therefore possess no fear of me?"

Glancing down at his cactus spine-studded fingers, Cupid pondered the answer he'd given to his sovereign. Love, being the truest of all emotions, never lied, and so he'd replied honestly: "You are the Almighty Jupiter, Lord of the Sky, but you have no command over matters of the heart. No one, be he mortal or immortal, is immune to my power, for I am love, and love knows no master."

As punishment for what the king considered unforgiveable insolence, Jupiter had devised a task for Cupid. "I am sending you to earth to bring love and romance to four mortal couples," the celestial monarch had decreed. "The people, places, and time periods will be of my own choosing. And I assure you, Cupid, that my choices will provide you with fairly insurmountable obstacles."

Cupid had smiled then. If there was anything Love enjoyed, it was overcoming all obstacles.

"You will be stripped of your youth and heavenly handsomeness," Jupiter had continued gleefully. "Furthermore, you may not take your bow or your arrows, and so you must devise another instrument with which to inspire love. To prove my benevolence, however, I will bestow upon you two gifts. The first is a bag that contains every sort of article known to mankind. From the satchel's depth you may pull whatever you need, be it large or be it small. The second gift is a watch that will tell you the date and where you are. Should you accomplish the challenge I have set for you, you may return to Mount Olympus, whereupon I will concede that Love is, indeed, the mightiest of all powers."

Cupid had seen the assignment as the perfect remedy for boredom and had readily agreed. His only request was that he be granted permission to take along his pet turtledove, Pompeii.

Jupiter had nodded in consent, a sly gleam glowing in his eyes. "But you might find yourself wishing the bird had stayed on Olympus."

With that final warning, Jupiter had sent Cupid speeding toward earth on a jagged spear of lightning that had unceremoniously dumped him directly into a cactus patch.

Flicking the cactus needles out of his fingers, Cupid dismissed Jupiter from his thoughts, examined his surroundings, and wondered where in the world he was. A dark wall of oak trees grew to his right, their branches like long fingers scratching the cloudless midday sky. To his left, verdant grass, pink basket flowers, and purple phlox waved in a warm breeze that carried waltzing butterflies along on its sweetly scented breath. Songbirds chirped vigorously from all sides, and bright sunshine poured down on the land, coloring the very air with a soft lemon-yellow tint.

The area was certainly beautiful, but its loveliness failed to clear up Cupid's confusion. Bowing his head, he started to look for the watch that would tell him the date and his location.

He found the solid silver timepiece swinging from his trouser pocket. Trousers? Quickly, he looked at the rest of his apparel. Gone was the flowing white robe he wore on Mount Olympus.

A red kerchief encircled his neck, dusty leather boots encased his feet, and he wore a light blue cotton shirt. His large, graceful wings were tucked beneath the shirt, creating a rather large hump on his back, and his curly black hair now stuck out of his head in wiry, stark white tufts. A swift touch to his face revealed handsome features that were now marred with a multitude of deep wrinkles.

The loss of his beautiful youth disturbed him sorely.

Cupid sighed and finally looked at the watch. "Flanders Mound, Texas; May 1870," the timepiece said.

*Texas.* "Well, howdy pardner!" Cupid exclaimed, hooking his thumbs into the waistband of his pants. "Been throwed off any bucking broncos lately?"

Chuckling, he reached for the red leather bag that lay nearby and thought about how easy it would be to fulfill Jupiter's edicts. Why, in less time than it took a heart to beat, he'd be back on Mount Olympus!

He picked up the red, gold-trimmed bag. While hurling toward earth on Jupiter's thunderbolt, he'd decided what sort of love-inspiring instrument he would use in lieu of his bow and arrows.

After sticking his hand into the bag, he felt around with his fingers and soon pulled out a white flask. Pasted on the pale bottle was a vivid red label that said, "Cupid's Delight." Since he was not allowed to utilize his godly powers, the flask contained nothing but cinnamon-sugar-flavored water.

But he was sure he could persuade the people to whom he sold the concoction that the sweet water was a love potion. A magical elixir guaranteed to create true love.

Anxiously, Cupid stuck his hand into the leather bag once more. When his fingers touched hard wood, he pulled vigorously.

A large object burst from the bag, knocking him down as it righted itself on the ground. Blinking and smiling, Cupid looked at the sturdy wooden pushcart and all the bottles of love potion that hung suspended from the poles that crisscrossed the top of the wagon.

Painted on the side of the cart in big silvery letters was the name, Cherubim V. Harper. Knowing that he couldn't very well introduce himself as Cupid, the God of Love, he'd invented a new name for himself, one which he thought sounded very much like that of a traveling salesman.

Yes, he mused, his idea would work splendidly. Before much longer, he'd be reveling in Jupiter's admission that love was, indeed, the mightiest of all powers.

First, of course, he had to find some sad and lonely mortal whose problems could only be solved by love and romance. With those ends in mind, Cupid struggled to his feet, brushed off his pants, and called for Pompeii.

But instead of his pet turtledove, a girl sped out of the dim oak thicket. A tall, graceful young woman whose curly hair looked like flames of fire licking at her freckled face and slight shoulders . . . whose exquisite buckskin-clad legs were well-defined with long, lean stretches of muscle . . . whose breasts were quite the most perfect he'd ever seen . . .

Whose large emerald eyes shone with tears.

"Halt, fair maiden!" he shouted, then paused. *Halt, fair maiden?* That sounded too medieval. "Hold on now, little gal! You're running like a bullet with feet! What's got you in such a frenzy?"

Panting with exhaustion and deep despair, Eulalie stopped and stared at the stranger. His stiff white hair didn't look like it would lay down even if he glued it to his scalp. And he was a humpback! She was sure she'd never seen his likes around here, and for a moment she felt frightened.

But his eyes . . . They looked like twinkling blue stars and drew her toward him in a way she found impossible to resist. "Who are you? Y'ain't hurt or in trouble or nothin' like that, are you?"

Her concern warmed Cupid's heart, especially since she obviously had problems of her own.

"Need me to do anything for you, mister?" Eulalie pressed.

Cupid smiled at both her kindness and the sudden realization that she was the first of the unloved mortals Jupiter had sworn to choose for him.

"There's nothing you can do for me, my dear," he answered softly, "but I suspect there is a great deal I can do for *you*. Tell me, have you ever heard of a love potion?"

# TWO

"Love potion?" Eulalie repeated, frowning.

"Cherubim V. Harper's the name; love potion's my game!"

Eulalie noticed the white bottles hanging on his pushcart, and understood the man was a peddler. "What's a love potion?"

Cupid took her hand. Maybe he needed to know her problems before he could assist her in solving them. "It's called Cupid's Delight, and I'll tell you all about the potion in just a minute. For now, though, suppose you tell me why you were crying? It breaks my heart to see such a young and pretty girl so sad and—"

He broke off when a large, cumbersome animal jumped out of the forest. On its long and powerful hind legs, the creature stood six feet tall, and its long ears rose straight up off its head. The animal held short front legs in front of its chest, beneath which was a furry pouch.

"Lord A'mighty, what the hell *is* that thing?" Eulalie cried, tightning her hold on her rifle.

Before Cupid could answer, the animal hopped toward him. Then, much to his wonderment, the ungainly beast attempted to leap onto his shoulder.

While Cupid fended the insistent creature off, an astonishing and totally absurd realization came to him. Only one animal he could think of would try to perch on his shoulder.

Pompeii.

Sweet ambrosia, Jupiter had turned the gentle turtledove

into a kangaroo! Well, Cupid mused miserably, the king of
the gods had warned him that he would wish Pompeii had
stayed on Olympus.

Cupid cast an angry glare at the heavens, then gave a
weak smile to the girl who stood staring at his pet.
"Uh . . . . This is Pompeii."

"I been livin' 'round ever here since I was small enough
to take a set-down bath in a half-full dipper o' water,"
Eulalie whispered, "but I ain't *never* seed a critter like that."

"Yes, well . . . he's my pet kangaroo," Cupid stammered. "I . . . I brought him over from Australia when I
was there a few months ago." Shaking his head, he rubbed
Pompeii's furry snout. "I don't suppose you have any
chocolate-covered worms, do you, Miss—Oh, I'm terribly
sorry, but I don't know your name."

"Eulalie," she answered. "Eulalie Bailey, but call me
Eulalie. I ain't never heared o' no worms covered with
chocolate. There's reg'lar worms all over. Watcha want
chocolate ones fer?"

"They're Pompeii's favorite food." Cupid looked at his
transformed pet a moment longer, then turned back to
Eulalie and clasped her hand once more. "Will you tell me
why you were crying?"

His question diverted her attention from the kangaroo and
reminded her of her dismal situation. Feeling about as bereft
as she ever had before, Eulalie spilled her entire story to the
only human she'd ever met who looked as out-of-place as
she did.

Cupid listened with growing compassion and concern. If
only he had his bow and arrows! He'd like nothing better
than to make Joyce Flanders fall in love with some
bed-wetting old man with warts on his nose and not a cent
to his name! "A pox be on the High and Mighty!"

Eulalie waded through a knee-high patch of grass and
orange lantana. "I ain't never figgered out what I done to
make her so mean-minded towards me. She was biggedy
even when we was young'uns, but now that we're all
growed she's dang right fractious."

Without ever having seen Joyce Flanders, Cupid suspected her cruelty stemmed from jealousy. Eulalie Bailey was one of the most beautiful mortals he'd ever met, and he'd been looking at women from the dawn of time.

He knew he couldn't convince Eulalie of her worth, however. Only a man in love with her could succeed in making her realize her enviable assets. And those assets not only included her beauty, but her sweet nature as well.

She needed a man to fall in love with her.

"Will you go to the Del Castillo fiesta, Eulalie?"

She kicked a stick into a small pile of rocks. "What fer? I've got about as much use fer them Del Castillos as I do fer a blowed-over outhouse." Her weariness and melancholy increasing, she sat down next to a large oak trunk. Rooney waddled toward her, and she stroked the raccoon's soft, warm back. "'Sides that, iffen I go to the git-together, the womanfolk'll jest fling sass at me all night long. And the menfolk'll jest fix their eyeballs on me. Don't none o' them men hardly never talk to me."

Sweet ambrosia, Cupid thought, he had to help this sweet girl. Smiling a mischievous grin, he reached for a bottle of Cupid's Delight and pressed the flask into Eulalie's hand. "This love potion is more powerful than anything beyond your wildest imagination. Use it wisely, for once its magic is released there is no way to stop the resulting love spell."

Eulalie looked at the red label on the bottle. "Y'mean iffen some man swallers this here tonic he'll fall in love with me?"

"Precisely."

Eulalie peered up into his blue-star eyes. "Mr. Harper, I 'preciate yore tryin' to hep me, but I cain't see how some love potion's gonna rid me o' my miseries. And I don't want no man no-how. I done tole you that all's I want is to stay on my little jag o' land withouten nobody pesterin' me."

"And who owns the bit of land you love so much, my dear?" Cupid asked slyly, softly.

"I do!"

"Very well, who *thinks* he owns the land? *Who* is going to come and try to throw you off of it? *Whose* uncle was responsible for your troubles in the first place?"

"Fernando Del . . ." Eulalie looked up from the white bottle and peered into the blue-star eyes that twinkled above her. "Y'mean—Are y'sayin' I orter git Fernando Del Castillo to swaller this here tonic so's he'll fall in love with me?"

Cupid feigned a look of confusion. "What? Why, whatever do you mean?"

"You said—" Eulalie gasped. Clutching the flask tightly in her hands, she bolted to her feet. "Oh, Mr. Harper, I jest got the mostest bestest idea in the whole world!"

"That good, huh?" he asked, laughing inwardly.

"Iffen I go to the Del Castillo party and git Fernando to drink this magic love potion, he'll take one look at me and fall plumb to pieces! Cain'tcha see, Mr. Harper? When Fernando's heart sets to pangin' fer me, he'll make me his bride. And once I'm his woman, the whole God-burned Del Castillo ranch'll be mine. Won't nobody never toss me offen again!"

Cupid clasped his hands together behind his back and fixed a serious look on his creased face. "But what about you, Eulalie? Could you marry and live with a man you don't love? You said yourself that you hated the Del Castillos. Think about that, my dear. Would you really be able to sacrifice your own personal happiness just to stay on this land?"

Her bright, excited smile faded into an expression of intense thought. Slowly, she surveyed her surroundings, her gaze missing no part of the landscape. "Wouldn't be no sacrifice a'tall, Mr. Harper," she whispered. "The only happiness worth havin' is the happiness I'll feel by bein' able to stay on this land. Y'jest cain't know how much this place means to me. There ain't a inch o' ground here that ain't feeled my feet on it. Ain't a tree that I ain't climbed, and ever' puff o' wind that blows here's got my breath clingin' right to it. No kind o' love fer any man could be deeper'n the love I got fer this land."

She pulled the small sack of dolls off her rope belt. "Iffen money was leather, I couldn't half shoe a gnat, Mr. Harper, so iffen it's all right with you, I'd like to pay fer this here romance tonic o' yores with the ten little dolls that's in this bag. Maked 'em myself."

Cupid accepted the sack. "Thank you." He slipped the bag into Pompeii's kangaroo pouch, then took gentle hold of Eulalie's chin. "Remember this, Eulalie: Love works his magic—I mean, Love works *its* magic in ways that are often impossible for people to understand. One might expect for Love to be born and live in a certain fashion, but when Love does come, he—I mean, *it* sometimes roots, grows, and flourishes in the most surprising ways. I realize that what I say makes little sense to you now, but I promise that one day soon you will see the truth of my words."

Her bright smile returned. "'Bye, Mr. Harper." On impulse, she kissed his cheek, then turned and ran back into the oak thicket.

Cupid smiled after her, dwelling on what she'd said to him.

*No kind o' love fer any man could be deeper'n the love I got fer this land.*

"We shall see, Eulalie Bailey," he murmured. "We shall see."


Astride his huge bay stallion, Fernando Del Castillo looked out over forty-thousand acres of grassland. No cattle grazed in the open fields. The animals had been sold after his Uncle Ignacio's death, and the family now expected *him* to replace the livestock. What did he know about cattle? He preferred fine, English thoroughbreds.

Frustration gripped him like a cramp he couldn't rub away.

"*No te preocupas, hijo,*" his father had told him. "Do not worry, son. You will feel deep affection for the land Ignacio left to you and will be proud that your uncle chose you to be the next *patron* of the hacienda that has been in our family for so many generations. Every Del Castillo is born with love of the land, and when you see the ranch in Texas, you will not remember your reasons for wanting to stay in Spain."

Ha! Fernando mused bitterly. He was looking at the ranch

now, and his desire to return to his life in Europe was growing stronger by the second.

*Dios mio*, how he missed London. Paris, Vienna, Florence, and, most of all, Madrid. How he longed for the cities' crowds of people, restaurants, buildings, art, symphonies, and social swirls.

Here, on this godforsaken Texas ranch, there existed nothing but scraggly trees, monotonous fields of grass, endless stretches of wooden fences, screeching birds, and an unbearably hot sun.

And he hadn't seen another living soul since his arrival a few hours ago. Of course, due to a sudden change in traveling plans he'd arrived a month early, and considering the vast size of the ranch, it was no wonder he hadn't seen anyone.

"And all forty thousand tiresome acres of it are mine," he muttered, his mood darkening at the thought of being forced to spend the rest of his life wandering through repetitious pastures.

Surely the life of a rancher was the most tedious on earth.

Tired, bored, hot, and thirsty, he toyed with the idea of riding into Flanders Mound, a nearby town about which his uncle had written frequently. Indeed, he was to hold a grand party for the township. His mother and father had both insisted, claiming the fiesta would provide him with the chance to become acquainted with his neighbors.

Fernando shrugged. What his parents really hoped the festivity would provide was a woman with whom he would fall in love, marry, and produce the heir to the Del Castillo estates here and in Spain. His mother had even gone so far as to give him the Del Castillo collection of gold jewelry. "Just in case you meet someone worthy of wearing it," she'd hinted.

As the last male of the Del Castillos, Fernando knew his responsibility was to ensure the continuation of the family name. But he'd never met a woman with whom he wished to spend the rest of his life. The truth was that he wasn't certain *who* he was looking for. And for that reason, he knew he had yet to meet her.

Dismissing his bedeviling thoughts, he concentrated on Flanders Mound again, wondering if there was a hotel there. He needed a place to stay until his ranch house had been prepared for occupancy. After having been closed for over a year, the place was in dire need of a thorough cleaning—a fact he realized during the quick walk he'd taken through the house a short while ago.

He stopped his horse over a mound of small pink flowers and deliberated. If he went into Flanders Mound, he would immediately be forced to play the part of rancher, a character he did not want to portray until he absolutely had to. But if he didn't go to town, he'd have no place to stay.

Damn.

With a light touch to his stallion's flank, he sent his stallion sailing over the fence that enclosed the pasture and began to follow the dirt road he thought would lead to town. But after only a short while the curving path came to an end, and he faced yet another dim grove of oak trees. *Santa Maria*, was his ranch so enormous that there was no way to pass over the boundaries?

Truly angry now, he urged his mount directly into the thicket. Surely the maze of tall trees would take him *somewhere*, and even if that somewhere was nowhere he wouldn't be any worse off than he was now.

Soon the dense trees began to thin, and Fernando spotted a small cabin in the clearing ahead. Strange. He was sure this was still his land.

As he rode closer, he decided the word *shack* more aptly described the dilapidated home. And the place was, indeed, someone's home.

Gray ribbons of wood smoke curled from the cabin's chimney, and the three small windows he could see sparkled in the sunshine that filtered through the treetops. The flower gardens of scarlet zinnias and yellow marigolds that colored two sides of the cabin were well-tended, a basket of plump, freshly picked blackberries sat on the porch step, and roasting meat filled the air with a mouth-watering aroma that made Fernando realize he was hungry as well as thirsty.

He stopped his stallion in the yard, dismounted, and

waited for someone to spot him. When no one did, he tied his horse to one of the porch railings and walked around to the back of the cabin.

What he saw there caught his full attention.

A young, shirtless woman knelt on the sandy bank of a rushing stream, washing the shirt she'd apparently just taken off. Her back was to him, and Fernando watched sunshine dapple her smooth, slight shoulders and flit through her soft and curly russet hair. A raccoon sat beside her, tugging at the fringe on her tight, buckskin breeches.

Fernando had never seen an unclothed woman outdoors before.

Without realizing his actions, he began to advance toward her, his boots crunching into fallen leaves and brittle twigs.

Instantly alerted, Eulalie grabbed her rifle off the ground, stood, and pointed the gun at whatever thing or person approached from behind.

Her narrowed, determined gaze met eyes so blue they defied description, and the dark-skinned man who owned them stood over six-feet tall. His black hair poured over his broad shoulders and down his chest like liquid midnight, and even the slightest of his movements produced a play of muscle in his chest, arms, and thighs.

An odd desire swept through her, making her light-headed with the feeling that she was floating.

"Hello, miss."

Eulalie thought his voice sounded like a mellow fire, husky, warm, inviting. The unfamiliar feeling inside her heightened, pleasant and puzzling at once. *Who are you?* she tried to ask, but could not find her voice. She could only watch him.

Fernando returned her unblinking stare, quite unable to look away. Accustomed as he was to silk-swathed, jewel-laden women, he could not comprehend his instant enchantment with this barefoot country girl.

But he was enchanted, and knew in his heart that he'd never encountered such beauty, not in all the glittering ballrooms in Europe.

Maybe living here wouldn't be as boring as he'd presumed.

He sent her a lazy smile. "You seem to have lost something, miss."

Her mind, that's what she'd lost, Eulalie thought. What was the matter with her, feeling this deliciously warm way over a man who quite possibly intended to rob her, violate her, or kill her?

"Your shirt," Fernando added, noticing the rag she'd been wearing drift down the stream. He waited for comprehension to come to her, realizing she'd forgotten the fact that she was naked from the waist up. After a moment, when she still didn't seem to understand, he decided to take full advantage of her absent-mindedness.

Slowly, he drew his gaze down to her chest. Golden rather than creamy, her full, heavy breasts appeared surprisingly firm. He'd shared intimate nights with large-bosomed women before, and it was his experience that such weighty breasts had a tendency to sag, if not a lot, some. And big chested woman normally had thick waistlines and plump thighs as well.

Not this woman. This woman's body was satin and sinew, a combination that Fernando found strangely and incredibly arousing. He took another step forward.

Eulalie stepped backward, into the stream. Lord A'mighty, she thought. Today was sure her day for meeting up with strangers. First Cherubim V. Harper and his love potion and kangaroo, and now this man and his vivid blue eyes, long black hair, and easy smile.

Fernando stopped when she backed away. "Miss, your shirt is floating down the stream."

"Floatin'," Eulalie repeated on a breath. "Yeah, floatin' . . ." Her voice faded as his words registered in her mind. Quickly she looked down at herself, saw her bare breasts, and then watched her shirt flow in the water.

She spun on her heels and, with a snap of her arm, she pointed to the clothing. "Rooney, fetch!"

The raccoon looked where she pointed, ambled into the stream, and brought his mistress a saturated stick.

Muttering a few choice profanities, Eulalie waded into the water, retrieved the shirt herself, and practically ripped the sleeves off in her haste to put the blouse on. Her rifle under her arm, she buttoned the shirt and turned back to the man. "Make one joke, and I'll grab yore tongue and turn you inside outen. I'm sick plumb near to death o' folks carrin' on 'bout my tits, hear? And don't y'dare make fun o' my hair, neither. I cain't hep that I got milk cow tits and this wild curly hair any more'n you can hep havin' them pieces-o'-sky eyes o' yours."

Fernando felt amusement slide through him. Joking about her breasts had never entered his mind. And as for her hair . . . True, her bright copper locks were quite unruly, but gloriously so. And the more she talked, the more convinced he became that her wild red mane suited her.

"What the hell do y'want, mister?"

She was the only woman he'd ever heard curse, but he did not feel offended in the least. Cursing seemed to suit her.

He looked at her breasts once more, which were clearly visible beneath her wet and clinging gingham shirt. "I stopped for water."

Eulalie saw him looking at her chest again. "Git yore dang water then and git goin', you God-burn tit-gawker."

Tit-gawker? Fernando repeated silently, more laughter bubbling inside him.

"Yore trespassin'," Eulalie warned.

When she cocked her rifle, Fernando sobered instantly. "Miss, this land belongs to—"

"Me," Eulalie finished for him. She sloshed out of the stream. "'Course, there's some who say it don't, but it does. Ignacio Del Castillo cheated my paw outen this here speck o' land, and cheatin's the same as stealin' iffen y'ask me. 'Course, not that y'asked me, but jest thought I'd tell you. Oh, and when y'leave my land? Well, be powerful careful 'bout where y'decide to wander. There's another God-burn Del Castillo on his way to take up where the last'un leaved offen, and I'm shore and sartin' he's as mean and selfish as his uncle. Iffen he finds you, he'll pro'bly commence to shootin' jest like his uncle was prone to doin'. Paw always used to say that ole Ignacio Del Castillo was mean enough to dip a ole maid in honey and stake her to a ant hill, so you'd best be long gone afore the new Del Castillo gits here. Even iffen you *are* a God-burn tit-gawker, I don't reckon y'deserve to die. Who are you, anyway?"

His mind spinning with her story, Fernando was hard pressed to answer. "Who? I'm— I . . ."

"Lord A'mighty, y'mean y'don't know?" Eulalie asked, seeing his confusion and listening to him stammer. "I heared that it's possible to lose yore mem'ry, but I ain't never meeted up with a person who really did."

Instant compassion filled her heart. How could she allow this sick man to leave in his condition? "Look," she said, then chewed her bottom lip for a moment, "y'can stay with me fer a while. God only knows what might could happen to you iffen y'don't got somebody to look after you till y'git yore recollections back."

She hurried to his side and took his arm. Solid muscle filled her palms. "Lord A'mighty, mister, I reckon yore strong enough to knock the white outen the moon, huh? Well, that's one thing we know about you. Whoever you are, you've muscled up some heavy loads doin' whatever it is you do." She gave the bulges in his arms a few squeezes and felt another wave of dizzying pleasure waft through her.

"Since yore name's a mystery," she said, her voice a bit shaky, "that's what I'll call you: Mystery. My name's Eulalie Bailey. My maw passed on when I was only three, but afore she passed on she had her a mind to be a poem writer. She couldn't write fer real, so she writ her poems in her mind. Paw said she loved makin' things rhyme. When I come along, she maked me rhyme, too. That's why I'm Eulalie Bailey. Some folks laugh at my name, but I try not to pay 'em no never mind. My name's special to me, y'see, on account o' my maw maked it up. Jest call me Eulalie."

Bewilderment still clouding his thoughts, Fernando could only gaze down at her.

Eulalie led him into her cabin, holding his arm as if he were a cripple. "Y'can wet yore whistler with that there bottle o' cider on the table," she said, shutting the door and

propping her rifle against the wall. "And whilst yore stayin'
here? Well, don't y'be gittin' no ideas, hear? I know yore a
tit-gawker and all, but iffen you even *think* about touchin'
me, that'll be the day when there'll be a new face in hell for
breakfast.

"I won't tell no lie, Mystery," she continued, her hands on
her hips. "Yore looks mess with my heartbeat. When I first
seed you outen there by the crick, I got a feelin' like I was
floatin'. Like there weren't no ground unner my feet. That
ain't never happened with no man I've ever seed afore.
Handsome s'what you are, but I'm fixin' to become Fernando
Del Castillo's mostest dearly beloved, so you'll have better
luck findin' a horse thief in heaven than you will gittin' any
sorter sexified jollies with me."

Fernando frowned. *Santa Maria*, what was she talking
about? "Did you say Fernando Del Castillo?"

Eulalie nodded and crossed the room. In the corner, she
turned her back and began to change into a dry shirt. "Seein'
as how Fernando's a Del Castillo, it jest ain't in me to ever
love him back. But it goes agin' my raisin' to go to my
weddin' bed with my virgin flower done plucked. I still got
it, y'know. Ain't never wanted to give it to no man I've ever
knowed, and I ain't real thrilled 'bout havin' to give it
to Fernando, neither. But I'll do it on account o' bein'
Fernando's wife'll mean the whole Del Castillo ranch'll be
mine ferever, and there ain't nothin' closer to my heart'n this
land. Hell, sometimes I think this ground runs through my
veins instead o' blood."

Slowly, Fernando sat in one of the two rickety chairs at
the scarred table in the middle of the one-room cabin. His
gaze riveted to Eulalie's back, he pondered her and all the
things she'd told him.

She hated the Del Castillos because she believed his
family had stolen her land. And yet, she fully planned on
marrying him, had even resigned herself to sharing his bed.
How she thought she would succeed with her outrageous
plans was beyond his imagination.

She was quite the most unusual woman he'd ever met.

And heaven knew she was the *only* interesting thing he'd found on his ranch since his arrival.

He decided not to divulge his real name to her. Not yet, anyway. Telling her he was the very man she professed to hate would undoubtedly end their relationship before it even began, the relationship *he* wanted to experience anyway. Not to mention that he was inordinately curious as to how she planned to get him to the altar.

And playing the role of Mystery with the beautiful— albeit outlandish—Eulalie Bailey seemed far more divert- ing than informing the township of Flanders Mound that he'd arrived early.

Smiling to himself, he reached for one of the two bottles on the table, slid the cork from the neck, and lifted the flask to his lips.

Eulalie turned back around just in time to see him pour the liquid into his mouth.

Horror nearly sent her to her knees.

Mystery was drinking the love potion.

# Three

"Mystery, stop!" she hollered.

Startled by her shouting, Fernando quickly swallowed the cinnamon-flavored water. "Stop what?"

Eulalie raced to the table and began beating him on the back. "Spit it out, dang it! Please spit it out!"

"But—I—al—read—y—swal—lowed—it!" Fernando yelled, each of his words jolted from his mouth by her pounds to his back. "*Dios mio*, what—"

"The love potion! Y'drinked the love potion I was gonna give to Fernando Del Castillo!" She ceased pounding his back, and jabbed a finger toward the other bottle that sat on the table. "*That's* the cider!"

Fernando looked at the white bottle in his hand and read the words Cupid's Delight on the red label. Surely Eulalie didn't believe in magic potions, he tried to convince himself. Such things were the stuff of fairy tales!

But when he peered up at her, he realized she did believe. Her gorgeous green eyes brimmed with despair so deep that he knew it stemmed straight from her heart. "Eulalie—"

"What am I gonna do?" She cupped her cheeks and shook her head. "Fernando Del Castillo was s'posed to drink the potion at the party he's gonna give when he gits here. He was s'posed to fall in love with me. Now I got only two chances o' weddin' up with Fernando—slim and fat!"

For the third time since meeting her, Fernando struggled with laughter. He'd known a great many women in Europe, but not a one of them had engaged him like Eulalie did. Just about everything that came out of her beautiful mouth struck his sense of humor. "I'm really very sorry for my error."

"Yeah? Well, *sorry* ain't gonna git Fernando Del Castillo's dang ring on my finger!" She grabbed the bottle from his hand, held the opening in front of her right eye, and squinted into the flask. "There's still some left! Not more'n a spoonful, but Mr. Harper didn't never say that Fernando had to drink ever' bit of it!"

"Mr. Harper?"

"The man who selled it me." She recorked the flask and dropped it into the front of her blouse. As she adjusted its weight against her belly, a sudden thought came to her. Her eyes opened so wide that her eyelids stung. "Near 'bout the whole dang bottle," she whispered. "Y'drinked near 'bout the whole dang bottle. No. This jest cain't happen."

Fernando watched hysteria take the place of her despair. "I said I was sorry."

Eulalie backed away. "Stay away from me, hear? I know yore itchin' somethin' fierce to throw yoresef to yore knees and kiss my feet. Yore set to give me yore heart, yore soul . . . yore very life! But I'll belong to another soon. You'll jest have to worship me from afar!"

"Worship you from afar?" What—"

"Better yet, fergit me!" In a dramatic gesture, Eulalie placed the back of her left hand over her forehead and held her right hand out as if to stop his potential advances. "You wouldn't want me, Mystery. Faults. I got more faults'n hell's got sinners and heaven's got angels. I . . . I cuss. Lord A'mighty, I cuss enough to singe all the grass within fifty feet o' where I'm standin'. And I ain't never been to school. Cain't read a lick, and I ain't much better with numbers. Y'deserve better."

Fernando rose from his chair and went to stand before her. "Do you think I'm in *love* with you, Eulalie?"

She clasped his shoulders and gazed into his clear blue eyes. "Y'shouldn't orter be, but I reckon y'cain't hep it, huh? The magic's jest too strong to fight."

Closing her eyes, she laid her forehead on his chest. "No

man ain't never been in love with me afore. I don't know how I'm s'posed to act."

Because she couldn't see him, he smiled a smile so broad that it moved his ears. "Just be yourself, Eulalie."

She nodded. "Go on and love me, Mystery. Enjoy me fer as long as y'can. Y'ain't gonna have a happy life, though, and it pains me somethin' awful to know that fer the rest o' yore days yore gonna be pinin' away fer somethin' y'cain't never have. I'll be forced to pitch a rock through the winderpane o' yore heart. Won't like doin' it none, but comes times when a girl's gotta do what a girl's gotta do, and I gotta marry Fernando Del Castillo."

Fernando felt restrained mirth rumble in his chest, and wondered how long he would be able to keep his laughter at bay. "I'll try to be brave."

Eulalie straightened and swept her hand lightly across his smooth, tanned cheek. "Y'can try to be brave, Mystery, but in the end it's gonna take a river o' whiskey to drown yore blues. I'll try my dangest to give you a lavish o' mem'ries, though. We'll do as much as we can together afore I—afore I give myself to Fernando Del Castillo. Then, once I'm gone, y'can live on them mem'ries fer the rest o' yore sorrerful life."

Her head hung low, she left the cabin.

And Fernando finally surrendered to the best laugh he'd had in years.


The woman went to bed at seven o'clock! How could anyone fall asleep so quickly at such an early hour? Fernando wondered. In Europe during this period of the evening, society was only just preparing for the night's activities!

But Eulalie *was* asleep, the last weak glimmers of daylight playing upon her features. She slept on the floor, a thick stack of blankets and furs her only mattress.

"There's room enough fer you, too, Mystery," she'd said before she'd fallen asleep. "Jest keep them britches o' yores on, and yore more'n welcome to stretch out right here beside me. It's the leastest I can do fer the man who loves me more with his ever' breath."

Fernando had never gone to sleep at seven in the evening, had never slept on a floor, and most assuredly had never slept with a woman without making love to her first.

Still gazing down at Eulalie, he felt a stirring of desire. Although he'd known her for only one day, he knew making love with her would be like embracing something beautifully feral. An untamed loveliness that evoked excitement and tenderness at once. She'd feign nothing. Her responses to his caresses would be as true and real as the heat of a flame.

His own thoughts further warmed his blood. *Santa Maria*, he had to find something to do! But he'd already read the Flanders Mound newspaper, Eulalie didn't have a single book in her cabin, and there were no nearby dinner parties to attend. There wasn't even anyone to talk to.

Except Rooney. The black-masked creature sat near the dying fire, watching his every move.

Fernando refused to converse with a raccoon, no matter how bored he was. Sighing, he looked around Eulalie's cabin.

The half-log shelves that hung on the walls were filled with flasks of flowers, whittled sit-arounds, shiny rocks, bird feathers, and empty nests. Faded orange curtains hung at the windows, and a blue-and-yellow-braided rug lay before the door. Another sat in front of the hearth. Above the mantel were no less than eight pairs of deer antlers, each pair decorated with strands of dried red berries and tiny green and purple bows. Besides the table and chairs, the only other furniture in the room was a battered pie safe and an old lopsided bench upon which was folded a colorful patchwork quilt.

Eulalie's cabin was very simple, and yet the room exuded a coziness Fernando found remarkably hospitable.

Having naught else to do, he took off his shirt and boots, and laid down beside Eulalie, but not too close, because as soon as he felt the heat of her body, desire returned. He tried to think unrelated thoughts.

He thought of Europe. If he were in London right now, he'd be at the opera. Or maybe the symphony. Music soothed him.

He doubted he'd ever hear stirring music again. Not here, on a Texas ranch.

He closed his eyes and waited for sleep to come to him. As he lay there, cricket chirps floated around him. At first the sound annoyed him, but after a while he found the melodic noise oddly peaceful.

The last flames in the fireplace crackled and whispered. He heard the deep and mystical call of an owl, and the rustle of tree branches. An evening breeze sang past the cabin bringing with it raindrops that gently pattered the window-panes.

And Eulalie's breathing came to him, a soft, rhythmic sound that stole through his senses.

Her sleepy sighs. The crickets, fire flames, and tree branches. Rain, night wind, and the owl song. All mingled gently, harmoniously, composing music no European symphony had ever performed, could ever imitate.

And Fernando slept.

After what seemed like only moments, Fernando awakened to the scent of baked apples and fresh blackberry muffins. He blinked, noticing that the cabin was no brighter now than it had been when he'd fallen asleep.

He rubbed his eyes and sat up just as Eulalie came in from outside. She held a string of fish in one hand and a bucket of sloshing water in the other. "What time is it?"

When Eulalie looked at him, she felt that same warm pleasure she'd experienced the day before. His turquoise eyes, long charcoal hair, smooth dark skin, and hard rippling muscles . . . Lord A'mighty, everything about the man sent her into a tizzy.

"Eulalie? What time is it?"

"Time? Danged iffen I know, and danged iffen I care. I don't never pay attention to clock stuff. Never seed much use fer it myself."

He stared at her. She never knew the hour, didn't care to know? He could hardly believe that!

He rose, retrieved his shirt, and withdrew a gold watch from the pocket.

Seven thirty.

Slowly, he raised his head and stared at Eulalie again. "You just went to bed, and now you're up. Was that only an evening nap?"

"Nap?" She laid the fish on a wooden cutting board that lay on the table. "What in the world are you talkin' about?"

"You went to sleep at seven o'clock, which means you slept for a scant half an hour. So did I."

She laughed. "Mystery, night's done over. That's daybust y'see creepin' through them winders."

"What?" *Dios mio*, he'd slept clear through the night without waking once! He'd never slept so soundly.

"Y'orter git up earlier," Eulalie advised as she began preparing the fish for frying. "I git up s'early that come times when I meet myself goin' to bed, but I git a lot done whilst I'm up. Don't waste nary a second o' no day. There's jest too much work to do."

Fernando wondered what sort of work she was talking about. All she had to take care of was her tiny cabin. How much work could that be?

"Come on and pad yore belly, Mystery," Eulalie said when the table was set with breakfast.

He moved to pull out her chair.

When he helped her be seated, Eulalie felt her heart turn over. No one had ever assisted her into a chair before; not even her father.

Mystery's gentlemanly behavior toward her made her feel more special than she ever thought she'd feel.

Of course, he was only acting nice because the potion had made him fall in love with her, she reminded herself. How would it feel if he'd fallen in love with her without the aid of the potion? Lost in her own dream, she sighed.

"I'm really not very hungry, Eulalie," Fernando said as he took his place across from her. In Europe, he rarely ate before eleven.

A moment passed before Eulalie was able to reply. Those

special feelings continued to drift through her. "Jest pick then," she finally said.

He ate four fried fish, three baked apples, half a dozen muffins, finished off the leftover meat pies Eulalie had made the day before, and washed everything down with a whole jug of fresh cider.

"Thought y'wasn't hungry."

He smiled a sheepish grin. "The food was wonderful. You're an excellent cook."

"Real—really, Mystery?"

At the mixture of disbelief and pleasure he noted in her eyes, Fernando realized she rarely received any compliments. "Yes, really."

He leaned back in his chair and folded his arms across his chest. "Do you have any friends, Eulalie?" he asked, his voice as gentle as he knew how to make it. "Anyone to talk to?"

"My critters," she whispered, still pondering the compliment he'd given her.

"No human beings?"

She picked up her fork and scraped the prongs around the edge of her tin plate. "I know some people in Flanders Mound, but . . . but they ain't never in no frenzy to talk to me. Mostly they like laughin' at my hair, clothes, the way I talk. They even poke fun at me havin' so many animal friends. Ole Joyce Flanders talks to me sometimes, but I can do withouten her kind o' talkin'. Her grandfather finded the town, and she thinks that makes her better'n ever'body else. She keeps her nose so high up in the air that I reckon she's got a double chin on the back o' her neck. I dread meetin' up with her on account o' she hates my innards somethin' fierce. I ain't never done nothin' mean a'tall to her, so I cain't unnerstand why she's always so riled at me."

She handed a scrap of muffin to Rooney. "Joyce is purty, though, I'll say that fer her. Yaller hair, big blue eyes, and she's real little. Menfolk like little women like her."

"Oh? How do you know that?"

"Well, Joyce is always sparkin' with somebody. Always got her a man. She's outen fer Fernando Del Castillo now, though. Even got her a length o' emerald green satin fer the dress she's gonna wear to the party. I got a blue and white gingham dress that I'm wearin'. Belonged to my maw. Ain't real fancy, but it ain't got no holes in it. And I ain't wearin' no acorn earrings and rock necklaces like Joyce thinks, neither. I'll make some jewrie with dried flowers. 'Course, there ain't really no need fer me to dress up real fancy seein' as how I got the love potion. Still, I'll dress good so's ever'body'll know I got manners same as them."

For some reason he couldn't fathom, Fernando felt irritated that anyone would mistreat Eulalie. "What about male acquaintances?"

Eulalie tugged at one red ringlet, then watched as the curl sprang back into a tight coil. "The menfolk don't pay me a nary jag o' mind, 'cept fer when they're starin' at me. Well, that's a lie. 'Bout three or four months ago ole Elwood Smutters, he wandered over here wantin' to know iffen I'd show him my tits fer two dollars and a set o' shiny red buttons. Said some o' the boys in town betted him that he wouldn't have the balls to ask me to do sech a thing. Them boys who dared him? Well, they was hid in the woods near my cabin just waitin' to see me lift my shirt.

"'Course, I didn't do it," she continued, pulling at another of her curls. "I could've used them red buttons, but I didn't lift my shirt on account o' I knowed fer shore and sartin that them boys only wanted to make fun jest like Joyce does. Joyce says I orter bind 'em up. I tried once, but I felt smashed flatter'n a fritter, and I couldn't take a decent breath to save my life."

Fernando didn't comment, but he suspected that Joyce Flanders was terribly envious of Eulalie's beautiful breasts. The woman's own breasts were probably the size of walnuts. And he knew also that the boys she spoke of hadn't had any intention of *ridiculing* her about her ample figure. Eulalie was simply too innocent to understand their real reasons for wanting her to lift her shirt. And why *wouldn't* she be so ignorant of her own charms? It was obvious to him that the township of Flanders Mound had spent years destroying whatever self-esteem she might have had at one time.

"Well, we'd best git started," Eulalie announced.

"Started?"

"Got wood to chop, Mystery. And we gotta haul water over to my garden."

"But it rained last night."

"That sorry rain didn't do nothin' but damp the air. It's so dry outside that the trees is bribin' the dogs."

At that, Fernando threw back his head and laughed.

But every trace of his amusement disappeared when he began helping Eulalie chop a mountain of firewood and haul bucket after bucket of water to the vegetable plants in her garden. Hours later, when they'd finished those chores, he assisted her with sawing off dozens of tree branches that had grown long enough to press down on the top of her cabin. After that, he repaired the two holes she found in the roof.

"Tuckered, Mystery?" Eulalie queried when they'd finished the tasks and sat in the forest shade drinking cool stream water.

He splashed a bit of the water on his face. "Some. And you?"

"Yeah, but it's a sight better to have two tired arms than one empty belly. You done good, Mystery. Worked s'hard, I reckon you had to be careful not to drown in yore own sweat. That's somethin' else we know about you. Wonder iffen there's more we can larn?" She examined his face and hair. "Y'know? Iffen it weren't fer them blue eyes o' yores, I'd say y'was Mexican."

Fernando thought of his mother, a dark-skinned, black-haired native of Mexico. The only features he'd inherited from his Spanish father were his blue eyes.

"Well, whoever you are," Eulalie continued, "y'know how to work, and that's somethin' y'can be dang proud of."

He glanced at the tall stack of wood, freshly watered garden, trimmed trees, and patched cabin roof. A feeling of self-satisfaction came to him, the same pride Eulalie thought he should feel.

He wondered if ranching would bring him the same sort of gratification. The prospect, for some reason, no longer seemed so absurd.

# Four

"Where are we now?" Fernando asked, guiding his horse along the twisting dirt path and feeling rather impatient with the unending miles of fence, fields, and trees. He'd finally agreed to Eulalie's pleas to ride over the ranch, but still didn't understand how she'd coerced him. It wasn't like him at all to bow to a woman's will so easily, especially a woman he'd known for all of one week. "Are we still on Del Castillo land?"

Sitting behind him with her arms curled around his waist, Eulalie smiled into the sunwarmed black hair that flowed down his back. Her lips tingled, her skin prickled. She allowed herself to enjoy the sensations for one short moment before speaking. "It takes near 'bout three whole days o' constant movin' to get from one end o' this ranch to the other."

He looked out over the empty fields. "And normally those pastures are filled with cattle."

"Yeah, but you know what? I always thinked that the Del Castillos orter breed and raise horses. From what I've heared, there's plenty o' cattle ranches around. But folks need good horses jest as bad as they need cattle. And I like horses. Ain't never had me one, but I've met a few in town that I jest loved."

Startled, Fernando shifted in the saddle and looked at her. He loved horses, too. Her idea about raising them on the ranch instead of cattle appealed to him. "Horses," he whispered, turning back around. "Yes, maybe I will."

"Whatja say, Mystery?"

"Uh . . . Nothing."

Eulalie watched the breeze sweep through the grassy meadows. "Ain't it purty? Don't somethin' about this land reach inside you and hug yore soul?"

Try as he did, he could not understand her profound love for his ranch. "The only hug I feel is the one you're giving me."

She relaxed her arms instantly. "I weren't givin' you no hug. I was only tryin' to keep from fallin' off."

"Of course."

She ignored the hint of amusement she heard in his deep, soft voice. "Up ahead's a real special spot. We can eat our picnic there."

He wondered what special thing could be found on his land. It all looked the very same to him.

"Here," Eulalie said after a moment, and pointed to a large area that was shaded by two ancient cedar trees. Quickly she slid off the horse and walked into the tree shadows, the picnic basket swinging from the crook of her elbow. "Like it?"

Fernando dismounted and examined the spot. "It isn't any different than any other place we've passed since leaving your cabin two hours ago."

"Y'ain't lookin' hard enough, Mystery. Cain't y'see nothin' different 'bout these here trees? Look at them two branches up there." She pointed toward the tree tops. "The highest branch on this cedar curves down, and the highest branch on the other tree does, too. Their tips meet together in the middle o' the curve, makin' a perfect heart shape. You ever see heart branches afore? I call this place 'Cedar Heart.' Ain't it special?"

She waited for him to answer, but only saw him shrug his broad shoulders. What was the matter with the man? Why was he so blind to the beauty of this land?

Troubled by his indifference, she lapsed into silence and sat down within the circle of cool shade beneath the trees.

Fernando joined her and watched her pet raccoon, Rooney,

tumble out of the picnic basket. "Something wrong, Eulalie?" he asked, noting her silence.

*Yore God-burned right somethin's wrong, and yore the one it's wrong with.* She handed him a meat pie and finished her own pie in three bites. After wiping the crumbs from her lips and chin, she decided to give Mystery another chance to recognize the beauty that surrounded him. Sticking two fingers into her mouth, she whistled loud and long.

The shrill and sudden sound almost caused Fernando to choke on his food. "What—"

"Shh. Jest sit still. Still as y'can."

He did, and in a few moments he saw a doe step out of the thicket of tall brush that grew behind the cedar trees. The graceful creature sniffed the air, seemed wary, but approached Eulalie when she cooed.

"This here's Dolly." Eulalie reached into the picnic basket, withdrew a handful of fresh blackberries, and held the dark, glistening fruit toward the deer's soft mouth. "Ain't she purty?"

Captivated, Fernando watched the wild animal eat from Eulalie's palm. When the doe had consumed all the berries, she licked Eulalie's wrist. Fernando tried to imagine what deer licks felt like, but failed.

Slowly, he held out his hand, dismayed when the deer drew away.

"She don't know yore smell," Eulalie explained. "Here, give me yore hand." When he complied, she rubbed her own hand all over him. "Now, try again."

He did, and this time Dolly gave his fingers a tentative lick, then returned her attention to Eulalie.

"She don't like the way you taste, Mystery."

Fernando didn't know whether to feel amused or insulted.

Eulalie rubbed the deer's velvety ears, then smiled when she heard a familiar chirp. She raised her hand, and in the next instant a bright red cardinal alighted upon her finger. "Mystery, meet Clarence. And over there, slower'n risin' cream, comes Tucker. Old s'what that turtle is. Paw always sweared that Tucker was born ten years afore Moses."

Fernando saw the turtle crawl right into Eulalie's lap.

Words failed him. He'd heard about people who had a special way with animals, but he'd never known anyone who possessed the gift.

"And looky there," Eulalie said, her grin widening as she noticed another forest creature nearby.

Fernando finally found his voice when a bristly-haired boar trudged into view. The grayish black animal appeared to weigh around two hundred and fifty pounds, and Fernando knew the long, sharp tusks protruding from its lower jaw could easily kill a man, even a horse! "*Dios mio*, Eulalie, that's—"

"Joseph," Eulalie said. "He's a javelina, and it's a God-burn miracle he's still alive. Ignacio Del Castillo shooted him 'bout three years ago. It would've been one thing iffen Ignacio shooted Joseph fer meat, but he didn't. Jest fired a bullet through Joseph's shoulder and leaved him to bleed to death. Paw watched it happen. Paw and me, we digged outen the bullet and nursed Joseph fer nigh on two months afore he was ready to git set free. 'Course, Joseph was ready to git set free after only one month, but he was enjoyin' all the attention s'much, that he put on like he was sick fer a spell longer.

"Y'ain't skeered o' Joseph, are you, Mystery?" she asked, noticing his stiff posture. "There ain't nary a need to be. Joseph, come swap howdies with Mystery."

In sheer wonder, Fernando watched the javelina arrive at Eulalie's side. The animal rolled to its back, stuck its feet in the air, and snorted in pure pleasure when Eulalie scratched its fat belly.

"See?" Eulalie said. "Joseph's as harmless as a bowl o' oatmeal."

"I see," Fernando replied, then broke into a broad smile when Rooney began licking the inside of the javelina's ears.

"Joseph don't never clean his ears," Eulalie explained. "Rooney does it fer him. Lord A'mighty, Joseph's ears is s'dirty that I reckon he could grow him a bushel o' taters in 'em."

At the thought of a boar growing potatoes in its ears, Fernando chuckled. "Do you come here often?"

"I make rounds. Joseph, Dolly, Clarence, and Tucker usually stick to this here neck o' the woods, but I got other pets scattered all over. It takes me 'bout a month to visit ever' one of 'em. 'Course, there's times when I ain't able to visit. When that happens, they come to my cabin."

Fernando pondered her intense love for her animals, then thought of the meat pies she'd packed for lunch. "How are you able to hunt?"

"Cain't on account o' I've done runned outen bullets."

"No, what I mean is how can you make yourself shoot and kill the animals you consider pets?"

Eulalie placed Clarence Cardinal on her shoulder. "I don't kill nothin' that I've give a name. Once a critter's got a name, I couldn't eat him even iffen my belly was empty enough to echo when I talked. But when I have to shoot nameless critters, I feel powerful bad over it. I always funeralize the bones. My cemetery used to be in a patch o' woods that always growed violets in the spring. It was so purty. But ole Ignacio got a God-burned notion to chop the trees down. I thought he was gonna build somethin' there, but he didn't. He was always fellin' trees. Whenever I seed the trees fall, it was like watchin' good friends git kilt. There was times when I swore I could hear 'em scream, and the sound was enough to clabber my blood."

Fernando felt her chilling sorrow as if it were an icy wind blowing straight at him. "Why did Ignacio fell so many trees?" he asked, surprised by his own sudden concern.

Eulalie picked a few dandelions and caressed Joseph's mouth with the brilliant yellow blossoms. "More'n likely jest so's he could see more wide open land. The man was mean, Mystery. Selfish and stingy, too. Paw always used to say that Ignacio pro'bly didn't never warsh in cold water on account o' goosebumps use up more soap. He didn't need mine and Paw's tiny plot o' land, y'know. Wanted it jest to have it. It was some four years ago. Paw couldn't pay his county taxes on the land. Somehow, Ignacio larnt that Paw couldn't pay. He rode over to the county seat and paid Paw's taxes. Convinced the tax man that the land didn't belong to Paw no more's what he done, and then said that

that was why he was payin' the taxes. Ignacio was slicker'n owl snot. And crooked? Lord A'mighty, he was so crooked that a snake would've breaked its back tryin' to foller his trail."

She sighed while remembering. "Anyhow, the tax man believed Ignacio's lies. That's how Ignacio got the name on the land deed switched over to his own. Weren't three days later when Ignacio come and ordered me and Paw offen our land. When we didn't leave, he set far to our cabin whilst me and Paw was out one day. Paw tried to make the mayor and lawman in Flanders Mound unnerstand the truth o' what Ignacio done, but they jest called him a dang liar. After that, me and Paw squatted wherever we could. Sleeped outside right on the ground, even in the winter. The Del Castillo ranch is s'dang big, Ignacio couldn't find us most o' time. When he did, he'd run us offen, but we'd jest squat someplace else. Paw couldn't even think on leavin' this land. He was borned here, and so was I."

Lifting her eyes, she watched a lacy swathe of white clouds ruffle through the late afternoon sky. "When Ignacio died, Paw rebuilded our cabin on the land Ignacio stealed. But he didn't git it finished afore his heart give outen. He passed on real quick. I cried and carried on, and then I buried him alongside the crick that runs behind the cabin on account o' Paw spended many a hour settin' bare-assed nekkid in that water. Jest set there, doin' nothin', like there weren't no better place in the world to be.

"When I'd done laid him to rest, I finished the cabin. It ain't maked as good as Paw could've maked it, but it's home. And y'know? Even after I'm Miz Fernando Del Castillo and livin' in that fancified ranch house, I ain't gonna tear down my cabin. It'll be my gittin'-away place where I'll go iffen I ever git the weary dismals."

Fernando deduced that "the weary dismals" were periods of sadness, and felt slightly ruffled over her assumption that she would become despondent while married to him. Of course, he had no intention of marrying her or anyone else for that matter. Becoming accustomed to the life of a rancher would be difficult enough; getting used to being a husband as well would only add to his troubles.

Still, if he *was* married to Eulalie, he would certainly do everything he could to keep her from running to her cabin with the weary dismals.

"I cain't me'mry the last time I talked as much as I've talked to you today, Mystery," Eulalie murmured, patting her turtle's cold head. "Yore easy to talk to. Y'listen good. 'Course, that's pro'bly on account o' yore in love with me." Feeling a warm blush color her cheeks, she bowed her head and stared at Tucker's shell.

With the tips of his fingers, Fernando lifted her chin, and smiled into her big green eyes. She was the very essence of simplicity, he mused. She seemed so innocent, and yet, when she spoke, her words held meaning; wholesome significance that he'd never thought upon before.

He found her rustic candor charming. "Eulalie," he said through his smile, "I would have listened to you even if I had not swallowed the love potion. I like the way you express yourself, and the stories you've told me have been well worth hearing. You say you cannot remember the last time you've talked to anyone as much as you've talked to me today. Well, I cannot remember the last time I've enjoyed a woman's conversation as much as I have yours."

As he spoke, he realized the truth of his own words. He truly hadn't ever met a woman who could hold his attention as long and fast as Eulalie Bailey.

"Honest, Mystery?" Eulalie asked, hoping with all her heart that this flattery had nothing to do with his being in love with her.

He smiled. "Not only do I enjoy hearing what you have to say, but I also like looking at you. You're wrong, you know . . . about believing that men like small women. Some do, I suppose, but not all. Indeed, I prefer tall women with long legs and large— Uh . . ."

"Tits?" she asked, urgent hope edging her voice.

"Well, yes. And I like big green eyes, a splash of tawny freckles, full, pink lips, and red hair that has a life of its own . . . that curls and bounces in happy chaos."

He played with one of her tight copper ringlets, then slid his hand down the length of her slender arm. "You're a very beautiful woman, Eulalie. A kind, generous, and compassionate woman as well."

She didn't dare believe him.

But she did because his eyes shone with a sincerity that could not be pretended. Her heart shook with unfamiliar happiness. "Whoever you are, Mystery," she whispered, "yore the nicest man I ever knowed."

He picked up her hand and brushed his lips across her fingers. The warmth and scent of her skin aroused him suddenly, fully, and irresistibly.

Lifting his gaze, he looked into her eyes and felt powerless to control the scintillating temptation to kiss her. "Beautiful," he whispered.

When she saw him lean toward her, every part of her screamed for her to flee. Every part but her happy heart, which longed for one true taste of the passion Mystery offered.

She closed her eyes. His warm lips touched hers. Lightly, like a whisper. She felt his hand circle the back of her neck, didn't resist when he pulled her closer, rather, slipped her arm around his waist.

Emboldened by her response, Fernando urged her lips apart and savored the velvet and sweetness of her mouth. Deepening the kiss, he lifted his hand to her breast.

Desire nearly rendered him senseless. She wore nothing beneath her shirt; the thin fabric was all that lay between his hand and her soft, feminine flesh. "*Santa Maria,*" he said, his words half whisper, half moan. "*Santa Maria,* Eulalie."

Only barely cognizant of her surroundings, Eulalie drifted on the hot and enveloping wave of desire Mystery's caresses had wrought within her. She yearned for something she couldn't understand, couldn't name, but knew Mystery could give her. "Don't stop," she breathed, her words absorbed by his kiss. "Please don't stop, Mystery."

He knew full-well what she wanted, longed to accommodate her, but dared not. She already hated the Del Castillos, and something deep inside him, some unfamiliar emotion, would not allow him to give her yet another reason to further detest him.

His lips yet clinging to hers, he opened his eyes and saw her cardinal still perched on her shoulder. He could have sworn the red bird had an expression of reproach on its feathered face. "Your bird doesn't appear very pleased with me, Eulalie. Indeed, I think he's angry."

"Angry," she repeated, mesmerized by the crystal blue depths of his eyes. "Yeah, ang—"

She frowned, finally realizing and understanding what she'd done with Mystery. "Well, that makes two of us!" Carefully, she placed her turtle on the ground, helped her bird off her shoulder, then sprang to her feet. "You low down, no 'count, slicker'n boiled okra, triflin'er'n a puddle o' spit *varmint*, you! Y'know dang well I'm as good as wedded up with Fernando Del Castillo! And what'd you do? You kissed me, and then went from a God-burn tit-*gawker* to a God-burnin'er tit-*feeler*!"

So as not to fluster her further, Fernando refrained from reminding her that she'd enjoyed the sensual encounter and had begged him not to stop. "Feeling just seemed more fun than gawking," he said, giving her a rakish grin.

"Yeah? Well, touch me one more time, and I'll hit you so hard yore young'uns'll be born shakin'!"

"I apologize," he said, and meant it. "I don't know what came over me."

At his explanation she recalled the love potion, and softened instantly. "Well, I'm sorry fer threatenin' to hit you. It's the Cupid's Delight. That stuff's powerful strong, and I reckon y'jest couldn't hep from wantin' as much o' me as y'could git."

She trailed her fingers down the buttons of her shirt, remembering the way his hand felt upon her breast. Would Fernando Del Castillo bring her the same pleasurable yearning she'd experienced with Mystery?

She couldn't make herself believe that he would.

"Eulalie? What are you thinking about?"

Shy once more, she busied herself by gathering the food back into the picnic basket. "We orter go, Mystery," she said so quietly that she could barely hear her own voice. "It'll be dark soon."

He waited for her to say good-bye to her animals, then walked her to his stallion. He mounted first, then reached for her.

His hands might as well have been made of flames, for when he clasped her waist, she felt heat spread through her body—a heat that became even hotter when he placed her in front of him rather than behind him.

Her shoulder and left breast pressed against his chest, and the backs of her thighs lay over the top of his firmly muscled leg. His long, ebony hair brushed her cheek, and his arms enclosed her waist as he held the reins.

*Lord A'mighty, I'm gonna catch on far and burn plumb to ashes.*

"I thought you'd be more comfortable this way," Fernando explained. He grinned, knowing that the word *comfortable* in no way described how she felt.

Urging his horse into a steady walk, he took one last look at the two old, gnarled cedar trees that meant so much to Eulalie. As he gazed at them, he realized he must not have studied them closely enough when she first pointed them out to him.

He'd seen many fine and precious sculptures during his travels through Europe. Sculptures that art collectors paid thousands of dollars to own.

But here . . . here in Cedar Heart there existed a sculpture so beautiful that only Mother Nature herself could have created it. And to think such a masterpiece belonged to him!

The heart branches really were special.

And so was the girl who'd shown them to him.

# Five

As the days passed, Fernando forgot to count them. By his best estimation he'd been with Eulalie for about three weeks, but he couldn't be certain. The tranquility he felt eased his perception.

He couldn't even remember when he'd last looked at his pocket watch. Before the first shy shimmers of dawn crept into the cabin, he was up with Eulalie, ready to participate in whatever plans she had for the day.

She taught him to whittle, and he taught her to waltz. The forest floor their ballroom, he swirled her through the thicket shadows, and the patches of glistening sunbeams that twinkled through the treetops provided light far more beautiful than any European chandelier he'd ever seen. Sometimes he hummed a melody, but more often than not he danced with Eulalie to the music of the songbirds who watched from the rustling oak branches above.

He rode over his extensive acreage with her, well away from his ranch house, as he suspected the townsfolk of Flanders Mound had begun preparing his home for his arrival. The empty fields and long stretches of trees that had once bored him no longer appeared as tedious. Colorful butterflies occupied the meadows, and he could have sworn that every time he rode past a grove of trees he could hear them whisper a welcome to him. Even the scent of his property began to affect him. Dirt didn't smell dirty; the soil smelled fresh and clean and alive. The fragrance, mingled with the rich perfumes of the grass, wildflowers, and sultry

breezes, brought him an odd exhilaration he'd never known
before and never wanted to lose.

In the evenings, while the dying light of dusk still
flickered upon the windowpanes, he was in bed . . .

With Eulalie.

He held her in his arms all through each night, touched by
the fact that she slept with the flowers he brought her every-
day. If she stirred in her sleep he awakened instantly and
murmured sweet words until she slipped back into slumber.

And while she slept peacefully beside him, he thought
about how right it felt to have her there.


"Y'got any bullets, Mystery?" Eulalie asked one morning
after they'd feasted upon sandwiches of hot biscuits and
fresh tomatoes. "Mr. Dawson over at the mercantile won't
let me trade fer 'em no more, and like I done tole you, I ain't
got none."

Fernando watched Rooney filch a whole tomato from the
vegetable basket that sat by the door. The raccoon carried
the bright red fruit to Eulalie's bucket of clean rinse water,
and washed the tomato before devouring it.

Fernando grinned, pondering the fact that he'd become
fond of Eulalie's animals. Besides Rooney, he'd made
friends with Penelope Possom, Sylvester Squirrel, Henrietta
Hare, Cody Coyote, and Tammy Turkey. He'd yet to
befriend Rex Rattler and couldn't supress a tinge of apprehension whenever Eulalie coaxed the snake to follow her
around the yard.

"Mystery?"

"What?"

"Ain't y'been listenin' to me? Lord A'mighty, yore so
slack-minded today that I reckon you'd kiss yore horse
good-bye and hitch yore wife up to the plow."

Smiling, he rose from the table and crossed to where she
stood by the fireplace. Noticing a smudge of flour on her
cheek, he kissed it away. "I'm sorry, Eulalie," he murmured,
his lips still nuzzling her cheek. "I wasn't listening. What
did you ask me?"

She trembled as if a strong wind blew through her insides.

During the past weeks, Mystery's nearness had begun to do strange things to her. Warm and tender were her emotions, and they dwelled in her heart, deepening every time he smiled at her, winked at her, held her hand, pulled out her chair, or brought her flowers.

Sometimes, like today, Mystery made her forget Fernando Del Castillo.

But she couldn't allow her feelings to overcome her plans. Mystery could not give her the land for which she harbored such passion. Only Fernando Del Castillo could.

She turned her face away from Mystery's kisses. "I asked iffen y'had any bullets."

"Yes. A rifle, too. Why?"

Eulalie untied her apron, hung it on a nail in the wall, and started for the door. "Much as I hate doin' this, we gotta hunt this mornin'. We ain't had no meat fer four days, and I'm sick plumb to death o' fish. With any luck a'tall we'll have roast venison tonight."

A quarter of an hour after they'd left the cabin, she spotted a young buck browsing within a thick tangle of brush. Examining the animal intently, she realized she'd never seen it before.

Slowly, she placed the stock of the rifle on her shoulder, sighted along the barrel, and curled her finger around the trigger.

Fernando, who crouched directly behind her, leaned forward and whispered into her ear. "He looks like a Benjamin, don't you think? Benjamin Buck."

Instantly, Eulalie lowered the rifle. "Benjamin," she murmured. "Mystery, why'd y'have to go and name that buck? Y'know dang well I cain't shoot nothin' that's got a name!"

When she turned to look at him, she saw that his shoulders were shaking with silent laughter. "This means we ain't havin' no venison tonight. We'll have to have fish again."

"Unless, of course, we happen upon Fred Fish, or his companions, Felicia and Floyd." At his own joke, Fernando laughed so hard that he lost his balance, fell, and lay sprawled on the ground.

Eulalie stared at him as though he'd lost his mind. "Mystery,

I ain't never seed you so silly." But his uproarious laughter soon proved contagious. She laughed until her stomach began to cramp, then collapsed upon Fernando's chest.

His laughter faded into a low chuckle, a smile, and finally his amusement ceased altogether. Sliding his fingers into Eulalie's thick, molten tresses, he thought about the things that had been so important to him before he'd met her: restaurants, buildings, art, symphonies, and social swirls.

Here, on his land, he mused, he was surrounded by crowds of animals, many of which were infinitely friendlier than European blue bloods. No restaurant he'd ever patronized served meals as delicious as Eulalie's, and he'd never seen any art or structure as breathtaking as nature's own. The melody of the wilderness was the loveliest he'd ever imagined, and as for the social swirls . . .

He'd conversed, laughed, and danced at those aristocratic gatherings. Had thought them exceedingly gay activities at the time.

But weren't his conversations with Eulalie far more entertaining? Didn't he laugh more with her than he ever had with any other woman? And their waltz through the forest . . . the wonderful memory still lingered in his mind.

He'd found her, he realized with startling and beautiful clarity. The woman he'd never met before, the woman with whom he wished to spend the rest of his life.

He knew who she was now.

Eulalie.

The most recent edition of the Flanders Mound newspaper under her arm, Eulalie raced into the cabin. "Mystery! Mystery, where the hell are you?"

He walked through the doorway behind her. "Where have you been? I've been looking all over—"

"I lost Rooney this mornin' and reckoned he'd wandered into town to steal him a apple from the barrel Mr. Dawson always has outside his store! He does that sometimes, but when I got there I couldn't find him nowhere. He—"

"He's washing a strawberry in the stream. What's that you've got under your arm?"

She thrust the newspaper into his hands. "Somethin's goin' on in Flanders Mound. There's banners ever'where, baskets o' fresh flowers hangin' all over the dang place, and the townsfolks is runnin' 'round town in a frenzified dither. I—I reckon a month's done passed, and I think Fernando Del Castillo's comin'!"

Fernando scanned the front-page article. "You're right. Mayor Perch expects the new Del Castillo to arrive within the next few days."

"Oh, Lord A'mighty, Mystery, this is it! The party—The love potion— Where the hell did I put that Cupid's Delight romance tonic?" In a complete panic, she began searching the cabin for the white flask.

Still standing beneath the threshold of the door, Fernando watched her, contemplating how much she meant to him. He hadn't spoken to her of his love, not because she believed his emotions to have been created by the potion, but because he'd hoped she'd admit to the feelings she felt for him.

He'd yet to hear her speak of them, but he saw them in her eyes. Tenderness filled her gaze whenever she looked at him, an affection Fernando had watched deepen as time passed.

Yes, she cared for him. He was certain of that. But the question was who or what did she care for more?

Him or his land?

He would have his answer the night of the party. She would either go to the ranch house and give Fernando Del Castillo the potion or she would give up her chance to have the land and stay with Mystery, a man she believed could give her naught but his love. No matter the outcome, he would give her as much of his property as she desired to have, but before he did she would have to choose between him and the land.

And he would not reveal his identity until she'd made her choice.

Dressed in her mother's gingham dress, her neck, wrists, and hair adorned with circlets of dried wildflowers, Eulalie stood by the small window. Night shadowed the yard. In only a short while longer, it would be time for her to leave

for the Del Castillo party. Another Flanders Mound newspaper printed the news that Fernando had arrived, had met
with the town council in his ranch house, and was holding
the reception this very night. Mystery had read every word
of the article to her.

Patting the flask of love potion that lay within the deep
pocket at the side of her dress, she turned from the window
and looked at Mystery, who sat at the table gazing into the
fire, his saddlebag in front of him.

She knew he was hurting. So miserable was he that she
was going to the party that for the past two days he'd taken
to leaving the cabin in the morning and not returning until
late at night. She had no idea where he went for such long
periods of time, and when she asked he'd answered only
that he'd been out riding, thinking.

"Mystery," she murmured achingly. Her heart beat frantically as she thought about how much he'd come to mean
to her.

She only wished she knew what to call the feelings she
had for him.

"Mystery," she said murmured again. "I . . ."

"I know," he answered, still staring into the fire flames.
"It's time for you to go."

Tears stung her eyes, but she blinked them away.
"Please . . . please try to unnerstand. This little piece o'
land belonged to my paw and his paw afore him. I got the
chance to git it back now. I cain't let it go. I jest cain't."

Her words sent misery surging through him. "I understand."

"It's the love potion, Mystery," she whispered. "Iffen it
weren't fer yore drinkin' the tonic, you wouldn't feel—"

"Wrong, Eulalie," he interrupted, finally turning his gaze
from the fire and looking at her. "Wrong. I was enchanted
with you before I tasted the first drop of your potion. The
second I saw you by the stream, I—"

"Don't."

He memorized every part of her face, wanting her love
more than he'd ever wanted anything in his life. "I have
something for you."

She watched as he withdrew handfuls of shine from his saddlebag. When he approached her, she saw that the brilliance dripping from his fingers was pure gold.

Without a word, Fernando dressed her in pieces of his mother's precious gold jewelry: a necklace, earrings, bracelets, rings, and an ornate hair ornament.

Eulalie touched one of the heavy gold earrings he'd attached to her ear. "Where did you get—"

"It doesn't matter."

"But I cain't take—"

"I love you, Eulalie," he ground out, clasping her upper arms and squeezing hard. "Do you hear me? *I love you.* And even though you are about to leave me for another man, I cannot allow anyone at that Del Castillo party to ridicule you. Adorned in this gold, you will be the envy of every woman at the party, most especially the high and mighty Joyce Flanders."

Tears poured into her eyes, swiftly running down her cheeks. In light of his profound love for her . . . his willingness to allow her to give herself to another man, she didn't know what to say to him.

Words of gratitude seemed grossly inadequate.

"It's a long walk to the ranch house," Fernando whispered, caressing the pink silk of her cheek. "An hour at least. Do you want me to take you on my horse?"

She shook her head.

"I love you, Eulalie."

She fled toward the door.

"Eulalie," Fernando called to her. "The arched sign to the entrance of the ranch . . . the one we rode by a week ago."

She knew the sign; it said *The Del Castillo*. "What— What about it?" she sniffed.

Fernando played the last card he held. "I'll wait for you there. If you change your mind about the land . . . about Fernando Del Castillo, I'll be waiting for you under the sign. I'll wait until nine. You can ask someone at the party the hour. If you don't come, I'll know—I'll know, and I'll leave."

Tears still blurring her vision, she nodded.

And then, in a flurry of gingham and a shimmer of gold, she left to meet Fernando Del Castillo.

# Six

Moonlight spilled silver on the ground when Eulalie finally arrived to the Del Castillo ranch house. As quietly and unobtrusively as possible, she entered the grand home and made her way down a short corridor that led to the room where the township of Flanders Mound had gathered. When she arrived at the threshold, astonishment slackened her jaw. Her mouth opened wide, she started at yet more evidence of the Del Castillo wealth.

Rich cinnamon-velvet covered the walls; antique-gold satin draped the tall windows. Beneath her feet lay a thick and luxurious brown carpet. The upholstered furniture was of cinnamon-and-brown–striped satin; arrangements of pale yellow roses were scattered throughout the room. The numerous intricately carved tables fairly bowed beneath the weight of fine foods and expensive wines and liqueurs. A multitude of elegant lamps and graceful tapers shared their light with the mellow fire in the marble fireplace.

The warmth and inviting feel of the room beckoned to Eulalie. Still mesmerized, she stepped forward.

"Eulalie."

Joyce Flander's icy voice broke through Eulalie's reverie. She took a deep, cleansing breath and turned toward the blond beauty, who had, indeed, succeeded in acquiring an emerald-green satin ballgown for the occasion. "Purty dress, Joyce," she managed to say.

Joyce could not reply. She could only stare. Gold blazed all over the red-haired heathen, the most magnificent piece a large heart-shaped pendant. Suspended from a thick and sumptuous gold necklace, the pendant gleamed richly upon Eulalie's lush cleavage, so beautiful and of such obvious value that Joyce had to curb the urge to reach out and touch the jewelry. "Where—Where did you get all that gold?" she demanded, her heart shriveling with envy.

Mystery's image flowed into Eulalie's mind. A long moment passed before her turbulent emotions calmed sufficiently for her to speak. "A friend give it to me."

"Oh? It was my belief that you had no friends. Where is this so-called friend of yours?"

Eulalie bowed her head, concentrating so intently on Mystery that she thought she felt his presence in the house.

But of course, he wasn't in this impossibly grand house. He stood beneath the arched Del Castillo sign.

Waiting for her.

"He's—he's somewhere, I reckon," she said lamely.

Joyce sniffed. "You are wearing far too much gold," she charged imperiously. "A few pieces are sufficient. More than that is vulgar. And to wear such heavy gold with a simple frock of faded blue and white gingham. . . . Really, Eulalie, is there no end to your ignorance?"

Eulalie raised her head and glared into Joyce's glittering blue eyes. "Joyce, iffen you belonged to me, I'd trade you for a flea-bitten ole hound dog, and then I'd shoot the dog! Now, git outen my way!"

She pushed past the cruel woman and walked further into the room. Every person in the assembly turned to stare at her. Some laughed, others whispered, all moved away.

Eulalie blinked back the tears that threatened. Mystery had been wrong. Not even the gold could keep the townspeople from ridiculing her.

She dipped her hand into her pocket and curled her fingers around the flask of Cupid's Delight. Soon, she thought. Soon, Fernando Del Castillo would make her his bride. He would give her his love, his house, his lands. He would—

Would he coo her back to sleep when she awakened in the night? Would he name strange animals in the woods and make her laugh?

Would he take her into his arms and waltz her through the forest?

"I suppose you think all that gold will catch Fernando Del Castillo's eye," Joyce speculated as she arrived at Eulalie's side again, a crystal glass of champagne in her pale, slender hand. "Silly girl. He'll see straight past the gleam of your gold and know you for exactly what you are—an uneducated, ill-bred squatter!"

Eulalie closed her eyes. Behind them yet lingered Mystery's image. Mystery didn't think her uneducated or ill-bred.

Mystery thought her beautiful. Kind and compassionate. He was the only man besides her father who had ever thought such sweet things about her.

Her gaze slanted with malice, Joyce sipped her champagne. "You'll see I'm right, Eulalie. Fernando has yet to make his appearance, but I just heard Mayor Perch say that Fernando will be coming down that staircase in only moments. No one but Mayor and Mrs. Perch and the town council has seen him yet, but Mrs. Perch says he is the most handsome man she has ever seen. I'm to have the first dance with him. Mayor Perch thought it only right that the granddaughter of the town's founder be the first." She patted her smooth blond chignon, then gasped with excitement when the crowd of townspeople began gathering around the landing of the staircase.

"It's time!" she exclaimed. "He's coming!"

Eulalie lifted her gaze to the top of the elegant winding staircase. In only moments, the wealthy and sophisticated Fernando Del Castillo would appear at the upper landing.

She thought of all the many times Mystery had appeared at the threshold of the rickety door of her cabin, his arms laden with the wildflowers he'd picked for her.

"Eulalie, for God's sake, get out of the way!" Mayor Perch flared as he tried to move past her. "What in heaven's name are you doing here anyway?"

Before Eulalie could answer the mayor, the large mahogany grandfather clock that sat in the corner of the spacious room began to peal the hour. Her gaze still raised to the top of the staircase, Eulalie counted each musical chime. One, two, three, four, five, six, seven, eight . . .

Nine.

*If you change your mind about the land . . . about Fernando Del Castillo, I'll be waiting for you under the sign. I'll wait until nine. . . . If you don't come, I'll know—I'll know, and I'll leave.*

As the memory of Mystery's parting words filled her mind, Eulalie felt rising panic. Hysterically, she tried to remember the land, the vast countryside she'd loved all her life. Try as she did, however, she could not summon that years' old passion.

But she did feel love gather and burst through her heart. A love so all-consuming that she knew she would die if she could not share it with the one for whom it existed.

*I'll wait until nine . . .*

Melting fear searing through her veins, Eulalie whirled away from the stairs, raced from the room, down the corridor, and out of the house. Passing the array of carriages and wagons parked in the courtyard, she fled toward the arched sign, which was at least three miles away.

"I love you, Mystery," she panted, her chest heaving as she ran into the night, "Don't leave withouten me. Please still be waitin'."

Just as Fernando stepped onto the upper landing of the staircase, the grandfather clock struck nine. Cheers of welcome floated up to him from the crowd below, but he could concentrate on nothing but Eulalie.

Was she here? Apprehension narrowing his eyes and scoring his face, he swept his gaze over every inch of the room downstairs.

And then he saw her. Her gingham skirts flying, she was running from the room as if Satan himself was chasing her.

He knew where she was headed and almost laughed aloud with his joy.

Taking the staircase steps two at a time, he arrived at the lower landing and was immediately surrounded by the townspeople of Flanders Mound. One woman, in particular, was obnoxiously insistent in her efforts to be near him.

"Mr. Del Castillo!" Joyce gushed, then batted her eyes. "Welcome to Flanders Mound. I'm Joyce Flanders, and I—"

"Miss Flanders," Fernando drawled, his gaze drawn to her chest. He nearly smiled. Her breasts *were* the size of walnuts. She'd padded them well, though.

*Too* well, he mused. One large wad of cotton had begun to come out of the bodice of her low-cut gown. "How charming you are, milady."

"Milady?" Joyce twittered with undisguised delight. Fernando Del Castillo surpassed her wildest dreams. The man was devastatingly handsome and so full of muscle that the mere thought of being held in his powerful arms almost sent her into a swoon. Smiling her most flirtatious smile, she offered her hand for his kiss.

Fernando touched his lips to her fingers, found them cold and clammy, then straightened. "Yes, truly charming. But have a care not to lose those charms." Grinning, he reached out and flicked his finger across the ball of cotton puffed upon her bare skin.

Joyce looked down, saw the white stuffing, and realized that the cotton must have come loose while she'd pushed her way through the throng. Mortified, she bent at the waist and tried to push the stuffing back into her bodice.

Her bent-over position, however, caused the bodice to gape, and before she could do a thing to remedy her embarrassing situation, every piece of the cotton floated out of her dress.

The soft padding landed directly upon Fernando's shoes. Casually, he picked the fluff up. "It would seem you have lost your charms. A pity you failed to heed my warning."

He deposited the cotton into Joyce's shaking hands, then turned back to the gaping townspeople. "Ladies and gentlemen," he said loudly, "I realize that what I am about to ask of you is rather unusual, but I would very much like for you to accompany me to the arched sign at the entrance of my ranch. My guest of honor is missing from this assembly, and I suspect that we shall find her there."

Extraordinarily curious as to who his guest of honor could be, the people trailed out of the house, stepped into their wagons and carriages, and followed Fernando.

But they found it impossible to keep up with him.

His long black hair whipping in the moonlit air, he rode as if a priceless treasure lay waiting at his destination.

# Seven

Eulalie had begun to lose all hope of ever reaching the designated meeting place when suddenly, just ahead, she saw pale moonlight illuminate the wide, arched sign. "Mystery!" Completely out of breath, she staggered forward and grabbed hold of one of the elegantly carved wooden columns that supported the wrought-iron sign. "Mystery, iffen yore here, please answer me!"

She heard nothing but the night breeze and the gentle sway of tree branches. Knees trembling so badly she could barely stay standing, she stumbled all around the area, searching for any sign of Mystery. To no avail.

Misery finally buckled her knees. As she collapsed beneath the sign, an armadillo waddled out from the shadows and nudged her arm. "Arlene," Eulalie whispered, staring into the armadillo's small black eyes. "Gone. Mystery—He leaved, Arlene, all on account o' I was too dumb to unnerstand how much I love him. He thinks—He thinks I wanted the land more'n him."

Silent tears slipped from her cheeks and splashed upon the armadillo's tough armor. "Oh, what difference does it make?" she cried. "He—He didn't really love me, no how! It was jest the potion! It was only that God-burn romance tonic—"

"You're wrong, Eulalie," a familiar voice said from behind her.

Turning around, Eulalie saw Cherubim V. Harper, his blue-star eyes twinkling with moonlight and benevolence.

Beside him stood Pompeii, his kangaroo, who held a mass of squirming worms in his furry paws. "Mr. Harper—"

"The love potion was but sweetened water with a dash of cinnamon added, my dear," Cupid said, reaching down to cup her chin. "Cupid's Delight possessed no magical powers whatsoever. You won Mystery's love all by yourself."

She frowned. "Me and Mystery . . . How do you know about us? How—"

"I have my ways," he replied mischievously.

Disbelief exploded through Eulalie, quickly followed by a sorrow so deep that she knew it would never fade. "He loved me. He loved me, and I let him go!" Choking on her grief, she covered her face with her hands and sobbed.

"There, there now, dear child," Cupid said, gently pulling her hands away from her face and smiling into her tear-filled eyes. "There is nothing that can conquer Love. Obstacles present themselves, yes, but I always find a way—I mean, *Love* always finds a way around them. You'll see. Love will win in the end, Eulalie, for there is no power mightier, not in heaven or on earth."

She was about to dispute his words when she heard the sudden sound of pounding hoofbeats in the distance. Swiveling in the direction from where the sound came, she saw a tremendous bay stallion thundering toward her.

And mounted upon the beautiful horse was Mystery.

"Mystery," she whispered. "Mr. Harper, it's Mystery!" She turned back to the white-haired peddler, only to find that he'd disappeared.

"Eulalie!" Fernando shouted. He brought his stallion to a halt, flew out of the saddle, and ran to take Eulalie into his arms.

"Yore here!" she yelled, wrapping her arms around his neck, and spreading kisses all over his face. "You didn't leave!"

"And you came," he responded. Holding her tightly, he buried his face in the fragrant mass of her wild curls.

"I love you, Mystery," Eulalie whispered into his ear. "Lord A'mighty, you mean more to me than this land, my cabin . . . I don't care nary a jag that I won't never own this land. As long as I got you, I—"

"The land is yours, Eulalie," Fernando said, his voice shaking with love. "The land, the house . . . Everything I have I give to you."

She drew back and peered into his sparkling blue eyes. "Everything *you* have? Lord A'mighty, Mystery, have you losed yore mind like y'losed yore memory?"

Gently, he set her on her feet, then enfolded her hands in his own. "Eulalie, I have never been without my memory. You just assumed I'd lost it. I realize it was wrong of me to allow your assumption to continue, but—"

He brought her closer to him, so close that he could feel the pelting of her heart against his chest. "You held me spellbound from the moment I first saw you by the stream. To be honest, however, my interest in you was only part of my deception at first. When I first arrived to my lands, the last thing I wanted to do was accept the role of rancher. I had a month before Flanders Mound expected me, and your cabin offered me a place to stay until I would be forced to oversee the lands that so bored me."

He released her hands and slipped his fingers into her vibrant copper curls. "After only a short while, your intense love for my ranch began to affect me. I started to see and recognize the same beauty of this land that you did. And . . . and I fell in love with you as well."

Eulalie didn't know what to say. Bewilderment, hurt, and incredulity played havoc with her thoughts.

"I knew you cared for me," Fernando murmured, "but you never spoke of your feelings, so I couldn't be sure how deep they were. The sole way I could be certain was to allow you to choose between the man you knew as Mystery and the man who owned the land you so desperately wanted to have. I never meant to hurt you, Eulalie, and I swear to you that no matter what you had decided in the end, I would have given you as much land as you wanted."

She tried to moisten her lips, but could not. Nor could she swallow. "Them two days . . . Them two days when you leaved in the mornin' and didn't come back till night—You was meetin' with Mayor Perch, his wife, and the town council."

"They were expecting me. I couldn't very well have stayed away."

Her emotions raging within her like a torrid fever, she fought to free herself from his embrace.

Reluctantly, Fernando let her go. He knew she was angry. She loved him, yes, but could she forgive his deception?

Eulalie walked well away from him, into the shadows cast by a grove of nearby oak trees. For days, weeks, a whole month, she'd been living with Fernando Del Castillo, and she hadn't even known it. Fury smashed into her.

But sweet and gentle memories gradually began to conquer her rage. Memories of Mystery waltzing her through the woods. Of Mystery holding her all through the nights. Of Mystery showering her with freshly picked wildflowers.

No, she amended. Not Mystery. Fernando Del Castillo.

They were one and the same, and she knew with sudden conviction that although she would always treasure her memories of Mystery, she would make a lifetime of new ones with Fernando.

When she turned to face him, Fernando saw a huge smile on her beautiful mouth. In the next instant, she ran toward him and threw herself into his arms.

"Marry me, Eulalie," he whispered, his plea filled with every shred of the love he felt for her. "Say you'll be my wife."

She laughed into his eyes. "Fernando, y'could rope a lightnin' bolt quicker'n y'could git rid o' me. I'll be yore bride, birth yore young'uns, and set on the porch rockin' with you when we're both old and gray!"

He let out a loud yell of sheer delight. "Horses, Eulalie. We'll raise the finest horses the state of Texas has ever seen. We'll—"

He broke off when the townspeople began arriving in their wagons and carriages. "May I present my guest of honor," he said when the crowd had assembled around the arched sign. "I believe all of you are acquainted with Eulalie Bailey."

Joyce Flanders stepped forward, her chest stuffing securely back in the bodice of her gown. "You brought us all the way out here to see this . . . this *squatter?*" she demanded, her gaze drilling into Eulalie. "Is this some sort of joke, Mr. Del Castillo?"

Fernando placed a warm and protective arm around Eulalie's shoulders. "A joke, Miss Flanders?" he flared with all the authority he possessed. "Do you think I would make sport of my betrothed?"

Clutching her well-padded breasts, Joyce gasped. "Be— *Betrothed*?"

Fernando bent and pressed a tender kiss to Eulalie's forehead. "Miss Bailey has done me the extreme honor of agreeing to become my wife. Her love and knowledge of this *hacienda* will undoubtedly assist me in countless ways in the future. And," he said, his gaze meeting every pair of disbelieving eyes in the crowd, "I'm sure everyone here is delighted to know that such a beautiful and warm-hearted woman will soon be the mistress of this vast and soon-to-be exceedingly profitable ranch."

Silence clung to the air like dense mist.

"Congratulations, Miss Bailey," one woman finally said, and gave a timid smile.

"Let us know if there's anything we can do to help you settle in, Miss Bailey," another woman added, her husband echoing her sentiment.

Many more of the townspeople wished her well—even Mr. Dawson, who added an apology for not letting her trade for bullets. "Hope you won't hold it against me," he murmured.

Never having received such kind words from the people of Flanders Mound, Eulalie wiped tears from her eyes. "Thank you," she managed to say.

Fernando handed her a handkerchief. All would be well, he mused with satisfaction. Once the township had a chance to know Eulalie the way he did, they would wonder why they never took the time to become acquainted with her sooner.

"Who here is a carpenter?" he asked.

A short, bald man raised his hand. "I'm the town carpenter, Mr. Del Castillo. Mack Grover at your service."

Fernando nodded. "Mr. Grover, I would like you to make a new sign for my ranch. I no longer wish it to be called The Del Castillo."

"No?" Mr. Grover said. "What will you name it then?"

Fernando smiled. "*The Eulalie.*"

"*The Eulalie?*" Joyce shouted. Oh, the unfairness of it all! While *her* name was the same as a tiny town of a mere two-hundred people, Eulalie's name was to grace a forty-thousand-acre ranch! A ranch owned by one of the wealthiest men in the entire world!

Her jealous fury too much to bear, she paled, swayed, and then fainted into a heap on the ground.

Arlene Armadillo sniffed the prone woman, quickly made a bed upon the soft cotton pillow on Joyce's chest, and squeaked with deep satisfaction.

Smiling, Fernando turned to Eulalie and took her into his arms again. His grin widened when he glanced at the gold heart-shaped pendant that lay upon her creamy breasts. "Gingham and gold becomes you, sweetheart. You should wear them together more often."

"Ever'day, Fernando," she promised.

"I'll have that promise sealed with a kiss," he teased.

As she tilted her head back to receive his kiss, Cherubim V. Harper's parting words to her burst into her mind:

*Love will win in the end, Eulalie, for there is no power mightier, not in heaven or on earth.*

She smiled, and just as Fernando's lips touched hers, she saw a sudden spear of lightning flash through the dark heavens. The tremendous thunderbolt illuminated the entire sky, then vanished almost as soon as it appeared.

And in its place there glittered a merry trail of twinkling blue stars.

# HEART'S DESIRE

## Lydia Browne

"He's here!"

The petite blonde stepped down from the footstool, gathering up the cream silk of her unhemmed wedding gown to keep from tripping. Like a cold caress, the heavy fabric brushed Rebecca's cheek as Leonora passed where she knelt on the floor. She smiled around a cluster of pins, watching the other girl sweep toward the narrow window.

"He promised me to come home before my wedding. Max has never forgotten a promise to me."

"Max?"

"You don't know him," Leonora said, not turning her head. "He's my brother."

"No," Rebecca said, rising. She took the pins from her tightly pressed lips and tapped them together, the tiny points prickling like frost against her fingers. "I haven't met him. Not yet."

"I *knew* I heard bells," Leonora said, tottering up on tip-toe to see farther. "Here he comes now!"

A curly-bodied red and green sleigh, pulled by a single bay horse, appeared at the end of the curving drive that led to the Dales' home, Elmloft. Rebecca, peering over the other girl's loosened curls, could see the driver only as a dark figure. When the sleigh stopped in front of the house, their downward view was blocked by the window sill. The bells rang a last wild time.

"Max home at last! I can't wait to see him!" Leonora said, racing across the wide planks of her bedroom floor.

"Not in that dress! You'd trip on the stairs and break your neck. Take it off and let me put it away."

"I'll be careful, Miss Clifton," Leonora said, looking over her shoulder. "Besides, if we stop now, you'd never get done. I've decided it must be finished today. I want to spend the rest of my time with Max. It's not every day he comes home from China or wherever he's been."

A male voice called, "Where's my little sister?"

"Up here, Max!"

The brass door handle turned. Rebecca knew already what kind of man she'd see. Her sister had described Max Dale to her so often—his white, winning smile, his deep-blue eyes and abundant wheat-colored hair—that she couldn't be bothered to look at him. Carefully, she inserted the silver needle she used into its worn velvet case.

"Max!" Leonora squealed.

"I beg your pardon, miss. I was looking for my sister, not a grown-up beauty." His voice could have inspired any girl to imagine herself in love if she were not forewarned. As Leonora giggled, he laughed with warmth enough to have broken the cold spell lingering over Concord, if such a thing were possible.

With a sideways glance, Rebecca could see nothing of the man behind Leonora, except the strong arms that lifted her kicking into the air as he embraced her in greeting. "Put me down," Leonora commanded. "You'll crush my dress."

As he placed his sister on her feet, Rebecca found her casual peep becoming a stare. Daphyne had described a young prince from a fairy tale, but this man did not quite fit that fantasy. Where the sunlight caught his hair, silver gleamed among the bright waves. His skin, dark from the sun, wrinkled cheerfully when he smiled, while his eyes, as blue as the sea itself, nested in many lines. Rebecca commanded her gaze away, though not before she'd met his look for one glancing second.

Her cheeks hot, she fumblingly collected her scissors and thread. Perhaps Daphyne had some reason for her raptures after all. Something inside her had leaped up alive at the laughter sparkling in his eyes. Rebecca sternly thrust the feeling aside.

Leonora primped her gleaming multi-flounced skirt, looking up flirtatiously. The ivory silk, sewn over with exotic flowers in golden thread, suited her giddy beauty. "What do you think of this dress?"

"Mighty fine feathers. Is it new?"

"Why, Max, it's my wedding dress. You sent me the silk by Captain Winston last spring."

"Did I? That was good of me." He chucked her beneath the chin with one finger. "You should see what gewgaws I brought for you this trip."

"What, Max? Show me!"

"I'll come back tomorrow," Rebecca said, interrupting.

"No, I told you. I want to finish it tonight," Leonora said. "Oh, I beg your pardon. My seamstress, Miss Rebecca Clifton. My brother, Captain Maxwell Dale."

"How do you do," Max said, with a straight look and a half-bow.

Rebecca nodded offhandedly. "There's not much to finish," she said addressing herself solely to Leonora. "I could take it home with me."

"I'll run you home in the sleigh," Max offered.

"No, thank you. I prefer. . . ."

"Max!" Leonora said on the same note as a puppy yaps. "You just got here!"

"It'll be all right, Leonora. I'm home this time to stay."

"Max! Do you mean it?"

He patted his sister's shoulder and asked, "Do you have a cloak, Miss Clifton?"

"I prefer to walk, Captain Dale. Thank you."

"If it's more than a step, you'll never make it before the weather changes."

"It seems to me to be a very pleasant day," Rebecca said, glancing toward the sunny game of naughts and crosses that was the nine-paned window.

"There's a storm coming from the southwest. It'll be here within the hour. Take a sailor's word for it."

To rebut his bold wink, Rebecca answered, "I've always heard that a girl who listens to a sailor is a fool."

"That's true. About everything but the weather." He grinned at her, with an engaging lift of his eyebrows that invited her to laugh with him. Rebecca fought to keep her stern expression. She saw his ebullience fade a little and knew a sudden shame for blighting his homecoming.

"Anyway," she said, "if you'll take off the dress, Leonora, I'll go at once. It was . . . a pleasure to meet you, Captain."

A few minutes later, he watched her as she came down the plain, highly polished staircase, her right hand moving smoothly over the bannister. She hesitated only an instant when she saw him waiting for her. Her steps continued downward, sure and solid. She would have walked right past him if he hadn't spoken.

"I'll drive you."

"It isn't necessary."

"For my own sake, Miss Clifton, I hope you'll allow me. How am I to sleep tonight if you freeze to death?"

Once again, he saw her full lips tighten as she repressed a smile. When he'd first seen her, a shadow girl behind his ivory-doll sister, she'd pleased his taste. He'd thought her a Quaker at first. Now he saw her clothes were merely old, though well kept. Nonetheless, from her maple-syrup colored hair, restrained in a high knot though shining gold where the sun had caressed it, to her slender waist, he had approved of the restraint of her beauty.

Yet she puzzled him by her coldness. Though he didn't consider himself an extraordinary gallant, he'd never met a woman before who seemed to hate him on sight. He wondered if it had after all anything to do with him; perhaps Miss Clifton never laughed or smiled at anyone. If so, it seemed a terrible waste.

Max said, "I must drive into Concord anyway, Miss Clifton. My grandmother has gone to visit a friend, and I wouldn't have her walk back in a snowstorm. I wish you New England women would take the easy way once in a while."

"We like exercise, regardless of the weather. It teaches us fortitude."

"Very commendable. But won't you allow yourself to be lazy just this once?"

Rebecca thought it over. If he only took her as far as the end of her drive, if Daphyne didn't see him, it would give her time to tell Daphyne he had come home before her sister heard it from someone else. . . . "Very well. It's good of you."

Behind the double-storied clapboard house, heavy clouds had mustered to challenge the still-shining sun. As she stepped up into the sleigh, wrapping the sides of her cloak over her skirt, the clouds advanced. She heard the mumbling voice of the thunder as the wind died.

"I think you are right, Captain Dale. It does look like rain."

"Not rain. Snow. A real blighter by the look of those clouds."

"Snow? With thunder?"

"It happens sometimes. It never means a mild storm. It's a good thing Roger didn't unharness the horse. Ready?" He snapped the reins.

Rebecca was thrown back as they started forward. She clutched at her bonnet, black like all her clothing, and gave him an austere glance. "Are you trying to outrace the wind?"

"Haven't you heard? That's what sailors do."

"That isn't all they do, or so I hear," Rebecca muttered. Fortunately, the wind whipped her words away. Yet, he gave her another grin as though he'd heard her. Rebecca turned her head to watch the trees flash by.

Daphyne had been right about one thing—he had good teeth. His mouth was good too, well-shaped and firm, and sailors tended to be clean-shaven these days. Rebecca could almost understand why her sister had so far forgotten herself to allow this man to kiss her. Remembering her own first, and only, kiss, Rebecca could recall little but the scratchy unpleasantness of an ill-trimmed beard and mustache.

The temperature dropped perceptibly. Rebecca wrapped

her arms about herself and wished she'd thought to wrap one of the beaver rugs around her when she'd gotten into the sleigh. Too late now, she thought. To try to stand up, even in a sleigh this smooth while traveling at this speed, would be a fatal madness.

The next thunder came as a crash, rather than a rumble. Rebecca's head jerked up in response. Almost at once, a second flash of lightning followed, illuminating the clouds from behind. Rebecca saw an immense rose in the sky, each petal outlined in blue electric fire.

When the snow began, it was no touch of an angel's feather but a sudden volley of snowballs, each landing in her face. She wiped her cheeks with her forearm and blinked the stickiness from her eyelashes. Turning blindly toward Max, she said, "We'd better stop!"

"Yes, but where?"

She peered into the suddenly white world. "There," she said, pointing at a dim gray mass that might have been the ghost of a building. "That's Mitchell's barn. We can stop there."

The horse had already turned its head toward the shelter. As they drove up the hill to the barn, the lightning exploded again. Each snowflake seemed to hang suspended in the quick flash of light. The thunder shook Rebecca, the concussion pressing on her chest, stealing her breath. Nevertheless, when Max jumped down from the sleigh to open the door, she followed.

Stuck fast with snow, dirt, and years, it needed both of them to force it open. Only his quick arm saved her from shooting over backwards when the door gave with a crack that rivaled the thunder. She grabbed at him, her fingers closing on the crusty snow on the front of his fawn woolen overcoat. It seemed to her that the wind died away for an instant. Then she stood on her own feet again, nodding her thanks with a tight smile.

Max led the horse and sleigh into the barn, accompanied by a swirling rush of wind-driven snow. Together, Max and Rebecca dragged on the door to close it. Brushing off his hands, he said, "We could leave the horse here and go into the house. We'd be able to light a fire, unless the chimney's too blocked."

"There isn't a house anymore," she answered. "They moved it two miles when Riah Mitchell got married."

"I don't even remember a Mitchell family. I guess I've been gone a long time."

"Well, it would be seven or eight years ago, now." She'd been kissed at that house-moving party when she'd been seventeen, and for a week or so, hope had bloomed in her heart that she'd soon be married. The man with the beard and mustache had wed another and gone west. She'd given up all hope now of ever finding another suitor.

"We should be thankful Mr. Mitchell built his barn to last," Max said, glancing around. "I haven't been in a barn since I was a boy. You know, it's almost the same shape as a ship. Turn her upside down and you could sail her across the world."

"I'm cold." Rebecca stepped up into the sleigh. Lifting one of the robes, she settled it over her lap and drew the edge up to her shoulders. The wind knocked and moaned at the walls, lost and hungry.

The barn seemed desolate without the constant small noises of cows, cats, and rats. Yet, even in the winter, a faint bouquet of long-ago summer grass lingered, an everlasting part of the boards and empty mangers. Rebecca closed her eyes and shivered deeper into the welcoming warmth of the rug. "I hope the storm won't last too long."

As though to reply to her hope, the thunder sounded again, a crash so loud that Rebecca cried out. She didn't feel the sleigh bounce as Max stepped up into it. For all his height and proportional size, he moved very softly.

Aware of nothing until the last tumult died, she came to herself in his arms, her face pressed against the lapel of his damp coat. He did not smell of close houses, of choking smoke, and dead air, but of the sea and the salt breeze. She jerked upright and away.

He patted her shoulder, smiling down at her. "There now. There's nothing to be afraid of."

"I'm not afraid," she said, giving him a icy glance.

"You screamed. Don't be ashamed. I'm none too pleased with loud noises myself. Reminds me of cannon fire. And that one was right overhead. I thought it would shake the barn down."

"Anyone can be startled. It doesn't mean I'm afraid. Afraid of thunder! What am I, a baby?"

"No, you're no infant."

Rebecca told herself sternly that he would not make her blush a second time. She was not a person who blushed. No doubt his voice warmed like that for every woman he met. She had reason to believe him a heartless trifler; now she knew it. Trying those games with her!

Pointedly, she scooted as close to the ornate brass rail at her right side as she could. Bringing her arms out from beneath the rug, she crossed them on her bosom. "Did I hear you tell Leonora that you are come home to stay, Captain Dale?"

"That's right. I'm giving up the sea for good. Tell me, are you interested, or are you merely making conversation?"

Rebecca knew her mouth hung open like a dead fish's. He was rude, too. Civilized people didn't ask questions like that. She primmed up her lips. "Really, Captain Dale!"

"Why don't you like me, Miss Clifton?"

Impossible man! "I have no reason to like or dislike you. We have only just met."

"I know, but I get the impression you didn't like me before you met me. Why is that?"

Though now the interior of the barn was nearly lightless, Rebecca felt his bright gaze fix on her. He had no business being perceptive, she thought, acknowledging the truth of what he said. She hadn't wanted to like him. Yet, now that she'd met him, she couldn't quite sustain her determination. His sense of humor appealed to her; she'd had a sense of humor herself once.

"You are wrong, sir," she said. "I neither like you nor dislike you. We are strangers."

"And you are always cold and formal with strangers?"

"I am naturally very reserved, Captain."

"You know, somehow I doubt that." She heard him sigh

and the creak of the sleigh as he shifted his weight. "So, to make conversation . . . I have no intention of going to sea anymore. An old friend of my late father's has offered me a partnership in a new manufacturing process for steel. He feels the American capacity for production is virtually untapped, and after what I've seen in Britain, I agree."

"It does seem a shame that we must import so much when all we need do is improve our own production."

"My dear Miss Clifton, do you mean to say that you understand steel importing?"

"My father is a great disciple of women's education, and I myself have no wish to be entirely ignorant of the basics of life. I have studied many interesting things—perhaps not steadily enough to equal a man's education, but I have not wasted my time."

"Your father isn't by any chance *Edgar* Clifton?"

"So you do remember us."

"No, I don't believe I've ever had the pleasure of . . . but I met a French priest in Canton who corresponds with an Edgar Clifton of Concord. Something about a new method of education?"

"Père Gascoigne? Father and he have written to each other for years. I always look forward to his letters. He has a gift for making the most exotic adventures sound as usual as going to the market in town." She fought to keep the wistfulness from her tone, but she must have failed.

"Do you long to travel, Miss Clifton?"

"It is best to be content with the things one has at home. You must learn that, Captain Dale, if you are to settle down."

"You give those words a very pleasant ring."

She did not need now to see his face to know that he beamed at her. He seemed to be closer, though he had not moved. "Are you never bored with your life at home?" he asked, his voice low.

She laughed nervously and despised herself. If she had faith in such things, she might have thought that some enchantment had been cast upon her, some evil spell that made her say and do things that ordinary, frivolous girls did when singled out for attention by a man. She heard herself say, with a hateful archness, "Concord is by no means as backward as you might think, Captain Dale. We have the railroad now. At least once a year we go into Boston—my father to visit the Athenaeum, my sister to the book shops. . . ."

"You have a sister too? Older or younger?"

She froze anew. "It's growing lighter and has been some time since we last heard thunder. Hadn't you better see if we can continue on? You must think about collecting Mrs. Dale."

Turning her head, she could see past his wide shoulders when he tested the door. A few desolate flakes continued to fall, but shone in sunlight rather than a blinding flash. "It looks clear," he said, leaning out. "That was the strangest storm. . . ."

"Weather at sea must be very different. At least we won't be delayed any further. I have dinner still to get."

He came back to the sleigh, but stood beside her. "Is your sister an invalid?" he asked with a stern line between his fair brows. "Is that why you sew for strangers?"

When she straightened up proudly, he touched her hand. "Don't think me prying, Miss Clifton. But when I see a gallant creature struggling, I must do something. It's an instinct that's gotten me into a sea of trouble before now."

"My sister, as you very well know, suffers from nothing more than an advanced case of disappointed romantic love."

"As I know?" He took a step back.

"You are the Maxwell Dale who seduced her, promised to marry her, and then abandoned her without a word?"

"I did what?"

"It was six years ago. She was only sixteen. . . ."

"I can promise you I've never seduced anyone under the age of thirty. How old are you?"

"This may be a laughing matter to you, Captain. . . ."

"No, indeed it isn't. What else have I done? I trust you don't think I've murdered anybody lately?" He thrust back the sides of his overcoat, uncovering the bright brass buttons on his short navy-blue jacket. When he scowled up at her from under the brim of his peaked cap, his hands on his hips, she could well envision him commanding ships and men.

She, however, refused to be intimidated. "My sister has often told me how you met and that your words upon that occasion left her in no doubt that she would shortly receive a proposal of matrimony. As no word was ever heard from you—I believe you left Boston somewhat precipitately?—I can only assume that you are a heartless cad."

"I left Boston six years ago because a berth opened on an outward-bound vessel. It was my chance to move up the chain of command to first mate. I wound up taking over from the master, and eventually. . . ."

"Please, spare me your excuses. If the weather has cleared. . . ."

"You can't make an accusation like that without listening to what I have to say!"

"Of course I can. There is nothing you can say. My sister has never lied to me in her life."

It was only the thought of walking home in fresh snow, with a hole starting in an otherwise stout left shoe, that allowed Rebecca to ride the rest of the way home beside him. His incoherent protests of never, to his knowledge, having even met Daphyne disgusted her. She would have respected him more, she told herself, if he'd owned up to his misdeeds, even if refusing to repent of them.

"You may stop here," were the first words that passed between them since they'd left the barn.

"Where's your house?"

"At the top of the lane. But I prefer to walk from here."

"Don't be ridiculous. You'd be buried up to your knees in a step," he said, starting to back up. The horse laid its ears back and stood as though rooted in place, shuddering. "What's the matter with you, boy?" Max called.

As she climbed down, Rebecca noticed, almost reluctantly, that Captain Dale did not take his bad humor out on the horse. No, she thought, with an inward gleam of wit, he would prefer to vent it on me.

"Where are you going?"

"Home," she said, starting resolutely up the path. The naked maple trees growing to either side had deep drifts about their trunks, but the path itself was not too bad.

She heard the emphatic crunch of the snow beneath his boots as he jumped down. With his long stride, he caught up to her in a moment. "Rebecca," he said, half-humorously. His fingers were strong on her shoulder.

Turning, she waited, her face set and her eyes cool. "Yes, Captain?"

"Nothing I say can convince you that I'm not a pitiless blackguard?"

"You'll pardon me for believing my sister rather than a person whom I have just met."

"The devil take it then!" With both hands on her shoulders he pulled her to him. Startled, she didn't even close her eyes as his lips blazed across hers.

Why weren't his lips cold? How could he laugh and murmur her name without suspending for an instant the exquisite fervor he imparted? How could she be so forgetful as to clutch and press closer to him still? Had she lost her mind?

Rebecca thrust herself out of his embrace, her hand pressed to her tingling lips. "You . . . you haven't the least cause to swear. . . ."

A last whip of lightning cracked and sizzled in the sky. It struck somewhere near, dazzling them both to blindness as the earth shuddered. The silence that came after weighed heavy as the snow.

She shook her head to clear it. He had behaved appallingly. Yet she admitted that her own behavior was even more blameworthy. She must have done something, all unwittingly, to encourage this outrage. And to have enjoyed it. . . .

Max sniffed the air. "I don't smell burning. Maybe it didn't strike anything. God, that was close! It's a good thing we hadn't any iron on us or we'd be laid out deader than Davy Jones right now!"

Finding her voice, Rebecca said, "Captain Dale, I haven't

anything further to say to you. I don't wish ever to meet you or even to see you again."

"If you're waiting for me to apologize, Rebecca. . . ."

"My name is Miss Clifton. . . ."

"I'm not going to."

She ignored his outrageous words. "I am supposed to come to Elmloft tomorrow to finish your sister's dress. I would very much prefer that you not be there."

It was not easy to turn on her heel in the snow and to march imperiously away. She stumbled once before managing it. She heard the sleigh bells dingling as he left, but she did not look around.

No living soul would ever hear of his treatment of her. She would take this secret to the grave. Who in any case could she tell? Her father never listened to a word she said, and Daphyne . . . how could she smash the wholehearted confidence her sister gave to her? "Never!" she said aloud.

Halfway up the drive, Rebecca paused. The voice she heard must have been the echo of her own, returning out of the stillness. But as she began to walk again, the cry was repeated.

"Help! Is anybody home?"

"Where are you?" Rebecca called in answer.

The path cut between tall pines, their usually outflung branches weighted down with snow. They seemed bent old men, and Rebecca could almost make out their benevolent faces amidst the shadowed green and white. She heard a bird singing joyously, as though spring had come and suddenly the air seemed warmer.

"Watch out!" the voice called. With a plop, a cracked and worn red leather satchel dropped before her feet.

Almost afraid to, Rebecca looked up. The gentleman hung by his knees from a branch, like a boy showing off for a girl in the schoolyard. Only the branch was far higher than any boy would dare go, and the hair falling straight down from the top of his head was a venerable white.

"I've been calling for the dryad," he said. "But she seems to be asleep."

"Well, it is winter," Rebecca answered inanely.

"Is it?" He turned his head from side to side as though only just noticing the snow. His clothes were not suitable for the weather, yet he seemed no more bothered by the cold than by his unorthodox position. "You must be Miss Clifton. I have a delivery for you."

"A delivery?"

"That is, if you can help me down?"

"I'll get a ladder."

Even as she ran up the path to the barn, she was thinking, "This whole day has been a dream. I am still asleep in my bed and it is not yet morning. If I try, I know I can wake up."

The ungainly apple-picking ladder was longer than she could gracefully handle alone. As she dragged it, the rungs caught on her skirts and she tripped at least twice, painfully barking one shin. The pain didn't waken her, yet she remained convinced that this episode was merely part of the same dream in which Max had kissed her. Perhaps I have a fever, she thought, tripping once again, and this is all part of my delirium. She found it an oddly comforting notion. She could not be responsible for what she did in a fever.

Returning, she heard the strange man's voice. He said, "At least you're bigger than you were the last time."

Rebecca came up almost all the way to the trunk before she saw the huge cat sitting at the base. "Oh, my," she whispered.

The black stripes on its pure white fur seemed like shadow branches falling on the snow. Its head turned almost all the way over its shoulder to look at her with preternaturally blue eyes, the color of the clear sky overhead. Then it yawned, showing the arch of slashing teeth in absurd contrast to the pinkness of a curling tongue, like battle-axes in a candy shop.

"He's quite harmless," the man in the tree said. "Practically a vegetarian!"

She could only stare. Her mother had once told her of seeing a similar beast in a traveling menagerie when just a girl. But she had described a tiger as a thing of flame, orange, and black, never to be mistaken for a fanciful sculpture of snow.

"Maybe you'd better wait for me over there, Pompeii."

The white tiger swiveled one black-tipped ear toward the voice. Then, with deliberation, he arose, each muscle rippling beneath the striped pelt. The enormous feet were set down so daintily that the sparkling crust was scarcely disturbed. In less than an instant, the tiger was invisible among the black trunks of the trees.

The man climbed down the ladder with notable nimbleness. "I do thank you. I am not so young as once I was."

"Who *are* you?" At least, that is what Rebecca meant to say. Somehow it came out as, "What can I do for you?"

"Now that is kind, Miss Clifton. I should be most appreciative—could you spare a modicum of cocoa? Not for myself, you understand. I am not partial to it. Nasty, sloppy stuff. But for my tur . . . my tiger."

This seemed to Rebecca a most reasonable request. After all, she thought, dreams are a form of madness, therefore a mad appeal must be logical. "I may have some in the house. It mayn't be very much. . . ."

"I do call that kind. If you could just . . . er. . . ."

Daphyne had left a scorched pot on the stove, and their father had obviously been rummaging through the pantry again, leaving desecration in his wake. These trespasses usually incensed her, but now she overlooked them. Fetching the box of chocolate powder seemed far more important just then.

Sometime later, she stood on the path, a small white phial in her hand. It seemed warm and curiously heavy for its size. As a rule, she could easily resist the fantastic offers of smooth-tongued peddlers, but there had been something particularly convincing about this one.

The label read, "To clear the sight of the drinker, one spoonful Heart's Desire." What insanity had possessed her to purchase such a thing! She'd never had any trouble with her vision, and if she had, a traveling oculist would not be her choice for a cure. Dr. Barton had always been good enough for her family and did not insist on payment in advance.

Ashamed of her gullibility, Rebecca thrust the offending

bottle into her cloak pocket. Throwing away good money on such nonsense! At any rate, the bottle would make a decent vase for a single flower, so perhaps the money was not an utter waste.

Funny, she couldn't seem to recall how much she had paid. "Too much, no doubt!" she said as she put her foot on the broken bricks that served as a front walk.

The paneled front door opened and closed, letting out a tall, gangling man. She fought the temptation to compare Thomas Rhode's figure to Max's athletic masculinity. Thomas, for all his shyness and the spectacles that slid relentlessly down a bony nose, had at least a constant heart. He'd been in love with Daphyne for months, even enduring philosophy lessons from Mr. Clifton—and paying for the privilege— merely to be near her once a week.

"Good afternoon, Mr. Rhodes."

"Is that you, Miss Rebecca?" He almost seemed to sniff the air to catch her scent.

"Yes, Mr. Rhodes. How was your lesson?"

"Oh, most interesting . . . interesting. Miss Daphyne brought us refreshments. I always enjoy her culinary arts."

Rebecca hoped true love had equipped Mr. Rhodes with a cast-iron stomach. "You've finished early today," she said.

He pulled his watch from his pocket and tapped it to see if it were running. "No, this is the usual time. Five o'clock."

"Five?" Glancing at the sky, she saw that the sun had indeed sunk appreciably since she'd left Max at the bottom of the lane. What had she been doing all this time? "Heavens, I better get busy with dinner!"

She entered by the back door, shaking her head over the smell of burning that still lingered. She hung up her cloak. When the edge swung against the wall, a rap reminded her of the bottle in the pocket. She was debating with herself whether or not to pour away the contents when Daphyne wandered in.

"What's that?"

"Just some nonsense I picked up." She shoved the bottle onto the shelf with the spices. Taking up her apron, she tied the strings behind her. "Couldn't you have cleaned out this pot?"

"Didn't I? I'm sorry. Father and Mr. Rhodes were talking about the German Romantic school and I had to hurry so I wouldn't miss anything. I'll wash it now," she said, looking about expectantly as though hot water and soap should materialize at any second from out of the cupboards.

"Never mind, it can get put in with the supper dishes."

The younger brunette, darker in both hair and coloring than her sister, rooted in the apple bin. "I'll have to read you my latest paragraph. Father says it's the best thing I've done yet! I really give Harriet Martineau pepper." As though to punctuate her statement, she took a decisive bite from a wizened apple.

"Don't eat that now, you'll spoil. . . ." She should save her breath. Besides, she hadn't the heart to scold the girl for anything, when she had such a serious disappointment awaiting her. Remembering how ill Daphyne had been when her novel had been rejected by every possible publisher, Rebecca decided to wait until after supper to tell Daphyne that Maxwell Dale had come home. Or else that apple would be all she'd eat for days.

Long ago, Rebecca had come to the conclusion that her father and sister were geniuses and that she was destined to understand no more than half of what they said. This supper was no different than any other. Even if the chief phrases hadn't been in German, she would have taken no part. Mr. Clifton had often tried to persuade her that philosophy was the most beautiful of the sciences, being pure thought, only to give up in despair. Rebecca knew Daphyne and her father pitied her for her earthbound mind.

After supper, Mr. Clifton returned to his study at the rear of the saltbox house, taking with him a slice of dried apple pastry and a mug of tea. "Don't sit up too late, Father," Rebecca called after him.

"Last night," she said to Daphyne, "I found him at two o'clock in the morning, almost frozen. His fire had gone out, and he hadn't noticed until I mentioned it."

Daphyne had taken her chair close to the window and

now sat, smiling at her own reflection, swinging one of her feet under her full skirt like a little girl. The ringlets that fell forward over her cheeks from a topknot half-screened her face, but she hummed a happy waltz.

Beginning to clear the dishes from the low plank table, Rebecca said, "You seemed pleased with yourself tonight. It must be a very good paragraph."

"Hmmm? Oh, it's not just that. Rebecca, have you ever reflected on destiny?"

Very slowly, Rebecca put the stacked plates down on the table. "Destiny?"

"That two souls can be so connected that nothing can separate them?"

"No, I haven't ever thought that. Daphyne . . . you should know. I saw Captain Dale today."

"Yes, I know. That's what I mean. He probably doesn't even realize yet *why* he's come back."

"He's here for Leonora's wedding."

"Dear Rebecca, always so practical. I don't know what I should have done without you all these years he's been away." She gave her reflection another slow smile. "That reminds me. Is my blue poplin clean? Remember I spilled that lemonade on it when Father and I visited Mr. Emerson."

"I don't know. It's on the thin side for winter wear, Daphyne. Why do you want it?"

"I need something light to wear to Leonora's wedding. Did I tell you she invited me? I wasn't going before, but now that Max is come home, I shall have an escort other than Father. He's certain to ask me." Her large eyes took on a soft dreamy expression.

Rebecca pulled a chair around so she could face her sister. Taking one of Daphyne's ink-stained hands in her own, she leaned forward, trying to capture her inward gaze. "Daphyne, will you tell me again how you and Captain Dale met?"

"He wasn't a captain then, of course. I believe he said he was what he called a second mate. He talked about the things he would do once he was the master of his own ship."

"Start at the beginning, dearest. Where was this?"

"But I've told you this before. You really should learn to listen, 'Becca, or you'll never improve your mind."

"That's probably true. Tell me again."

Now that she had met Max Dale, Rebecca found it easier to picture the scene. He had come to Miss Standard's Academy for Young Ladies to visit his sister. Daphyne had never really been happy there, finding the emphasis on deportment and fine sewing oppressive when she longed to be home, taking Socratic lessons at her father's knee. However, an aunt on their mother's side had given the money for Daphyne to take two years and the opportunity could not be wasted.

Daphyne sought refuge from the frivolousness of her teachers and fellow students in books. "I should have preferred works by the great thinkers, but there was little choice in the bookroom. I had never read novels before. They do draw one in."

"And so you were reading when you met Cap . . . Mr. Dale."

"I am ashamed to admit that I was sniffling with sentiment. It was one of Mr. Cooper's romances, and Alice Munroe and Uncas, the Indian who loved her without speaking, had just gone off the cliff. I glanced up and there he was. He wanted to know why I was crying."

She sighed. "When our eyes met, I knew he was my fate. His eyes were so kind, so happy that I knew he felt the same as I."

Rebecca sighed too. She had learned that look today, but she mistrusted it. "What then?"

"Then? Why, nothing. Everything worth saying had been said in the first instant."

"But in your novel. . . ."

"That was fiction, though based on my own story."

Comparing the high-flown speeches indulged in by Daphyne's hero to the real Max Dale's humor, Rebecca could see that her sister's poetic license had all but run its limit. She wondered at the sudden upward swoop her heart took, as though some great weight had been lifted from it. "Then he didn't kiss you. It was all made-up."

"Kiss me? Oh, yes. He did."

The younger but taller girl stood up, stretching out her arms in their tight sleeves as though waking from a long sleep. "I think I shall write for a little while longer before bed. During supper, I thought of two more things to call Miss Martineau. I must hurry and get them down on paper before they fly out of my head."

"Daphyne! Wait!"

But, with the same single-mindedness of purpose that powered her father, Daphyne walked from the room with her long, unhurried and unhurriable stride, saying, "Later, 'Becca."

Defeated, Rebecca drummed her fingers on the table. There was only one thing to do. Taking up one of the half-inch tall candles that had lighted their meal, she went up the straight, narrow stair that divided the hall. She passed Daphyne's door, paused to hear the vigorous scratching of her sister's steel-nibbed pen, and continued up to the attic.

Here was no dusty jumble of boxes and trunks, broken furniture, and outworn toys. Everything usable had found an application. Brocade from a dress her mother had worn as a young bride had served to cover her father's chair. Chairs with splintered backs were now stools, the damaged parts burned for fuel. Rebecca had remade and reused so often that she no longer even considered it a virtue, but a necessity.

However, one item still remained in its original form. The manuscript of Daphyne's only novel lay in a tin box. In the bleakest hours of despair, she'd been instructed to bury the poor, neglected thing with her sister. Fortunately, that extreme had never been reached.

Downstairs, Rebecca cleared and washed the dishes. Then, after listening to her father's snores and Daphyne's continued writing, she sat down at the kitchen table, drew the candle closer and began to read.

She'd been her sister's only reader. Knowing praise was all that was wanted, she had concealed her doubts. After all, what did she really know about literature? Perhaps violent passion, nature taking on shades of sympathy with the heroine's every emotion, and people who never took action but who talked a lot was indeed what publishers would pay for.

Rebecca read the densely written pages again, this time focusing on a different aspect. Half the ideas were obviously culled from Goethe's *The Sorrows of Young Werther,* which depressing novel had encouraged morbid sensibility in more than one naive young lady. But how much of "The Maiden's Aspiration" was based on the author's life?

Finally, she tied up the manuscript again with its faded pink ribbon, her question still unanswered. The story had definitely been written at great speed, as though the author had been under some strong compulsion to get it all down. Certain scenes sprang off the pages, while others were merely an excuse for fine language. Once or twice there was even a glimpse of the real Max Dale, rather than the tediously dramatic Rollo Ward.

Daphyne would simply have to be made to answer questions about Max. Only then would Rebecca know what action she should take. If there had been some honorable proposal of marriage, then Captain Dale would have to live up to his promise. She did not dare ask herself why the prospect of seeing her sister married to a handsome, successful gentleman made her feel like smashing something.

"What a pleasant surprise," he said.

Rebecca blushed the moment Max came into his room. Even though her back was to the door, she knew that he stood looking at her. The more she told herself that she had no reason to color up, the hotter her face burned.

Leonora, of course, had chattered like a magpie all during the final hemming of her gown. She'd had all her new treasures spread out on her bed and insisted that Rebecca admire each trinket. If anything, she seemed more excited by her gifts than by her impending wedding, now only two days away.

Mrs. Honoria Maxwell Dale also wanted to show Rebecca the fine embroidered shawls and ivory combs her grandson

had brought home for her. Rebecca had great respect for
Mrs. Dale. She raised two sons alone after the death of her
husband. Though she never spoke of that hard time except
to make some charming reminiscence, Rebecca felt that the
older woman understood many of her own struggles. Today,
when Leonora's dress was finished, she asked Rebecca to
measure Max's new mattress as the old sheets did not quite
fit it.

"I'll be out of your way in a moment, Captain Dale."

"Take your time."

She glanced around at him. He leaned against the wall,
his arms crossed, looking very much at ease. He wore no
jacket, only his vest over his white shirt. Behind the laughter
in his aqua eyes, she glimpsed an interest that renewed the
carnation in her cheeks. Leaning over his bed, her tape
stretched between her outstretched arms was perhaps not the
most graceful position.

Straightening up and blowing the hair out of her eyes, she
said, "I can't do this if you are watching me."

"Let me help you, then."

"No thank you. I can manage." Her voice came out so
husky. Something must be wrong with her throat. She
backed up until the edge of the bed was behind her knees.

Very gently, he pushed back a freed lock of her hair with
his forefinger. "I like you better in brown than in black."

"I don't dress to please anyone but myself."

"Your hair is coming down. You ought to fix it. Borrow
my brushes if you like."

"I just want to . . . to. . . ." Rebecca couldn't recall
what she'd been doing a moment since. When she looked up
into his eyes, all she could remember was the way his mouth
had felt on hers, so hot that she had forgotten to be cold.

"Give me the tape. I'll measure; you write down the
figures. We can be done in a minute."

She handed the string to him without a word. Obviously,
his memory did not have the same force as hers. Just as
well, she thought, shaking herself. He probably kisses so
many women he can't remember by now if I'm one of them.

"Write forty-four and a fifth by seventy-two and a

smidgen. Then diagonally . . . eighty-four and a quarter. Let's see. By my calculations, that should put us somewhere east of the Maldives."

A laugh escaped her lips before she could muffle it. When she looked up from writing the last figure, he was rifling through his desk under the sunny window. He pulled out a blue-leather diary.

"Today is the fifteenth of March. I must circle the date. A momentous occasion like making Miss Rebecca Clifton laugh must be noted for posterity."

He looked so ridiculously earnest scribbling in his book that Rebecca couldn't help laughing again. Picking up her measuring tape, she slung it around her neck and said, "I'll leave you to be my biographer, then. Who knows? Perhaps you'll make me famous despite myself."

"Rebecca," he said, his tone becoming serious. "Close the door. There's something I want to ask you."

"What is it?"

"Come here so I don't have to shout."

She pressed her hand against the panels and the door slowly swung to. Clutching the paper, she crossed the heart-of-pine floor, her feet oddly heavy. Was he going to confess?

"What had your sister to say when you asked her about me?"

"What makes you think I asked her anything?"

"Didn't you?" A man's eyes, however rich a blue, should not be able to see right through one's defenses.

"She had already heard you had come home. She told me . . . the same story as before."

"Obviously I need to have a talk with her."

"I think you must see her. To refresh your memory."

Suddenly, the ends of her measuring tape were clasped in his large brown hand. He began twisting them around and around with supple circles of his wrist, pulling her nearer. "Do you think I could forget her? Especially if she were anything like you?"

"But. . . ." She was about to protest that Daphyne was

nothing like her when Max touched her chin. He lifted and
brought her lips under his.

Rebecca melted. She could feel his kiss everywhere, from
the soles of her feet to each individual strand of hair. When
he teased her with the tip of his tongue, she smilingly
opened her mouth for him and pressed her body more firmly
against his heat.

Somehow they crossed his bedroom from the desk to the
bed. The edge of the bare mattress was once more behind
her knees. He stroked her throat and the ruffled corsage of
her old dress with calloused fingertips that roused every
nerve. Rebecca heard new sounds burst from her lips,
sounds of divine pleasure, and did not try to hold them back.

He pushed her dress back from her shoulder. His lips
burned there. She drew his head down to the soft white
roundness below, utterly shameless, and shivered with
delight when he tasted her. He said her name on a hoarse,
hungry whisper. Then, with a half-laugh, "Thank God we
shut the door."

"Hush, don't. . . ." Rebecca wanted nameless things, the
deeds she'd dreamed of him doing last night but could not
understand. Talking had nothing to do with it. She sat down
on the bed, her eyes raised to his. Though his chest rose and
fell to hurried breaths, he stood back from her, an expression
of puzzlement so great as to amount to anger on his face.

"This isn't right," he said. "I'm not surprised you don't
believe me when I say I've never seduced a girl who didn't
know what she was doing as well as I did. You have a
strange effect on me, my dear. I'm not certain that I like it."

A slow wave of burning color washed over Rebecca. She
did not know how to return to the mindless passion that he
had created in her body, not without his cooperation. "I'm
not like this either," she said, rubbing down the gooseflesh
on her arms.

Max stepped forward and tugged the collar of her dress
over her shoulder. His hand curved over her collarbone, and
he dared to look down into the depths of her eyes. Whatever
he had been on the verge of saying died unspoken when a

soft knock sounded at his door. Directly upon the knock, the knob turned and his tiny, elegant grandmother came in.

Had Rebecca suddenly glowed white-hot, Max could not have snatched his hand away more quickly. Mrs. Dale's bright brown eyes flicked from one hot face to the next. "Here you are, Max. The Reverend Mr. Jobb is here and would like to see you."

"Old Rob Jobb? The last I heard he was trying to live on some kind of Utopian farm. When did he become a minister?"

"The farm failed," Rebecca answered. "My father and Mr. Jobb learned that people cannot expect food to grow by itself while the so-called farmers talked ethics."

"Your father?" Max asked.

Mrs. Dale said, "Don't be bitter, dear. Their hearts were in the right place."

"Regrettably, their experience was in other fields. I believe Mr. Jobb is an excellent minister, though."

"Very solid in his doctrine," Mrs. Dale agreed. "Now, about the wedding, Rebecca. You're sure you don't mind serving? Emma will do the heavy work, as usual. But if you'll hand around the Madeira and. . . ."

Max frowned. "Certainly not, Grandmother. Miss Clifton will be my guest."

Rebecca answered Mrs. Dale, not him. "Of course I'll help Emma with the service. Does she want me to make my cheese popovers too?"

"I'm not certain . . . I'll ask her."

"This is preposterous!"

"Will five dollars be enough? I hope you can stay to clear up afterwards."

Five dollars would nearly pay the butcher. At least it would keep him from scowling so dreadfully every time she went in. "You're always so generous to me, Mrs. Dale."

"I'll give you ten dollars," Max said, "to come with me."

Rebecca gave him a slow up and down glance. "I am not for sale, Captain."

"I didn't mean that." Heedless to his grandmother's

interest, Max seized Rebecca's wrist. "You're not a servant! I can't have you working like a kitchen slavey."

With a firm jerk, she freed herself. "There is nothing wrong with being a servant! And it's not as though I'm kept locked in the cellar until needed, you know. I've been of use to your grandmother on more than one occasion. . . ."

"Yes, I'm so grateful. . . ."

"And to be perfectly frank, we can use the money." She turned to Mrs. Dale. "I'll come by at three on Friday."

"Excellent. Really, Max, I don't see why you are making such a fuss. Miss Clifton has been invaluable to me. I can no longer sew as I used to, and you certainly don't suggest that I or Leonora should serve our guests."

"Of course not, Grandmother. But. . . ." His big shoulders lifted and fell.

Leonora appeared in the doorway, wearing part of her trousseau. "What's the row? Miss Clifton, you know the hem on this traveling dress *still* isn't straight. And when I tried on my blue batiste nightdress, I'm afraid I tore a little hole in the sleeve. Could you fix it please?"

Max said, "Go away, Birdie. We're having a discussion."

"The discussion is over, Captain Dale." Rebecca crossed the room to the door.

"So there," his sister added, poking out a little red tongue. "And you won't be able to talk to me like that much longer, Max. When I'm married, I mean. I don't think John would care for it."

"I've already told Philpot your pet name."

"Oh, you didn't! You're teasing! You know how I hate it!"

Max only grinned at her. Rebecca tried not to respond, though her heart gave a bound. He had the devil's own smile, and she was all but helpless when he used it. There must be some sort of sorcery at work, for what else could explain her dizzying response whenever he took her in his arms? Rebecca reminded herself sternly that this was 1848. Witchcraft belonged to another time and another part of Massachusetts.

She'd followed a stomping Leonora halfway down the

hall when she realized she'd left her sewing box in Max's room. After only a few steps, she could hear Mrs. Dale speaking, her voice slightly raised as though to compensate for her own hearing loss.

"Of course she's a dear girl. I don't know how I should have managed the last year or two without her. Leonora's sweet, but, as you know, handless. I'm glad John Philpot has enough money that she won't have to do her own housework, for she'd do a very poor job of it."

Max said something which Rebecca could not make out. Hating herself for eavesdropping, she stepped quietly nearer. She caught only the last few words. ". . . wrong with her?"

"Nothing, except her family."

"Well, if we are going to count families, your own father. . . ."

"He was never convicted of anything and you know it."

"Of course not, darling. But the Cliftons at least never ran guns to two sides at once."

"No, they haven't the energy! I shan't mention her father. Concord is used to eccentric gentlemen. Did I ever tell you what that Thoreau man said to me? Well, he was very offhand. But the oddity in the Clifton family is also in her sister."

"Yes, I've heard about Daphyne."

"I should hate to see any of that bluestocking trait in any descendant of mine! And Rebecca's a dear child, but far too self-sacrificing. She'd make a selfish tyrant out of any man she married, and very few men have the strength to resist that sort of spoiling."

"You think it's better to be like Leonora and her John? She'll never be anything more than decorative, Grandmother."

"What more would any sensible man want in a wife? As long as he is rich enough to enjoy her, that is. I used to be rather decorative myself."

"And still are."

Mrs. Dale laughed. "Well, we mustn't leave Mr. Jobb alone any longer. He'll think it very odd I've been away this long."

Rebecca turned and tiptoed lightly away. When Mrs. Dale came out, Rebecca seemed to just be coming down the hall. "I forgot my sewing box," she said breathlessly.

"I do hope Leonora hasn't ruined that nightdress. She is so careless!"

He stood frowning out the window, his hands clasped behind him as though he stood on his own deck. Come to think of it, the sparsely furnished room was somewhat like a cabin—everything neat and in its proper place, save for where he'd disturbed the papers on his desk. Moving as quietly as possible, Rebecca crossed the room and reached out for her little mahogany box. She had just lifted the brass handle when he swung around and took a step toward her.

"Rebecca, I want to talk to you."

She thrust out her hand. "You stay where you are."

"Why?" he asked, taking another step. "Don't you trust me? Or is it yourself you don't trust?" The light was behind him and his fair hair glowed like a halo. Rebecca knew better than to believe his saintly appearance.

"What did you have to say, Captain Dale?"

"Isn't it time you called me Max?"

"Stop!" she ordered, snatching up her sewing box. She backed away, her insides quickening with excitement as he pursued with slow steps.

"You can't deny that there is something powerful between us, Rebecca."

"I can't deny it, but I can't explain it either. And something without an explanation cannot exist." She misnavigated, for instead of exiting through the open doorway, she backed up against a wall. "That's . . . that's what my father says."

"A very learned gentleman, I'm sure. But in this case, wrong." He planted his hands on either side of her head. She had to look up into his eyes or shut her own. The scent that was so uniquely his surrounded her. Had the sea sunk into his very being that she could still smell its freshness?

He did not begin the delicious assault upon her good sense that she trembled to experience again. "Tell me truthfully. Have you ever known anything remotely like this before?"

"Never," she confessed. "Nor ever wanted to."

"Neither have I. It could be that I have been at sea too long, and yet . . . I spent a week in Charleston before coming home and met half a dozen young ladies, the daughters of men I had business with. Not a one of them inspired such. . . ." He shook his head as he sought for a word.

"Lust?" Rebecca could hardly believe she knew such a word, let alone understand what it meant. That she said it to a man who was virtually a stranger only convinced her more that she had lost some vital piece of moral machinery.

"Lust," he repeated.

Hearing that word spoken by his deep voice did things to Rebecca. It called up in her mind a kaleidoscope of images as uncontrollable as a swirl of leaves in a windy lane. Meeting his eyes, she felt he knew exactly what she was thinking. She licked her dry lips, unable to move when his gaze fell to her mouth.

Inch by inch, he lowered himself, bending his elbows. More lightly than a breath, he skimmed her lips with his own. He must have felt the tremor that passed through her as her eyes closed in surrender.

Then he straightened his arms, drawing away. "If it's only lust," he said, in a voice striving for normalcy, "then we should be able to fight it off."

"Yes, we must fight it."

"The best thing for me to do is to take some religious instruction. It may be somewhat difficult. After all, Rob Jobb and I did used to steal apples together."

"Did you?" She wanted to press her lips to the side of his throat, to steal from his lips the kisses he withheld. Perhaps he read her desire in her eyes. His arms trembled as though he had to struggle to keep his elbows locked.

With sudden strength, he pushed away from her. "I never suspected I was a coward until this moment. But if I don't leave now. . . ." In the doorway, he looked back at her. "I

don't understand it any more than you do, Rebecca. Maybe
you're right and I should just stay away from you."

When he'd gone, Rebecca let out the breath she seemed
to have held forever. Without the wall to support her, she
would have slid to the ground in an exhausted heap. If this
was how tired unfulfilled passion left a person, no wonder
lust was a sin. Marriage must change things, she thought, or
else husbands and wives would do nothing but sleep.

Realizing her left hand was painfully cramped, she
glanced down in wonder. She'd kept her clutch on her
sewing box, the brass handle leaving a deep red score across
her fingers. It reminded her Leonora waited for her. Walking
down the hall, she had to skim the wall with one hand to
keep on a steady course.

As soon as Daphyne came back from Leonora's wedding,
she ran up the stairs to her sister's bedroom, making more
noise than a blacksmith competition. "Oh, 'Becca, you
should have come with us. The Sewing Circle had decorated
everything with evergreen garlands and holly—it looked
just like a druidic temple."

Rebecca sat up, taking the damp cloth from her eyes.
"I'm sure that didn't occur to them."

"I know. They didn't seem at all pleased when Father
pointed it out to them. Leonora certainly looked happy. I
don't think much of her new husband though. He doesn't
look like he has much soul—if anything, he's running a
little to fat. She'd do well to make a Grahamite of him."

"Living on graham flour crackers and vegetables wouldn't
appeal much to Leonora. Any more than it appealed to me
when Father made us live on that regime for a year." Pushing
the coverlet aside, Rebecca sat up.

"Were you sleeping?" Daphyne took off her hat and
sought the pins in her hair. The dark waves fell onto her
shoulders. Frowning, she began to vigorously brush out the
fluffy softness, aiming as always for perfect smoothness.

"No, only resting. I shall be on my feet for most of the
evening." Coming behind Daphyne, she took the brush from
her hand. "Sit down and I'll do the back."

After pinning up a knot, she began to brush a section of Daphyne's hair round and round her finger to make a dangling curl. "Did you . . . see Captain Dale?"

"He was a groomsman. I'm tired of ringlets," Daphyne said. "They're frivolous."

"I'll braid it then and pin it in loops over your ears. That's a more serious look." If she had to envy one thing about Daphyne, it would be her hair. It could be fixed in any style and could be counted on to stay as arranged. Remembering how Max had touched her hair, she spoiled a braid with her shaking hands and had to do it over.

"Did you speak to him?"

"No, he was much too busy. Mr. Philpot seemed to be having trouble with his knees. But I think Max recognized me. At least, he stared at me."

"Did he? Hold this," she said, giving Daphyne the end of a braid. "I'd better put my wrapper on before I catch my death. There's a draft."

"The church was stifling. Father wanted to leave in the middle of the ceremony for fresh air, and I must say I agreed with him. It'll be a wonder if everyone there doesn't come down with the typhoid."

"Don't say it! Even as a joke."

"All right," Daphyne said, looking up hurt. "I still think they should have opened the windows."

"It's not exactly a summer's day. What will you say if you see him tonight?"

"I'm sure to see him. But I don't think I'll have to say anything. He'll say everything." She took up the maple hand-mirror. "That is more like a serious scholar's coiffure. I like it. You are always so good to me, 'Becca."

"It's easy to be good to you. Daphyne . . . if everything shouldn't go as you want. . . ."

"Why shouldn't it?" The younger girl stood up. "It's like you to try to protect me. But you know, destiny is a force like gravity or the wind. It can't be stopped. Captain Dale merely needed more time than I did to see where his destiny lies. I know he'll discover what's right tonight."

In the face of such sublime confidence, Rebecca could do

nothing. She was very much afraid that Daphyne was about to be hurt. Yet perhaps this letdown would be a blessing in disguise. She couldn't be allowed to dream any more of her life away.

If Max could make it clear, gently, that he had no intention of fulfilling Daphyne's fantasy, then Daphyne would be free to find someone near her own age and outlook. Someone like Thomas Rhodes, for instance. They would make a perfect couple, though Rebecca knew it would mean one more person she'd have to care for. Mr. Rhodes had about as much sense when it came to practical matters as her father.

Rebecca began to brush her own hair. She prayed that her hopes for Daphyne's future happiness were not selfish ones. Max and she had agreed that there was nothing between them but an animal attraction. She had no business wishing for more.

As it turned out, Mr. Clifton decreed that he'd suffered enough social congress for one day and decided to stay home from the Philpot's wedding levee. He had deputized Mr. Rhodes to escort his daughters. "You young people can never get enough pleasure," he said. "Yet remember that with age comes reflection and regret for the wasted hours."

"Yes, Father." Rebecca supposed he just hadn't noticed that it was three o'clock in the afternoon and that the wedding reception was not due to begin until six. Nor would he have noticed that she wore a plain black dress, hardly suitable for a festive occasion unless one was to be present at but not actually *attending* such an occasion.

She added a pinch more mustard to the beans baking in the oven. The rich brown sauce bubbled up with an aroma of molasses and ketchup. Putting back the cast-iron lid, she pulled on the chain, and the stubby-legged pot rose far enough above the fire not to scorch, but near enough to remain warm. Putting the mustard back, she turned to her father.

"Listen," she put her hand over the page he was reading. He tried to read between her fingers before looking up with the air of a startled owl. "Father, listen. At six o'clock, when

Mr. Rhodes comes for Daphyne, you are to eat your dinner. At six o'clock, Father."

"Ah, yes. What happens at six o'clock?"

It wasn't really his fault, she reflected, her cloak billowing about her as she walked. Her mother had thought him a young god, destined to take his place between Socrates and Aristotle, the Plato of the nineteenth century. When she died, there'd been no one with enough influence to drag Mr. Clifton into life's struggle. The young god turned into a befuddled man, desperately searching in his philosophy for the reason behind the death of his wife, the one event he'd never imagined.

Arriving at the Dales' home, Rebecca went around to the back door. The cook, Roger's wife, opened to her. "Thank goodness it's you, Miss Clifton! Everything's going wrong!"

"What's the matter?"

"The cake didn't rise—there must of been something wrong with the saleratus soda. And the cat's been at the cream!"

Rebecca tied on the calico apron Emma handed to her. There was another one, spotlessly white and trimmed with lace that would go on over her plain dress when it came time for her to serve. Unbuttoning her sleeves, she pushed them up to her elbows. "Do you have any pearl ash in the house? And send Roger down the road to Mrs. Haney. She's been bragging that her cow gives as rich a milk in winter as in summer. Now's her chance to put her money on the line."

She was in the midst of beating rosewater into her own favorite cake recipe when Max came in. Giving him a level look, she said, before he could speak, "I haven't time to talk."

"I haven't come to talk," he said with a wink. "Emma's running around in hysteria, shrieking that the sky is falling. What can I do to help?"

"You can peel and core those quinces if you want to. I thought you'd be visiting the groom's family." She beat the cake more vigorously, hoping he hadn't noticed that she'd admitted thinking about him. Trying to concentrate on her task, she fought her eyes for they wanted to peer at him as he removed his coat and rolled up his sleeves in imitation of her.

"Grandmother made me bring her home early. She complained that her head ached but, privately, I think she doesn't care much for the Philpots. They treat her like a piece of valuable porcelain with a crack in it. Always trying to make her sit down and asking if she'd like a shawl."

"I would chafe under such treatment, too. It must be hard enough to forget one's years without being reminded every moment by the well-intentioned. Did you like them?"

"I like everyone." He stood back and brushed his hands together. "All done. Now what?"

"How did you do that so fast?"

"On a ship, you learn to do nearly everything quickly, or you may not have time to finish. There are few leisurely moments when you're under sail. What now?"

"Do you really want to help or are you just . . . because I'll make use of you if you stay. Any help at all is welcome at this point."

"Even mine? You flatter me. But, please, make whatever use of me you want to."

The glint in his eye was impossible to mistake. To cover her confusion, she said briskly, "You'd better put on an apron or you'll ruin your clothes." She pointed out the drawer where they were kept.

Max held the bright print against him and turned his back. "Tie it for me?"

Her hands trembled as they brushed his back. The white shirt was smooth linen and she could see the powerful molding of his muscles beneath it. Quickly, she made a bow and dropped her hands, curling her fingernails into her palms. They itched with a desire to run along the furrow his spine made, to give him pleasure that would make him turn and renew his bold possession of her lips.

"Those . . . those silver spoons need to be polished. That will keep you out of my way."

He entertained her with stories of his travels; of jungles teeming with brilliant birds and gigantic butterflies, of ceremonial feasts on islands where volcanic smoke still issued from the mountains, of the strange, man-made hillsides of Siam. He told her about receptions where Chinese mandarins looked past the barbarians as though they weren't present only to wager heavily with them later at dragon-boat races.

After touching on porcelain vases twice the height of a man and figures on lacquered screens that almost seemed alive, Max said, "I've never seen so much that was as beautiful and yet utterly mystifying as in China. A man could spend two lifetimes there and never know any more than when he came."

"I've heard," Rebecca said carefully, "that the women are especially lovely."

"You never heard that from Père Gascoigne!" He chuckled and then said, "Yes, some of them are as lovely as dreams, but it's a difficult thing to court a lady when you don't speak her language and she thinks you smell like rotten cabbage."

"No one could think. . . ." she started to say and then thought the better of it. "Surely, no one told you so to your face?"

"Do you have to tell someone when you find them offensive? It doesn't matter where you live; some things cannot be hidden." He wrinkled his nose and crossed his eyes while waving an imaginary fan in short strokes.

Rebecca laughed at his game and shook her head. Replacing the nutmeg, ginger, and cinnamon on the shelf kept for such things, she froze, her hand drawn back in midair.

"What is it?" Max asked, rising.

"Nothing." Rubbing the back of her neck, she studied the painted floorcloth almost as if she expected to find the answer there. She gave the shelf a quick, suspicious glance, then shrugged. "Something struck me as odd, but I think it's just one of those mental lapses. Maybe I forgot something and putting things away half-reminded me."

"You're tired, aren't you, Rebecca?" He came up behind her and laid his heavy, warm hands on the top of her shoulders. With strong thumbs, he began to rub away the tension that kept her back straight and her head resolutely up.

"No," she said, her eyes closing. "No, I had a good rest before I came."

His breath stirred her hair. He used his palms now, pressing in firm circles over her shoulder blades and spine. She sighed and leaned against the delightful pressure. The magic his touch wove around her stole bit by bit over her body and mind. If Max had been even an eighth as compassionate toward Daphyne as he was toward her, it no longer surprised Rebecca that her sister fell in love strongly enough to outlast six years of silence.

Summoning up all her moral fiber, Rebecca jerked away from his wonderful hands. Facing him, she said forthrightly, "You saw Daphyne in church today, I think."

"Was she there? You never did tell me what she looked like."

"You ought to remember. I'm shorter and my hair is lighter, but our noses are the same."

"I can't say I've spent a lot of time looking at your nose. It's seldom the first thing a man notices about a woman. Now that I consider it, however, . . ."

"Are you going to say that you didn't see Daphyne?"

He shrugged. "Not if you don't want me to. 'Course, I was fairly occupied. You would have thought John was going to his execution, not his wedding. And Leonora suddenly seemed to realize why she was wearing white and panicked. Oh, it was a wedding to remember all right. I had little time to check the house, as the actors say."

Taking her hand in his, he stroked the back. "Come now, you don't believe any longer that I seduced your sister."

When his laughing blue eyes fixed on hers, Rebecca wanted to believe that he hadn't. Yet, didn't he know women all over the world? Perhaps Daphyne had been his girl in Boston, to match the one in Caracas, and others in Bergen or New Orleans. Rebecca knew how close she was to becoming his light-of-love in Concord.

Possibly he read the doubt in her eyes for he lifted her hand to his lips. He kissed the red knuckles one by one, then turned her hand over and pressed a kiss into the palm. "Even if I had," he said, "it was a long time ago. And I didn't know about you."

Rebecca snatched her hand away. "You did see her!"

"No, I swear it." The laughter faded from his eyes, and she saw him grow stern and uncompromising. "You may believe me or not, but I never lie, Rebecca."

His smile came back. "Besides, when I did look around the church, it was only to see what that madman was up to."

"That was probably my father," she said, feeling as though lightning had struck her. Was it possible that Daphyne's novel had been made of whole cloth?

"Then your father was drunk, or next door to it. He kept looking under the pews, claiming to have lost his pet cat."

"My father abstains from alcohol."

"I doubt tea would satisfy the man I saw. He had shaggy white hair and carried, into the church, mind you, a leather satchel that looked old enough to have been Noah's luggage aboard the Ark."

Rebecca frowned, for something in that description teased her memory as had the sight of Emma's spice shelf. "Well, it wasn't my father. He hasn't much hair anymore, at least not on top. He wears gray side whiskers."

"The funny thing was," Max continued, "the gentleman I saw sat through the whole ceremony and then came up to offer me his felicitations on *my* marriage. He seemed very surprised when I told him I hadn't a bride in mind. Come to think of it, I didn't smell alcohol on his breath. Maybe he was mad."

"Of whom are you speaking?" asked Mrs. Dale from the doorway. She had changed into her evening dress, an elegant pearl-gray silk lavished with pure white lace. A matching lace cap sat upon her painstakingly waved hair.

Max turned to her, this time without displaying any discomfiture at being seen talking with Rebecca. "Of that odd man at Birdie's wedding."

"What odd man?"

Describing him again, Max said, "You must have seen

him, Grandmother. He was looking for his cat. And he asked me if I had any bait. As if I always carry some."

"Bait?" Rebecca asked.

"Yes, you know. Worms. He really was very peculiar."

"No, I saw no one like that," Mrs. Dale said. "How are the arrangements coming, Rebecca?"

Though she'd overheard Mrs. Dale's opinion of her family, Rebecca couldn't find it in herself to dislike her. If anything, she had to acknowledge the justice of what she'd heard. "I'm sure Emma told you about the cake. I've made a new one, flavored with rosewater and orange."

"It should be delicious. Did you hide the tokens in it?"

Rebecca put her hand to her mouth, screwing up her eyes in self-condemnation. "No, they're in the first cake and I forgot. I'll dig them out now."

Raising her eyes to her grandson, Mrs. Dale said, "I can understand how you might forget."

The little holes where Rebecca had pushed the good luck charms into the cake with a clean broomstraw were easily hidden by the icing. At the reception, after the bride had cut the cake, the young people sought earnestly for the silver ring, the sixpence, and the baby. No one seemed to mind spoiling their gloves as they laughed and teased one another. The older folk shook their heads reminiscently.

Rebecca could understand how a stranger might mistake Max for the bridegroom. His blue frock coat made him look even taller than he was, and the gold watch chain festooned across his flat stomach gave him the air of a respectable citizen. Poor Mr. Philpot, whose clothes were made by a London tailor to his measure, looked like a boy beside him.

Balancing a tray, Rebecca moved among her friends and neighbors. If they spoke to her, she smiled and answered, yet always continued moving. She was not paid to socialize, she told herself. Her white apron over the black dress, no matter how charmingly bedewed with lace, marked her out from among the debutantes and matrons as if she wore a placard around her neck.

Returning with the empty glasses to where Emma stood behind the punchbowl, Rebecca noticed that the cook looked as heated as something from her own ovens. "What's amiss?"

"It's not as if there weren't enough good things on this table. It's not as if I haven't been slaving all day—and you, too, Miss 'Becca—even though she is your sister, I'd give that girl a piece of my mind if we were private."

"What's Daphyne done?" She'd seen the younger girl for only a moment as she came in, her dark dress of slightly worn velvet as out of place as Rebecca's own. Not that Daphyne would have noticed what other women wore or fussed over her own clothes.

"Just brung her own bottle, that's all! As if Mrs. Dale hadn't broken out the port her husband put away fifty years ago."

"Daphyne brought spirits? That doesn't sound like her. Where would she get such a thing?"

"Said she made it herself—some kind of cordial." Emma pulled a small white bottle from her pocket. Traces of red sealing wax over the lip showed where the cork had been. "Said she wanted Mr. Max to try it. Something about it being an old family receipt."

Rebecca wasn't listening. She'd taken the phial, now cool and light, and ran her finger over the card still attached with golden thread to the neck. "To clear the sight. . . ." Suddenly, she remembered the strange old man in the wood.

"Where is Mr. Max now?"

Emma scanned the parlor. "I don't know, Miss 'Becca. Maybe in the library?"

"The library. Of course."

As quickly as she could, Rebecca cut through the crowded room. The library was down the hall from the parlor, and the sounds of gaiety faded into disembodied noises once the door was shut. Daphyne was just closing the double mahogany doors to the library, letting herself out.

Rebecca caught her roughly by the arm. "What have you done?"

"Stop. You're hurting me!"

"Where's Max?"

"In there. Asleep."

Fearful, Rebecca jerked open the door. The firelight danced on the spines of the books, bringing out the gold-leaf titles and designs. All she could see of Max were his pantaloons and shoes, for his legs were thrust out and the rest of him hidden by the enfolding wings of an armchair. To her lasting relief, she saw one foot lift and cross over the other and heard a contented sigh. She quietly closed the door so as not to disturb him.

Turning to her sister, she asked, "Did you give him something out of that white bottle? How could you? You don't even know what's in it. It could be poison for all you know."

"Of course it isn't," Daphyne said with fine disdain. "Anybody can tell it's a love potion."

"A love . . . Daphyne, have you lost your mind? There's no such thing. Listen," she said, halting the girl's half-uttered protest. "That bottle came from some half-cracked man I met. It could be anything. We'll hope it was harmless. Did you drink any of it yourself?"

"No, my sight is already clear," Daphyne said with sublime confidence. "It was Max that needed to have his eyes opened. Now he knows I am his true love. Or at least, he will as soon as he drinks."

"He hasn't. . . . Thank God. Daphyne, get back to the parlor. I'll talk to you later!"

"All right, Rebecca. I don't understand why you're so angry, though. Obviously, that potion was meant for me."

"Potions, my dear foolish sister, are only in fairy tales and such rubbish. They don't exist."

"Many eminent authors. . . ." Daphyne began. She broke off and said, "Mr. Rhodes will explain it to you. I saw him arrive a few minutes ago. I'll put it to him and he'll tell you."

"Do what you want," Rebecca said, dismissing her. She opened the library doors and went in.

No other man, it seemed, had sought the refuge of this quiet study, away from the gabble and gossip of the women. Only Max sat and slumbered. There was no cup or goblet on the table at his elbow, nor let down to the floor by nerveless fingers.

She stepped closer to him. His breathing seemed clear and his color was good. With luck, if he had drunk the "potion," it proved to be a harmless jumble of flavorings or even the cordial that Daphyne had claimed it to be. Dragging her gaze away from the thick lashes that shaded his cheeks, telling herself that she did not feel any tenderness toward him asleep, she searched the room for the glass.

On the white marble mantelpiece, she saw a clear glass goblet, like a cone set into a base. John Hancock and Samuel Adams had drunk toasts to their new nation from this set of glasses. Mrs. Dale was immensely proud of them and of the fierce eagles her future father-in-law had ordered incised into the glass to mark the occasion.

Rebecca cradled the goblet in her fingers. A drain of cherry-red liquid swirled around, clinging somewhat to the sides of the glass. Whether sipped or gulped, the drink was gone.

"Should I have saved you some?" he asked, his voice rumbling in her ear.

Surprised, Rebecca let the precious goblet fall. Almost too quickly for her to see, Max stooped and caught it, juggling it upright. The last few drops of liquid splattered on the red brick hearth and glittered like rubies in the dancing firelight.

Max put the glass back on the mantel. "I had a talk with your sister," he said without preamble.

"Do you remember her now?"

"Yes, I do."

Rebecca braced herself to hear the truth. He must have sensed her tension, for he chucked her lightly beneath the chin. "Don't look like that. I'm not confessing to a murder, you know."

"What are you confessing to?"

"It's very simple," he continued. "I went to school that day to visit Leonora. I visited her all the more eagerly because I knew that there would be at least half a dozen young ladies, all willing to admire a dashing sailor. At twenty-four, I was somewhat susceptible to a pretty face and cared little what lay behind it. I must say in all modesty that pretty girls liked me then about as much as I liked them."

"I can believe it," Rebecca muttered.

He gave her an engaging smile. "However, the easy conquests are never the most satisfying. My taste cast around for something more piquant."

"You can't say Daphyne isn't lovely. She was pretty even at sixteen. I remember how I envied her. At that age, I had spots."

"Oh, Daphyne was a beauty. But of a serious mind. I suppose I found her intriguing. It must have pleased me to steal a kiss or two from her."

Rebecca didn't know whether to be amused or exasperated by his impersonal description of his actions of six years ago. "And it never occurred to you that she might take you seriously?"

"I can't say that at the time much made me consider the future. For all my time at sea—I first left home at thirteen, you know—I was woefully green. Especially where girls were concerned. I've learned a great deal since then."

"I haven't noticed. You still love to flirt." She could now see their embraces in that light. She would have been as big a fool as Daphyne if she gave into the temptation of thinking he meant anything else by them.

"Oh, but I have," he said, a light in his eyes she knew. "I've learned never to kiss a maid when I can kiss her mistress, and never kiss a girl when I can kiss her older sister."

The fire behind her burned less intently than the heat that flared between them. A deep trembling shook her. She wanted to kiss him, wanted to melt into his arms until sanity and principle swirled away. Yet, for the moment, she was still sane.

"No! I don't. . . ."

He stepped away from her, hurt etching lines of confusion in his brow. Unable to meet his look, Rebecca felt unaccountably ashamed, as though it were she who had owned to a fickle heart.

Max drew her again into his arms, resting his cheek on the plain cap that covered her smooth red-brown hair. She heard the smile in his voice when he said, "I think you've misunderstood me, my dear. All that, my volatile affections, my roving eye, no longer exists. I think I have found the one woman to make with me a safe harbor."

Very gently, he tipped her face back. Rebecca couldn't help but open her eyes. "You're the one," he said steadily. "Don't ask me how I know it. Will you marry me?"

The thing that bewildered her the most was her longing to agree. She did not think of the hardship of her life or the difficulties that marriage would solve. To say yes would make Max happy and somehow his happiness had become indescribably important to her.

Then she seemed to hear again Daphyne saying something about a love potion. Rebecca fought to dismiss the ridiculous notion but certainly Max's proposal was astoundingly sudden. If there really were such a thing as a love philtre. . . .

"Why do you want to marry me?" she asked.

"If you don't take the . . . I don't know why. Why does the sun rise every morning? Ask me why the mountains don't fly off into the stars. I only know that you have brought something special into my life."

"What?" By now they stood some feet apart. Max leaned with his elbow on the mantel, studying her. Rebecca wished she had the power to accept at face value his abrupt proposal. Far from looking at her with love, he seemed irritated.

"Does there have to be a reason? I want to marry you."

"You're feeling quite yourself?"

He laughed, with little humor. "Do I have to be a lunatic to want you for my wife?"

"It might help."

He reached out and caught her hand. "I'm waiting for your answer."

She was mute. She told herself that he couldn't possibly be in love with her. Therefore, either this proposal of his was a cruel joke—which she did not choose to believe—or he truly was in love with her—which she found hard to believe. Finally, his offer could come from the elixir he drank, in which case she would have to accept the existence of a love potion—which she utterly refused to believe.

"I see," he said, gently putting her hand down and turning aside.

"No!" Rebecca grabbed hold of his sleeve. "I need . . . time. I don't know what to say. I need to talk to my father, to see. . . ."

Max's face lightened. "Of course you do. Shall I ask him formally for your hand?"

"I don't think that will be necessary. You'd only confuse him." She couldn't imagine that her father and Max would have very much in common. Max had roamed the world, had given and taken commands, and had found adventure even in mundane Concord. Her father had always claimed that brains were better than brawn, although he'd probably never met anyone like Max, who combined the best of both qualities.

"What are you smiling for?"

"I didn't know I was."

"You have an enchanting smile, Rebecca. It was that, I think, that first made me love you. Don't look so shocked. I intend to say 'I love you' often over the next thirty or forty years."

"I haven't said I'll marry you."

"Oh, I'll go on saying it to you whether you marry me or not. Every time I pass you on the street, I'll lift my hat and say, 'I love you, Miss Clifton.' When you see me in church, you'll know what I'm saying to you, or in a shop, or . . . so you see, it'll be much less a strain if you marry me."

Laughing despite herself, Rebecca said, "You know, I sincerely doubt it."

A few minutes later, during which Max said things to make her cheeks burn, they emerged from the library. He said, "You better put your cap straight."

She stopped in front of a round mirror, thick with gold leaf and surmounted by another eagle. Her reflection was no more than a squat face at the bottom edge of the convex surface. "You go ahead," she said, moving back and forth to find herself. "I'll be a few minutes."

Her cap looked as though it were on backwards, probably from when he laid his cheek against it. Rebecca was unprepared for the surge of tenderness that arose in her at the thought of his doing that. She could almost feel her heart expanding and growing softer. It unnerved her.

Rebecca knew she had to talk to Daphyne. Though Max believed Daphyne had accepted what he remembered of their meeting, Rebecca had seen no sign that her sister was willing to surrender her dreams so easily. Rebecca dismissed from her mind the nonsense about a love potion. Such things were for fools who believed in *Grimm's Fairy Tales,* fools like Daphyne.

She hurried back to the table where Emma had done valiant service alone since she'd gone looking for Max. The tray, full of filled glasses, stood near the punchbowl. As she lifted it, Rebecca said, "I'm sorry I was so long."

"Hmph! All the same to me! So far as I care, they can all scud up to the table and get their own."

Rebecca wasn't listening. She stared at two objects on the white-linen-swathed table, willing herself to stop seeing double. She blinked hard and shook her head, but still the plain white bottles refused to merge into one.

"Where did that come from?"

"I'm surprised you asked. It's yours 'course."

"Then what about that one?"

"Yours, too . . . oh, no wait." Fortunately, Emma never stayed mad for very long. "That good Rhodes boy left it here. I thought I'd offer it to you. They do make a nice decoration sitting there together. 'Course, if you don't want 'em. . . ."

Rebecca would have been satisfied never to see anything like them again. "Where's Mr. Rhodes?"

"He and Miss Daphyne . . ."

Still carrying the tray, Rebecca went in search of her sister and the tall, thin boy who loved her. People stopped her now and again to take a drink. She smiled, nodding, her eyes always moving for the ones she sought. Then she saw them enter the room, snow sparkling and melting on their hair and shoulders.

Dangling from Thomas's hand were two goblets, a trace of clear red refracting the candlelight. The way her sister inclined toward Thomas, the new smile of adoration that curved her lips when she looked up at him, deeply troubled Rebecca. She clutched the tray as the foundations of her life shook with the force of a new idea.

Max appeared beside her. "You look as if you've just seen a ghost. Is everything all right?"

She looked up at him with dawning horror in her eyes. "Dear God, no!" The tray fell from her nerveless fingers with a shattering bang. Everyone stopped talking to stare, fans paused and glasses still raised.

Her hand flew to her lips as Rebecca backed away from Max, afraid to take her eyes off him. "I . . . I. . . ." Desperate to escape, she seized the slack of her skirt and twirled around, running out through the door to the kitchen. Stopping only to throw her cloak around her shoulders, she dashed out the back door and down the steps, hearing Max calling after her.

In the morning, she sat, white-faced, while Daphyne rapturously described her newly discovered love. "And of course, he's so intelligent, such a pure soul. I know I could never be happy with anyone unrefined or materialistic. Can you imagine anything worse than having to listen to someone prose on and on about tons manufactured and shipping and . . . that sort of thing? I'd have no soul left if I'd had to marry someone like John Philpot. Oh, he's all right for Leonora. . . ."

"What about Max? Captain Dale?"

"Who? I can see now that was just a girlish fancy. Thomas has so many good qualities. He's patient, kind, and, though it shows a want of pure spirit on my part, such beautiful brown eyes. Don't you think brown is really the best color for a man's eyes? Who'd want them to be hazel or blue?"

This certainly seemed like enchantment. The first thing

Rebecca had done last night, coming home half-frozen and thoroughly miserable, was to make sure that one of those mysterious white bottles had indeed come from here.

"Daphyne, did you take that bottle of Heart's Desire that was here?"

"I didn't know you had any heartsease."

"Not ease; desire. I had a bottle of it and now it's gone."

"No, I haven't seen it. Maybe you put it somewhere else. Thomas says that everything should have a specific place and that mine is in his heart. Isn't that a wonderful sentiment?"

Rebecca remembered how all memory of the strange man in the woods had apparently been wiped out of her thoughts. The same impenetrable fog that now enraptured her sister worried her. Could it really be that Daphyne had forgotten everything that had happened before she agreed to marry Thomas? There had to be some explanation besides—she almost feared to think it—magic. Rebecca decided that she needed to have a talk with her future brother-in-law.

Daphyne sat up, listening. "Is that a horse? Maybe Thomas has come by. Is my hair neat?"

"You look very nice," Rebecca said. "Go and let him in." Actually, her sister gave off a radiance like the moon's, soft and spiritual. Rebecca let her head sink into her hands, her elbows propped up on the table. The words that had pounded in her brain all night long repeated. "There's no such thing as magic, but if there were . . . if there were. . . ."

A pound of rich, shining fudge suddenly appeared before her on the table. Rebecca jerked back, looking up to see Max grinning down at her. "I asked Emma what you liked."

It had been more than twelve hours, but his besottedness showed no signs of wearing off. He sat down and smiled across the table at her. "You left suddenly last night."

"I had to," she said, falteringly.

"That's all right. Grandmother had me bring you your five dollars. I'm glad you won't have to work anymore. I'm going to take care of you, now and always."

"Max . . . about that. . . ."

"I'm just waiting for your father to finish with Thomas Rhodes. He, I think, came for a similar reason."

"Max, I can't marry you."

He went on smiling at her. "Why not?"

"Well, it's a little difficult to explain." She decided it was impossible to say, well, you don't really love me, you just think you do because of that drink my sister gave you last night.

Leaning toward her, Max said, "You're amazingly lovely in the morning, Rebecca. I can't take my eyes from you."

"Please don't. I don't know how to answer you when you say things like that."

"Leonora simpers when someone compliments her; I don't think you'd want to do that. Just smile at me."

She couldn't keep from smiling at him. When he had walked into the kitchen, she felt the same as when she threw open the doors at both ends of the house to the first warm breeze of May. Her heart was full of envy of his sister, his grandmother and of the lowliest sailor in his crew. They could see him anytime.

"I'll get you some coffee," she said, remembering her manners.

"I'd rather look at you."

"You can look and drink."

Safe in the kitchen, Rebecca gripped the edge of the dry sink, feeling as though she were about to fall off the edge of the world. *She* hadn't drunk any of that potion, so she had no excuse. If her pulse leaped high the moment she'd seen him, if she felt flushed and hot, why, then, she must be sickening for something. A good dose of sulfur and molasses would set her straight. Perhaps she should give some to Max—it might prove an antidote.

He followed her. Rebecca turned, instantly defensive. He came up close to her, his shoulders like a wall. "You have to stop running away from me. How 'bout a good morning kiss?"

As he brushed her temple with his lips, Rebecca drove her nails into her palms, they itched so with the longing to ruffle his bright hair. She couldn't feel the pain. The soft warmth of his lips against her cheek drove out every other sensation. She fully meant to protest, to push away. Instead, she found her arms about his neck.

She strained upwards, all of her body pressing firmly against his. She gave him all her passion with her lips, because, she knew, she might never have the chance again. Once the potion wore off, he might kiss her as he had before, but never again with love.

He did love her, no matter why. He kissed her with such tenderness, not unmixed with a fervent longing. Holding her gently, he whispered, "You must be mine. I won't hear of waiting. If you haven't a napkin or tea towel to your name, I'll buy whatever you need after we are wed."

Though every nerve in her body protested, Rebecca moved back. "I still cannot marry you."

But he had heard the front door close. "Who's that?"

"Father. He's going out to read *Ivanhoe* to the cows. He says they like it better than Dickens." This must be sorcery. "Did you hear what I said, Max?"

"Of course. And I understand. After all, we haven't known each other but a few days. Don't be nervous, though. You'll have thirty years or so to get used to me."

She stopped him from going outside, her hand on his sleeve. "Tell me this, then. Why do you want to marry me?"

"Did anyone ever tell you that you ask a lot of questions? Why, indeed!" But he didn't quite meet her eyes, looking off slantingly out the window. Then slowly, the words came. "It was when you came down the stairs, that first day, so calmly, one hand on the bannister, not clutching it or disdaining it. You set your feet just so and I knew. That's all. I just knew."

Rebecca sighed. If only it were true. "Are you sure you didn't fall in love with me yesterday?"

"Only deeper in love, Rebecca." His engaging smile returned. "I'll go see your father." Halfway out the door he turned and said, "Where and why did you fall in love with me? Think it over. It's not an easy thing to answer."

That she knew already. It must be a comfort to swallow a potion and immediately have all doubts and conflicts wiped away. But such an easy path wouldn't do for her. Firmly she put down the temptation to take his love at any price. If she could not have Max's love without magical trickery, she didn't want it at all.

Determined, Rebecca marched into the library. Daphyne flew off Thomas Rhodes's knee like a startled dove. "Father's gone out to the barn," she said.

"I don't want to talk to Father. I want to talk to you, Thomas."

Daphyne asked, "What about?"

"Never mind. You run up and put on your cloak and bonnet. Perhaps Mr. Rhodes will take you for a drive into town later. We are out of tea . . . and cocoa."

"I'd enjoy that," Thomas said, his spectacled gaze fixed on Daphyne. Even after she left the room, he stared at the open doorway as though willing her to return.

Rebecca closed the door, first making certain her sister had actually gone upstairs. Then she faced Thomas, her fists on her hips. "I suppose you also met that man in the lane."

Thankfully, he didn't dissemble or ask her what she was talking about. "He offered me what I wanted most and didn't charge very much."

"No, he doesn't charge much at all. He just takes your peace of mind. How could you do it, Thomas?"

"The same reason you did it to Captain Dale."

"*I* didn't do it. Daphyne did it!" she declared, pointing up at the ceiling. "About fifteen minutes before you gave it to her, near as I can figure it."

"Oh," he said, running his nervous fingers back through his hair. "I didn't know that. Once she drank the elixir, she never mentioned him again."

Rebecca let go some of her righteous indignation. "I know you're very fond of Daphyne. . . ."

"I worship that girl. I . . . I always have, even when she and I were children. She's not like other girls."

"That goes without saying. But I'm not like other girls, either. I won't marry Max Dale under these circumstances. And you're going to help me."

"What can I do?" Thomas asked, shrinking back.

Looking around at the tall shelves that lined the walls of her father's library, Rebecca said, "Somewhere there must be something to say or do that will break this . . . this spell. Daphyne tells me you're a well-educated man. You can find the answer more easily than I can."

"But I don't want to know it!"

"Personally, I think Daphyne should have married you a long time ago, Thomas. But don't you want her to love you for yourself and not because you gave her a potion?"

"I'm weary of waiting for her to love me that way. When the Heart's Desire was offered to me, I couldn't seem to say no."

"That man in the lane was very persuasive. You didn't *send* for him, did you?"

"No, I wouldn't know how."

"I wish you did. He'd know how to undo it. Max said he saw someone like that at Leonora's wedding. When you go into town later, you look around for him . . . what was his name? Harper?"

"I think so."

"Should be Archer. Yes, you find him. I want to give him a piece of my mind. Playing Cupid is dangerous."

When Thomas and Daphyne drove into Concord, there were several heavy and ancient-looking tomes on the floor between them. Rebecca handed Thomas her shopping list. He said quickly, pushing his glasses up, "These books may have what you want. I'll read them over tonight and let you know."

"I certainly hope you find something right away," she said, looking past him. Max and Mr. Clifton were returning from the barn, the sailor towering over the scholar.

"You shouldn't be out here without a wrap," Max said to her. "You mustn't catch cold."

"It's turning warmer," she said, waving as the small brown carryall started down the path. Daphyne wore an expression of such delight that for a moment Rebecca felt confused over the tack she'd taken. Surely anything that made someone so happy couldn't be all bad?

"Is it warm enough," Max asked, "for you to walk with me?"

Rebecca hesitated. Yet a sneaking voice whispered that a walk could no do harm. When she gave Max the antidote to the potion, she could hope that their time together would be a pleasant memory for him, if one to be wondered at. As for herself, if memories were all there were to be for her, she would store up as sweet a treasure as she could.

"I'd love to come walking with you. Let me take off this apron and get my cloak."

A moment later, she sat on the bench that ran along one wall of the hall, her rubber galoshes beside her. "Let me," Max said, suddenly kneeling before her. He took a somewhat smelly black bootee in one hand and gently grasped her ankle with the other.

"You have pretty feet, Rebecca." Glancing up, he said, "Remember, just smile at me when I compliment you."

She tried, but her eyes were shimmering with tears and her lips trembled. When he looked up at her laughingly, she realized how much she loved him and exactly what her principles demanded she sacrifice.

"Dearest, what's wrong?" he asked in alarm.

Impulsively, Rebecca touched his cheek. He pressed her palm to his lips, never taking his eyes from hers. "Nothing," she said, knowing her smile wavered. "Let's hurry before it turns cold again."

Outside, she caught a glimpse of her father looking out his window. She lifted her hand and saw his slow wave in return. "Poor Father," she said. "He must be very confused right now, with suitors suddenly pursuing his daughters. He hates changes."

"That's not what I just heard. He told me in the barn how much healthier and happier we'd all be if we'd give up beefsteaks and earning a living. That sounds like a revolution to me."

"Father's very fond of revolutions. It's change he doesn't care for."

They stayed out late—not doing very much, wandering around the snowy woods. They saw the first snowdrops and crocuses, deer tracks, and the marks of hares and small, anonymous animals. Max told her about growing up at Elmloft without appreciating his advantages, for his heart had somehow been given to the sea.

"Won't it pain you to give up your wandering life?"

He didn't make a lover-like reply, to her relief. "I'll probably find it difficult at first. Who knows, I might be off again in a year. But I'd like to try. These steamers they have to cross the Atlantic; I'm impressed by their speed, but they're not the ships I've learned to love. If I must live with steam, I'll do it on dry land."

Daphyne had returned with the shopping by the time Max and Rebecca came home. She hardly glanced at the man who had been the focus of her dream-life for the past six years. "I put the corned beef on to boil," Daphyne said. "Is the captain staying for dinner?"

"No, thank you," he said, looking at Rebecca. "I promised Grandmother I'd be back by now. Shall I see you tomorrow?"

"If she doesn't need you."

"I'll make time." He aimed a hasty kiss at her lips, touching her cheek instead. His whistle came floating back on the still air as he went away.

Thomas Rhodes came back several hours later. Both Daphyne and Mr. Clifton had already retired, so Rebecca did not let her sister's lover in. Wrapping a shawl more tightly about her shoulders as she stepped outside, she asked, "Have you found something already?"

"Yes, in an old book about Hispaniola. Apparently the slaves there hold certain magical beliefs. Here." He handed her a small bag. "I wrote down the instructions. Burn this red candle."

"Where on earth did you find a red candle?"

"It's one of mother's beeswax ones. I've been dipping it in cranberry juice ever since I read this passage. Of course, it's more pink than red but it should do."

"Thank you, Thomas."

His thin shoulders shrugged. "It's marked off in inches. Every time the candle burns down an inch you say . . .

well, you can read it off the paper if you like. There was a lot of stuff and nonsense about graveyard dust and whatnot, but the principal effect seems to come from the candle."

"I'll begin first thing tomorrow morning."

"No, no," Thomas said. "According to this book, the magic works at night. You did seem in a hurry or I shouldn't have bothered to come back tonight."

"I'm very grateful, Thomas. If it works, I shall be sure to let you know."

"Don't bother. *I'm* completely happy with my choice."

In the morning, Rebecca felt sluggish and heavy-eyed. Even Max commented on her appearance when he arrived. "Were you dreaming about me? Or couldn't you sleep because you were so excited about marrying me? You still haven't given me your answer, you know."

The expression in his eyes told her the counterspell had not worked. Perhaps she should not have burned the candle in her room. After staring at the single flickering flame, she could not resist lying down for just a moment. When she awoke again, the candle had burned down some distance below the measure. She'd hurriedly repeated the incantation, yet the failure must have been enough to invalidate the spell.

"Would you like breakfast?"

"I'd rather have my answer. But if you need more time, please take it. As I said, I'm willing to wait as long as you need."

When Thomas Rhodes appeared, he looked offensively well-rested. "Didn't work, eh? Well, a Greek quoted in a manuscript clumsily translated by a fifteenth-century monk suggests . . . garlic." He thrust into her hand a papery bundle, the natural wrapping of the clove head.

"Garlic?" She hated the stuff. With a heavy sigh, she asked, "Eaten or worn?"

"Both."

That night she put it in the chicken, sprinkled it on the potatoes, and hid it in the bread dough. Daphyne was appalled. "Captain Dale will never want to marry you if this is your idea of a first dinner. Don't you want to impress him with what a good cook you are? He's going to think you can't cook anything without garlic!"

"That's what I hope," Rebecca replied. "Now, how can I make a pie with this stuff?" Though she wracked her brains, she couldn't think of a way to do it without making everyone ill. So she left the garlic out of the dessert, hoping that enough would be enough. She did manage to sprinkle a little on Max's collar while they kissed.

The next morning, the house still reeked of the herb. And Max had not fallen out of love with her yet. On the doorstep sat a Chinese puzzle box, left that morning with a note that turned her heart into a pincushion.

She sat down right there, heedless of the cold. After pushing on the satiny wood and then tugging, the box opened in her hands like a rose in bloom. Nestled at the heart was a gold ring with a turquoise stone. Rebecca knew that if Max saw the ring on her hand, he'd know he'd been accepted as her husband.

Deeply troubled, she put on the ring. It fit only her smallest finger. Clasping her hands behind her, she plodded along the path to the road, due to meet Max there for a sleigh ride. Thomas Rhodes had come up with another antidote, but her whole soul shrank from the idea of pushing Max into fresh cow droppings.

"Really, you know," said a voice she recognized, "I've almost never had a dissatisfied client with that particular formula before."

Her misery was such that not even the sight of Mr. Harper's massive companion, curled up with twitching tail at his feet, could rouse her. "I can't help it," she said. "It's wrong to trick someone into loving you."

"Ah, you modern girls! Things were different when I was young. Then it was every man—or woman—for himself. I suppose you want to know how to overcome the potion's power?"

"Very much." She sat down on a stump, noticing idly the green shoots of grass sprouting around the base. Concentrating hard, she prepared to memorize every step of the process.

Mr. Harper leaned back, closing his eyes as though to focus his thoughts. "Tell him," he said.

"Tell him . . . what?"

Even the tiger gave her a look of scorn before beginning to wash one gigantic paw. "Tell him," Harper said, "exactly what happened. Only very powerful love can withstand the truth."

"That's all? No incantations, no herbs, nothing but the truth?"

"Well, that's done the trick in the past, more often than not." Both man and tiger turned their heads toward the road. "Here he comes now."

Rebecca also looked to her right. "I don't hear. . . ." The two of them had vanished, as if melted into the silence and the snow. The hairs pricked up along her arms. Very slowly, she stood up and edged away down the path. Now, she heard the bells on Max's sleigh and began to run.

She sat in a daze for some time in the sleigh. Max seemed to realize that she didn't want to talk. When she looked up at last from her cold hands, she realized they were arriving at Elmloft. "Are you bringing me to see your grandmother?"

"No, she's in town with that friend of hers that is always having palpitations or lumbago or some other thing. What I need you for is—well, I've had some things sent for from the last trip I made. I thought you might like to pick out a few rugs, draperies and such for our house."

Standing above him, her hand in his as he steadied her for descent, she said, "I still haven't said that I will marry you, Max."

He touched the ring on her finger. "But you will. Say you will."

The tears in his eyes rent her heart. "We'll settle that before I leave here today," she said miserably.

She walked before him into the house. The big rooms echoed with emptiness. Rebecca was glad that no one else was there. It would be hard enough to tell Max her story without interruptions.

"Grandmother insisted I have all the crates taken up to

my room so the excelsior wouldn't litter the parlor. I hope you don't mind."

In his room, dominated by the old-fashioned tester bed, he held up the treasures he'd brought home. With pride, he showed her a tea set made of jade, so thin that she could see her fingers through the green stone. There were screens from the Coromandel coast, golden lacquer mellow against satin black wood, and curious ivory figurines made of revolving balls, each inside a fretwork of incredible skill. The rainbow silks he draped over her shoulders, and Rebecca marveled at the different woman she saw in the mirror and in his eyes.

"You're made for silk," he said, his hands caressing her shoulders. "But even these are dull and lifeless compared to your skin." He bent his bright head to kiss her.

Rebecca pulled away. "Don't . . . there's something I have to tell you. I don't want to, but I must. You see, you're not really in love with me."

His chuckle only made her feel worse. "Who am I in love with, if not you?"

Only by holding herself as rigidly as a statue could she resist the longing to give in to his embrace. Max let her go to the length of his arms. "I don't know what's wrong, Rebecca. Come sit beside me and I'm sure we can fix whatever it is."

The deep sill of the window was hard, and a trickle of cold air from the glass blew down her neck. She did not forgo the comfort of Max's arm about her waist, though she knew in a moment it would be withdrawn. Slowly, every word a stone, Rebecca told him about the man in the woods and the potion.

"Come now," he said, tilting up her chin. "You don't believe in that kind of thing? I thought you were a rational. . . ." He pressed his lips to her temple and her cheek.

Rebecca couldn't keep from offering her lips. In her desperation, for in a moment surely the spell would be broken and he'd look at her as a stranger, she gave him her heart as well.

Max tightened his arms around her. Her hands were trapped between them as she began to burn with the fires he alone could create. Somehow, she found her way between the buttons of his shirt, and the hair of his chest scoured her fingers.

That maddening touch drove her to explore further, shamelessly. Had she untied his cravat and undone each button, or had they flown away by wizardry? Rebecca only knew that she had never seen anything so exciting as his naked chest, golden from the sun.

He murmured words to her, poetry broken by kisses that inflamed her mind and body. The tight molding of her dress offered no barrier to his hands. Kneeling on the broad sill, she reached out to him, with a simple "Please?"

Rising, he swept her up and carried her to his bed, the lustrous blue and gold silks floating like wings from her shoulders. For the first time, Rebecca began to hope that the spell would last but a little while longer. Taking up all her courage, she whispered, "I love you."

"You're the only magic," Max answered.

Slowly, he sought to uncover her beneath the black wool dress and white petticoats. She tried to aid him, but he urged her to lie still. "You do everything for everyone. Let me do this for you."

Nothing could have prepared her for the sensation of his velvety tongue against the virgin rose of her breast. A haze like smoke obscured her eyes as wildness mounted in her blood. When his hands, the hands she loved, traced down over her body to part her thighs, she could hold nothing back. She flew among the clouds, reaching heights only the gods had known before her.

Rebecca hadn't a blush left by the time he slipped off his breeches and lay down beside her. He was warmer than she was, though she was by no means chilled. How could she be, when he lay his hair-enriched thigh over hers? She felt a wild tremor in her stomach, knowing that he was hard and eager. Soon she'd be lost. She couldn't wait.

"Rebecca?" he asked with the grin that had won her the

first time he'd used it. "You wouldn't take advantage of a poor sailor. Will you make an honest mate of me?"

Suddenly bold, Rebecca rolled onto her side, and urged her hips closer to his. She reveled in the raggedness of his breathing, even as she lost all sense of balance. "I'll always love you . . . always."

They came together so easily that she could not have said afterwards whether he had thrust or she had impelled. Her maidenhood was as insubstantial as the finest cambric veil. In a moment, they rocked in a rhythm far older than mere civilization. Rebecca had never felt so proud as when Max locked her in his embrace, calling out her name on a new note of passion.

Afterwards, she said idly, stroking his back, "I haven't ever yet made your new sheets."

"You've made me a new life, Rebecca. Sheets can wait."

When she awoke, it was to find him, propped up on one elbow, gazing down at her. "Why, Miss Clifton!" he said, shocked.

Rebecca froze. Crushed, she rolled away from him, pulling a corner of the silk over her nakedness. "I knew it couldn't last," she said. She felt as empty as a hollow seashell.

"What couldn't?" He lifted up to see her face. "Rebecca . . . Rebecca, I was only teasing." Shaking his head, he said, "I don't understand all this potion business. You can't really believe. . . ."

"Daphyne believed in it and thought that by giving it to you she could make her dreams come true. When you suddenly claimed to love me, I didn't want to think . . . but what other explanation is there?"

"What has Daphyne to do with it?"

She faced him. "Daphyne gave you the potion at Leonora's wedding. Don't you remember? In the library, just before I came in."

"That filthy red stuff? I didn't drink *that*! I detest sweet drinks. I like my liquor straight."

"You . . . didn't . . . drink. . . ."

"No. I chucked it in the fire as soon as she left. I didn't want to hurt her feelings."

Pushing her hair off her face, Rebecca repeated, "You didn't drink it."

Taking her hand, he laid it over his thudding heart. With utter sincerity shining in his aqua eyes, he said, "If I am enchanted, it is only you who have enchanted me. And this spell will never be broken." He pledged his love with a kiss.

"Now," he said, trying to be severe, "for the last time, are you going to marry me?"

"A practical woman would never marry a sailor. But I suppose I'm just a romantic fool, so yes. Yes, yes, yes!"

# MUSIC FROM THE GODS

## Elaine Crawford

# One

"Sweet ambrosia, Pompeii!" Cupid yelled into face-flattening wind as he and his pet hurled through space and time astride Jupiter's thunderbolt. He clutched the lump beneath his coat where the turtledove huddled in the hollow of his neck. "We're headed for a street! Just a plain ordinary street! Brace yourself!"

Pompeii dug his tiny claws into Cupid's bony shoulder.

The street looked empty, too, Cupid noted, not a single buggy or pedestrian anywhere to be seen. Jupiter was apparently showing some mercy this time. *For once.* Cupid tightened his grip on the handle of his red leather satchel and readied himself as the fiery bolt sped them toward the center of the tree-lined strip, a wide avenue, where lush lawns and flower gardens spilled away on either side to large brick houses with steep slate roofs. A lovely street . . . that *swallowed him. Engulfed him. In darkness.*

He plopped on his rear with a thump and a splash. "What the—!" His cry echoed through the hollow bowels of . . . *where?*

Slipping and sliding, he scrambled to his feet on a slimy surface. *What a horrid smell! A sewer! He was in a blasted sewer!* Jupiter had shot him with unerring accuracy, all right—right into a manhole.

Cupid raised a lanky arm and shook a fist heavenward into the light shafting from the opening above. His feet started sliding again. He grabbed a rung of the metal ladder

leading to the street and steadied himself. Then with a huff
he started climbing.

Halfway up, Pompeii sprang past Cupid's lapels and
clamped onto his head. Four sets of sharp nails dug into his
neck, and what felt like a warm furry body spread down
over his face, blinding him.

With one hand on the ladder and the other holding his
indispensable valise, he couldn't snatch the frightened
creature away. And, of course, Cupid groused, the gods only
knew what Jupiter had turned his pet turtledove into this
time. He could fairly hear the great bearded one bellowing
with laughter now. Probably so hard the god would start an
earthquake somewhere or erupt a volcano. At times like
these Cupid wondered if returning triumphantly to Mount
Olympus was really worth all the indignities he was
compelled to suffer.

"Shh, Pompeii. If you'll let go, I'll have us out of this foul
hole in a wink."

Pompeii's body relaxed slightly, but the animal did not
relinquish its grip.

Blindly fumbling for the next rung, Cupid's ire at the
supreme god spurred his flagging determination. Jupiter
wouldn't be laughing nearly so loudly when Cupid returned
with his irrefutable evidence. Love *was* the greatest power
of all. More powerful than all the gods. More powerful even
than the mighty Jupiter.

Cupid climbed with yet more resolve. Juipter hadn't
foiled him yet by assigning him *the most impossible* of love
matches. And he wouldn't this time either.

Feeling the rounded rim of the manhole, Cupid shoved
his carpetbag through and set it on the street. Then, pulling
Pompeii from off his head, he raised the animal out of the
hole to get a look at whatever his pet had become.

A fluffy brown creature with horror-filled eyes and a
button-nose stared back as it clung to his arm.

It took a moment for Cupid to identify the strange
round-faced animal. "A koala. Australia?" He peeked over
the manhole rim and studied his surroundings. "Georgian-
style homes in Australia?" Cupid returned Pompeii to the

inside of his coat and retrieved his silver pocket watch. Flicking open the cover, he read the date and place in which he'd landed. Virginia. Richmond, Virginia, June 27th, 1904.

Cupid shoved his timepiece back into his vest pocket and began to climb out, then halted. A rumbling vibrated the street beneath his hands. He looked up and saw a hulking mass of steel and wheels chugging straight for him. An automobile.

He ducked below, then remembering his valise, pulled it in after him.

He'd expected the vehicle to drive over him, but it didn't. It halted at the side of the road mere yards from him with a screeching of brakes and the sound of throaty female laughter. "Oooh, Jack," the voice sighed on a giggle.

"I told you it would be grand fun, Sophie," boomed the enlivened voice of a young man.

"My heavens, yes," she agreed with what seemed like stage-trained airiness. "And did you see the way everyone gawked at us as we passed? They virtually dripped with envy." From the added smugness in the young woman's tone, it was obvious she'd thoroughly enjoyed the attention.

Pompeii, regaining some of his curious nature, scampered out of his hiding place, up the side of Cupid's face, and popped his head out the hole.

Catching a handful of thick hair, Cupid pulled the rascal back.

"It is a wondrous automobile, isn't it?" From the young man's continued enthusiasm, it was evident he hadn't seen Pompeii.

Cupid shoved his pet farther down for good measure.

"When I asked my brother, Bill, to bring back the best from Europe," the young man, Jack, continued, "I never dreamed he'd find anything half so big and stylish. And the engine! The power of eight horses are here at my fingertips."

A vintage auto! This time it was Cupid who couldn't resist a peek. Edging his head up above the manhole, his gaze quickly roved past the young man gripping the steering wheel with leather-gloved hands to the splendid horseless carriage. Parked, yet still idling at the side of the road, its brass lanterns and horn sparkled in the midday sun. Uphol-stered black leather seats front and rear added to a mascu-line richness as did the forest-green exterior. Yes, Cupid concurred, an automobile truly worthy of admiration.

"Of course Billy would find the *perfect* horseless car-riage, Jack. When have you ever known your big brother to fail?"

Cupid caught the hint of a taunt in this Sophie's voice, though it still poured out as sweet and smooth as stove-hot honey. He shifted his attention to the delicately rounded strawberry blonde who shaded her porcelain complexion with a lace parasol. Her pouty lips continued to move slowly, aimlessly, even after she'd stopped speaking. Cupid guessed she was not one who would allow her overabun-dance of pink feathers, frills, and flounce to upstage her own very ripe presence.

Jack vaulted up, the expression on his tanned features no longer a jaunty match for the sporty tilt of his summer straw.

Cupid started to duck, then realizing he'd not been spotted, he remained. After all, this was undoubtedly the couple he'd been sent to assist. And, of course, any insights he could gain in advance would be to his advantage as well as theirs.

Jack stepped down onto the running board and took a moment to smooth the creases in his white linen suit *and,* Cupid was sure, to regain his confidence—by lauding the older brother, Sophie had trimmed his sails with what appeared to be practiced expertise. The young man then dropped down to the brick paving and strode around the auto.

By the time Jack reached Sophie's side, he'd regained his smile. He held out his hand to her. "Since you enjoyed our ride so much today, perhaps you would care to join me Sunday afternoon. We could take a run out into the country. Have a picnic. I know it's short notice . . ."

"Oh, darling, I'd love to." Ignoring his proffered hand, Sophie twirled her parasol and smiled enticingly beneath a fringe of lashes.

Jack's face brightened.

"But, didn't I tell you?" she continued after a theatrical pause. "Mother and I are going up to Old White Sulpher Springs for a month. After all, it is almost the Fourth of July. And anyone who is anyone will be there. My other beaus are all going. Two are even taking their thoroughbreds up for the races. I'm surprised you haven't mentioned it yourself."

Cupid had to admire Jack's self-control. Totally the gentleman, he took her lace-gloved hand to help her down without so much as a twitch of the jaw as she gazed up with exaggerated innocence. "I really can't," he said in a smooth baritone, "now that I've taken a position at my father's law office. And as low man on the totem pole it's only fair that the others take time off first."

"Oh, Jackie," she said, coming to her feet. She swept her skirt aside, showing a considerable amount of ankle as she stepped onto the running board. "What good is it to be the boss's son if you can't take advantage of it once in a while? In fact, I have an idea. An extraordinary idea. And I'm sure I could get Mother to agree." Then, keeping him in suspense, she reached out and brushed a strand of his wheat-colored hair from his brow.

As she did, he caught her hand and kissed the tips of her fingers.

She smiled down at him with a saucy tilt of her head that set the plumes on her wide-brimmed bonnet to fluttering. "Wouldn't it simply be the biggest lark if you would drive us up to Old White in your new automobile. What an entrance! I can just see the other girls' faces."

This time Jack didn't maintain his self-possession. His face became a mix of emotions. "But, I— My father—"

"Nonsense. I can handle your father. Just give me five minutes alone with him."

Jack's jaw stiffened. "That won't be necessary. If Father knew I would be escorting the wife and daughter of Henry Monroe, he'd be more than glad to give me the time off." He cocked a brow and his gaze hardened. "Anything to enhance his standing with a client."

Sophie obviously hadn't noticed the coolness in his

lowered tone. She smiled with triumph. "Absolutely, darling. Mother and I are set to leave early the day after tomorrow. Do be prompt. Now, be a dear and help me down."

The rumble of an approaching horse-drawn phaeton caught Sophie's attention, and she pulled back. "Pris is coming with Gordon and Harry to take me to tea. Wait until they've pulled up before you help me down. I want them to see me getting out of this—this—Who did you say built it?"

"De Dion and Bouton."

"Ah, yes. *Very* French. *Very* sophisticated."

Jack glanced up the elm-shaded street at the carriage bringing the gayly laughing threesome and took a breath deep enough to stretch the white linen across his wide shoulders.

Evidently, Cupid noted, there was no end to the competition over the flirtatious belle's favors.

Then, complying with Sophie's request, Jack handed her down just as the small carriage, its bonnet folded, drew up alongside.

Sophie descended languidly, playing the moment to the hilt.

Her friends' laughter died away as they watched, obviously enthralled.

The driver, darkly handsome, tossed his reins aside and hopped down. Acknowledging Jack with no more than a curt nod, he swept the pink-swathed confection up to his carriage. Then, while gathering the set of traces again, he looked at Jack and called, "Tally ho, Stuart." A smug grin slid into place as the driver snapped the leather across the team's backs and sent them off at a smart trot.

Sophie turned in her seat and blew Jack a kiss as the carriage drew away, then lifted rapt eyes to her new escort.

Left standing in their wake, Jack watched until they rounded the corner at the end of the block. Then, his shoulders sagging slightly, he started around to the driver's side of the auto.

It sputtered and died.

"Great. Just great," he growled.

Cupid couldn't blame young Stuart for his ill temper. It was no easy task to crank one of those contraptions to life in the best of circumstances. But to have the engine choose to die while one could still hear the laughter of the departing competition? That was a bit much.

Grimacing, Jack bent to turn the crank.

Bringing those two young people together would be quite a task, Cupid realized. And actually, from what he'd seen of the vain and flirty belle, he didn't feel she even made a good match for this young man who seemed to be instilled with forthright honesty. But if she weren't Jack's soul mate, why had Jupiter sent him to this very spot at this precise moment?

She must be. Cupid shook his head. Oh, sweet mystery of love.

Noting that Jack was still occupied with the crank, Cupid sneaked out of the manhole, then glanced about for a place to hide just long enough to replace his sewer-slimed clothing.

The engine roared to life.

"Mercury's wings!" Cupid swung toward the auto. The young man would get away before he could speak to him.

Just as he predicted, Jack straightened and dashed around to the side of the vehicle without so much as a glance Cupid's way. He climbed up and sat down. Then, while pumping the gas pedal with one of his highly polished boots, he reached for the gears.

Cupid looked at his own murky shoes then back to Jack's and wagged his head.

Jack, seemingly still unaware of the man standing in the middle of the road, started working a gear into its slot.

"Can't be helped," Cupid said, surveying his stained attire. After a couple of quick slaps at the wild flare of his snow white hair, he strode toward the side of the auto, toting his red satchel along. "Young man . . . Mr. Stuart," he called.

Jack shot a startled glance his way, then eased back in his seat before answering. "Yes?"

Stopping beside the front fender, Cupid bent into the most gracious bow he could manage, considering the disrepair of his appearance. "Pardon my untimely intrusion, but I must have a word with you."

The Stuart lad's nostrils flared.

"Sorry, my young friend, but I just met with a very unpleasant accident as you can see *and* smell. But please let me introduce myself. Cherubim V. Harper at your—"

Before Cupid could finish, Pompeii, the scamp, pick that instant to pop out his fuzzy head.

Jack stared at what was surely a very odd-looking creature, his clear blue eyes mirroring his puzzlement.

Shoving Pompeii back into his coat, Cupid attempted an offhanded chuckle. It did nothing to forestall the frown creasing Jack's brow.

Cupid shrugged. "Bothersome little fella. Pay him no mind while I borrow a moment of your time. Concerning your dilemma, I've been sent here to help you."

"You've been sent? And exactly to what *dilemma* are you referring?" Jack's scowl deepened.

"Poor choice of words," Cupid said, spreading his hands. "What I'm trying to say is, I understand completely the frustration, the rejection you're feeling right now. I know how painful it is to be rebuffed by the one true love of your life. But take heart, I have here in my valise the very thing that will solve all your problems."

Jack's eyes narrowed. "I'm in no mood to be accosted by a flimflammer today. Step out of the way, sir." He revved the engine, filling the still afternoon air with its roar and plumes of smoke.

"Wait! You must hear me out. Never in all my travels have I known my love potion to fail. It's—"

Jack grabbed the brake handle. "What do you take me for, some ignorant backwoods bumpkin?" Abruptly he released it, and the auto sprang forward.

Cupid leapt out of the way just in time to save his toes from being smashed by the rear wheel. Staring after the escaping young man, he shouted, "But, you don't understand. My 'Cupid's Delight,' it's guaranteed."

# TWO

"Cut it out, Pompeii." Cupid attempted to lift the pesky Aussy varmint away from himself to stop it from digging through every pocket of his neatly pressed three-piece suit.

His pet clung onto him with long-nailed stubbornness.

"I told you, that was the last chocolate-covered worm I had. Now stop wrinkling my clothes. I made a bad enough impression on Mr. Stuart the last time, and he should be driving by here any minute."

Ignoring him, Pompeii continued to rifle his conservative gray gabardine.

Cupid grasped the long fur at either side of the koala's head and stared his sternest. "If you'll be good until after I get a chance to speak to the young man, I'll hire a dozen boys to dig up worms for you. And I'll buy every ounce of chocolate in that general store we passed a mile or so back to dip them in. *If* you'll settle down and keep out of sight."

Pompeii looked sheepishly away, obviously well aware of his impetuous behavior. Removing his claws, the animal slinked down Cupid's body to curl up behind his master's feet. Another nap. Since becoming a koala a few days ago, Pompeii wanted to prowl all night then nap away the day.

Cupid grimaced at the thought of all the sleep the scamp had cost him. He might as well have taken the risk of unbinding his wings and flying out to this coaching inn during the night. In the wee hours he probably could've landed unnoticed. Instead, he'd just spent three long miserable days bumping along in a rented rig to reach the last stopover on the road up the Allegheny Mountains to Old White Sulphur Springs.

Unthinking, Cupid rubbed his sore rump. Catching himself, he glanced back at the fieldstone inn to see if anyone had come outside and noticed. Thank the stars, no one had. He checked the tilt of his dapper felt bowler, then tugged at the hem of his coat until the only bulge remaining in front came from the small white flask of Cupid's Delight in his coat pocket. But, of course, no matter how much he pulled or how straight he stood, he could never completely conceal the humpbacked appearance caused by wings folded beneath his shirt. But he shouldn't complain. They had come in quite handy from time to time.

"And when I'm in control of my flight," he muttered, with an arched-brow glance skyward, "I don't end up in sewers and the like."

The hot sun caused him to squint, and trickles of sweat started sliding down his temples. Also, to his dismay, he felt his starched shirt collar beginning to wilt. He tapped his foot and looked down the road again, becoming irritated that the dense undergrowth of the woods prevented him from seeing past the first curve.

*Where was that blasted auto?*

As if on cue, the put-put of an engine drifted his way on a balmy breeze.

A rush of excitement coursed through Cupid. He glanced around. Where exactly should he be standing when they drove in? Maybe he could be getting a drink, he thought, looking at the quaint stone well beside the walkway. Or sniffing the roses that formed an arbor over the inn's door.

The automobile came into view, gleaming from brass and green enamel. And Jack Stuart was at the wheel, with Sophie Monroe in the other bucket seat beside him. Another woman, most likely the mother, sat behind them.

Cupid swiveled around, eyeing the old coaching tavern again, realizing inside would have been the best place to "bump into them." But he couldn't trust Pompeii to behave.

Fraught with indecision, Cupid swung back. The vehicle hadn't slowed one iota. It barreled toward him at a good twenty miles an hour.

*They weren't stopping.*

Heedless of his own safety, Cupid stepped into the road and pulled out his love potion. He waved the scarlet-inscribed flask as if it were a red flag.

The Stuart lad's eyes widened to a startled blue, and he whipped the steering wheel to the right, narrowly missing Cupid as he sped by.

Left to hack on a cloud of powdery dirt that was settling on his sweat-streaked face, Cupid watched the auto disappear around a curve. Leaving him behind. Again.

As he cleared his throat, dispelling the dust as well as his disappointment, his pet scampered up to his shoulder. "Well, my friend," Cupid sighed, stroking the animal's soft fur. "It looks like this calls for stronger measures."

"For pity's sake, Sonny, you almost hit the poor man."

Although Jack knew Mrs. Monroe wouldn't miss a chance to harp at him as she had at every turn for the past three days, his beleaguered ears still recoiled from her latest shrill outburst. Also, he noted, she never failed to call him Sonny, a childhood nickname he detested.

"And did you see that strange looking animal creeping up behind him?" She must have leaned forward as she continued—her words blasted closer. "I do hope it wasn't going to attack him. One can never be too careful, you know, out here in the wilds. I trust you brought a weapon, Sonny."

"Actually, no, Mrs. Monroe," he answered, knowing he'd regret it. "Neither bear nor any other dangerous animal has been sighted in these mountains for decades."

"There are far greater dangers than some mangy old bear. I've heard tales concerning these backwoods folks that would set your hair on end."

Jack shot a glance to Sophie, hoping for some sign of support.

She sat in the bucket seat beside him, looking exceptionally delectable in lemon-yellow from head to foot as they drove beneath a shady archway of sugar maples. And, as usual, she seemed totally unaware of her mother's badgering *or* anything else, including him.

"There's really nothing to worry about," he offered her mother in his defense. "I've never heard of any trouble along this road. Ever."

"You're just a boy, Sonny. What would you know?"

Why he ever allowed himself to agree to a motor trip with this overbearing matron he'd never understand. Even winning the favor of Richmond's most sought-after belle couldn't possibly be worth the torture. Could it? Jack took another look at Sophie.

She held a lace hanky to her nose in an effort to breath dust-free air, and with her other hand she worked to keep her parasol tipped into the wind at the precise angle that would thwart any stray sprinkles of sunlight. She was solely preoccupied with her comfort as she had been for the most part during the trip. The only time she had ever acted as if she enjoyed their adventure was when they were forced to slow to a snail's crawl while passing through a town along the way. Then, with the certainty of a freshly wound-up toy, she laughed and flirted and teased, much more, he knew, for the benefit of the bystanders than her escort.

Jack couldn't decide if her aloofness was some female ploy or brought on by the fact she truly wasn't interested in him. He quickly forced the last thought from his mind. Sophie would never be seen with anyone she didn't care about. Would she?

The auto began nosing up a rather steep pine-covered incline, and Jack shifted into a lower gear. It coughed, then lurched before digging in for the climb.

"Mercy. This smelly contraption will make it, won't it?" came Mrs. Monroe's piercing jibe from the rear.

"It hasn't failed us yet," Jack shot back while eyeing Sophie, hoping for the tiniest bit of concurrence.

The picture-perfect redhead lowered her handkerchief to her lap, then plucked a stray pine twig from her voile skirt.

"How much longer will it be?" Mrs. Monroe asked, her voice this time edging toward a whine. "You said we'd get to Old White in time for supper."

Jack took a calming breath. It couldn't be more than a minute past two. "We're just now starting into the higher mountains. It's still a good thirty miles."

"*Thirty*. That'll take forever."

"Not more than two or three hours."

"*Watch out for that pothole.*"

"Yes, ma'am." The battle-ax must have been a drill sergeant in some past life.

"*Look!*"

This time her sharp cry nearly shattered his eardrum. Resisting the urge to massage the bombarded spot, Jack studied the winding road ahead, but saw nothing.

"Daughter," the woman demanded. "Surely you saw it."

Sophie lowered her parasol and peered over her shoulder. "What, Mother?"

"You didn't see it either? It was the biggest bird I've ever seen. Three times the size of an eagle. Four. And fast. So fast I didn't get a good look before it vanished behind the trees."

Sophie rolled her eyes. "I think the heat's getting to you. Dampen a cloth and cool your face."

"Don't treat me like some feather-headed dolt. I know what I saw."

Turning forward again, Sophie shrugged. "As you wish, Mamma."

The auto coughed again. Sputtered ominously.

Maybe the carburetor needed a richer mixture. Jack pulled out the choke.

Cupid clung to the flimsy tree branch with one arm while he worked a snared wing loose from a tangle of others. "Sweet ambrosia, I can't believe how suddenly the wind shifted."

Pompeii hopped off Cupid's shoulder and onto another pine branch and peered down to the ground that was a good forty feet below. He looked back at his master with round-eyed amazement.

"Too sudden a wind shift, if you ask me. And just where the jumpin' Jupiter did I drop my valise? Do you see it?"

His pet scampered farther out on a limb, then after glancing around, turned back to Cupid with a happy face and a squeak.

It must be nearby, Cupid decided. With both wings now freed, he climbed down to a lower branch and edged out. He could still fly down to that secluded glen up the road and be waiting to "help" as he'd planned when the auto came to a chugging stop.

Pompeii's ears perked up.

Cupid heard a backfire, then the vehicle sputtering into silence. Peeking through the branches, he saw the oversized monstrosity coast downhill to a stop no more than ten yards away. How would he ever get out of this tree without being noticed? And where was his red valise? He needed to retrieve his shirt and coat to conceal his wings.

Seconds later he spotted the bulging bag in the middle of a berry patch. It would be a sticky bit of business to retrieve it. He glanced from it back to the automobile.

The older woman sitting in the rear edged forward. "What is that foul smell?"

The Stuart lad leaned out over the side. "Oh-oh. 'pears like we've sprung a leak in one of the fuel hoses."

"I told you to be more careful of the ruts. But would you listen to me? Heaven forbid." All decked out in iris-purple, the older, plumper version of Sophie Monroe looked as much like an explosion of spring as her daughter did in yellow. But her tone was frosty winter.

And this was the mother-in-law to be? Cupid wagged his head.

Jack, coatless in the hot afternoon, jumped out, removed his cuff links, and started turning up the starched white cuffs of his pinstriped shirt. "I can't imagine what happened. I checked the fuel hoses before we left. And—"

Mrs. Monroe lurched forward, clutching the back of the front seat. Her delicate skin began to blotch with anger. "Are you telling me that *you* fooled with the engine? There are professionals for that."

Although Jack angrily rammed his rolled sleeves above his elbows, he judiciously said nothing.

"Oh, Jackie, did you really?" Sophie's tone duplicated her mother's, down to the same demanding whine.

Cupid slumped against the tree trunk. There had to be a

mistake. Jupiter couldn't expect him to foist that shrew-in-the-making on the poor lad.

Jack tossed his straw hat on the driver's seat, then raked his fingers through his blond hair as he eyed first the mother, then the daughter. "For one with a working knowledge of the combustion engine, the operation manual is not that difficult."

"All I know, Sonny," Mrs. Monroe countered, "is that we're stuck here in the middle of nowhere with a dreadful leak. And not even a gun to protect ourselves." She puffed up into a self-righteous pout, ignoring Jack as he walked to the rear of the auto. Then, opening her lavender silk parasol, she deliberately cocked it between her and the young man.

The daffodil also tilted her parasol backward, treating Jack to the same rebuff.

Cupid pursed his lips as he watched young Stuart stoop to search for the leak's source. "Perhaps," he murmured, "I'm judging the women too harshly. They're probably just reacting to a frightening situation. Causing a crack in the fuel tank might not have been such a brilliant idea after all." How could he "save the day" if he couldn't get out of this tree to fetch the soldering iron from his valise? How?

"Pompeii," he whispered as an idea popped into his head. "Climb down. Distract them."

His pet peered over the branch to the scene below as if he'd been asked to jump into a fire, then dug his nails into the limb and shook his head.

Cupid made a grab for the recalcitrant imp.

Pompeii scooted beyond his grasp.

A pinecone dangled temptingly close. "Go, you little dickens, or else." Cupid reached for it.

In the still muggy air, a sudden cool breeze blew it off.

Cupid's startled gaze followed its descent to the forest floor . . . and saw a young girl running among the trees with the lithe grace of the Huntress Diana.

A doe loped along beside her.

The girl hesitated, darted behind an oak, and the doe swerved into some brush and disappeared.

Cupid pressed back against the rough bark. Had she spotted him?

Obviously not. She peeked around the tree at the automobile in the road.

Cupid wiped beads of sweat from his brow—the air again hung hot and heavy. Yet around the girl a strange wind played. It flirted with her, licked the hem of her skirt, swirled tendrils of hair about her face . . . hair as richly brown as the loam beneath her feet.

Cupid glanced at the auto. The two women sat, fanning themselves as Jack checked a gas can strapped to the back of the auto. Returning his attention to the girl, Cupid was not surprised they hadn't noticed her. She blended with the woods as intimately as any wild creature. From the warm glow of her skin to the gold-flecked green of her autumn eyes she seemed at one with the forest. Even the muslin shift she wore lent itself to the varied hues of bark and stem as the breeze molded it to her slender body.

When she passed beneath Cupid's tree, Pompeii skittered down on flying feet and landed on the ground before her.

She halted. Then after the slightest hesitation, she knelt and held out her arms. The scamp leaped into them as if he'd known her all his impetuous little life.

As the deserter cuddled against the gentle swell of her bosom, the girl smiled with loving eyes, then rose and continued on toward the vehicle where Jack looked up and saw her.

Surprised at first, the young man's features relaxed into those of someone viewing an awe-inspiring sunrise.

Cupid quickly shifted back to the girl. Although her face was now beyond his view, he noted that both the hair flowing down her back and her strides became more liquid—if that were possible—as she moved unwaveringly toward Jack.

"Sweet ambrosia." Cupid rocked back against the trunk and chuckled. What a fool he'd been. No wonder he'd been thwarted at every turn. This was the one. The one meant for Jack.

# Three

"*Ja . . . ckie.*" Even from high up in the tree, Sophie's wail pierced Cupid's ears. She wrenched around in her seat. "*What are you doing* just standing there? Mother and I are burning up, and. . . ." She spotted the girl. Her eyes narrowed to angry slits as she swung her attention back to Jack.

Young Stuart, Cupid noted, looked like he'd just been caught doing exactly what he had been doing—openly admiring the loveliest of creatures.

"*Ja . . . ack,*" Sophie repeated in that irritating whine as she aimed shards of her icy glower at the girl. "How much longer is it going to take you?"

His attention, now prudently fixed on Sophie, Jack never wavered for an instant as he dusted his hands, then raked one through his hair. "Actually," he began in a low drawl Cupid had trouble hearing, "the most impossible thing has happened. The fuel tank, solid iron, has cracked. I can't repair it. Not without the proper implements. I need to find a smithy.

Mrs. Monroe, who'd been hiding behind her parasol, cast it aside and came to her feet, striking a formidable pose, despite looking like an overgrown iris. "*Then, Sonny, why are you still here?* We passed a town about—" Her words stopped, but her mouth remained open as she also caught sight of the girl. Too soon she regained her voice. "Where did that half-dressed hillbilly come from?"

With a hunted look in her eyes, the girl hugged Pompeii tighter and turned, no doubt, to run.

"You. Over here," Mrs. Monroe commanded.

The girl froze for a second, then took a hesitant step toward the auto.

Mrs. Monroe leaned out. "Which way to the nearest blacksmith?"

The girl pointed down the road from whence the auto had come, then lowered her head, half-burying her face in koala fur.

"Surely," Sophie broke in, her lips stretched into a tight smile, "there's someone closer who could fix one little old crack."

The girl peered up, her gaze wandering until it found Jack again.

He smiled with what Cupid knew was tender encouragement.

She took a swift breath. "My gramps," she said in almost a whisper. "He likes to tinker. He can fix most anything."

"What's that you said?" Mrs. Monroe intruded harshly. "Speak up."

Taking a backward step, the girl again appeared ready to take flight.

"Does your grandfather work with things made of iron?" Jack asked, his voice a deep soothing contrast to the old shrew's.

"Yes," she answered. Though slightly high pitched, her voice now held more confidence. "Iron and tin. Copper."

"Wonderful," Jack replied. "Where do you live?"

She glanced over her shoulder. "In the holler two ridges over."

"Two ridges you say, my dear?" Sophie's words had regained that staged sweetness Cupid had overheard the other day in Richmond. "Could you be more precise? Just exactly how far is it to this *holler* of yours?"

Pompeii, fool that he was, sprang out of the arms of nature's most perfect gift and raced pell-mell for the auto. In a flash, he hopped up on the floorboard and leaped into Sophie's lap.

Screeching, she batted wildly at the koala.

To escape, the ball of fur dove over her shoulder and landed, claws-first onto the skirt of the still-standing Mrs. Monroe.

The plump matron gasped, stumbled back, and fell onto her seat. Then, snatching Pompeii by the scruff of his neck, she flung him out of the car.

His feet were scrambling before they hit the ground. He shot past Cupid's tree and, a few yards farther, fled up a maple.

All the while, Sophie continued to bray as if she'd been attacked by a vicious beast.

Jack rushed to her. Jumping up on the running board, he captured her flailing hands. "It's all right, sweetheart. The animal's gone. You're fine now. You're safe."

Cupid groaned. That's all he needed—Jack turning into Sophie's knight in shining armor.

And the blasted female calmed almost instantly . . . *just as Cupid expected she would*. She batted her lashes at Jack, then woefully slid her gaze in the direction of the escaped culprit. An instant later she zeroed in on the girl, and her expression turned brittle. "*You*. You did that on purpose."

"No, I—" The girl glanced about helplessly, spreading her hands, then inhaled some of the cool breeze still playing lazily about her. "I'd better go fetch Gramps." Whirling away, she vanished as quickly as she'd appeared.

"That's the last we'll see of her," Mrs. Monroe predicted with finality. "So, young man, I suggest you hoof it back down the road for some help. I don't intend to spend the night out here at the mercy of heaven-only-knows what. And neither does my daughter."

"Mother," Sophie said, her tone surprisingly sharp-edged. "We're really making far too much of our predicament."

Jack stepped down from the running board and at eye level, stared at Sophie. He seemed as amazed as Cupid by her charity.

Gently, she tapped Jack's cheek with her closed fan, then looked back at her mother. "You remember the Barker's landau we passed a mile or so back. They should be coming by any minute now. We'll simply catch a ride with them on up to Old White, and tomorrow Jack can send back a mechanic to take care of this bothersome business."

Jack stood at the side of the road, watching Sophie and her mother disappear over the rise in the Barker's carriage. When Mrs. Monroe had flagged her friends down, Jack couldn't believe how quickly she and Sophie had jumped ship. And worse, how they'd not objected in the least to his staying behind when he'd said he couldn't trust his De Dion's repairs to an unsupervised stranger. As worried as they'd been about their own welfare, they hadn't seemed concerned in the least about his.

No, Jack denied as he climbed up to his seat, he wouldn't let himself believe that of Sophie. If it hadn't been for her mother's presence, she probably would've enjoyed sharing a few hours here alone with Jack in the cool shade of the woods. Encouraging his fantasy, he saw himself easing her and all her yellow fluff onto the grass, saw himself, at long-last, kissing those pouty lips.

He lounged back against the black leather. "Yes, and if I'd taken that flimflammer up on his offer of a love potion, there's no telling where that dress might have ended up." Smiling lazily, he closed his eyes and began to play out the rest of the scene in his mind.

A loud crack and a stirring high in some branches snapped Jack to attention. He glanced up but saw nothing, then remembered the nameless furry animal who'd escaped up a tree. "Damn critter," he muttered, punctuating his frustration by delivering a slap to his steering wheel. "Sophie might've stayed if it hadn't been for that . . . whatever the blamed thing was." Vaguely, he recalled seeing one before. But where? When?

He pulled out his timepiece and checked it. Almost three. The girl had been gone more than half an hour now. Hooking the fob over a gear handle, Jack decided he'd give her another fifteen minutes. Then he'd start walking.

"But what in blazes could've caused my tank to crack? And of all times."

His latest outburst must've startled the animal again. More leaves rustled, and this time he caught a glimpse of gray fur up in a sugar maple. "That's right, you little devil," he yelled. "You'd better stay out of reach if you know what's good for you."

After a moment his gaze drifted to the spot where he'd first seen the mountain girl, and the remembrance sent a shock to his heart. As hard as he'd been trying to dismiss from his consciousness what had surely been a romantic illusion, it returned with full force. In no way could he deny it. The unexpected appearance of that unadorned nymph had virtually taken his breath away—the very sight of her, her hair whipping freely about her. And that sack of a dress . . . *my God*, it had molded so completely to her body, he'd been able to make out every silken curve, every swell, as surely as if she'd been naked.

Jack shook his head, in an attempt to dislodge the image. Such raw sensuality could only have been a figment. Nonetheless, he couldn't keep it from intruding, despite having been with Richmond's most sought-after belle.

Think about Sophie, he told himself, *and* the competition that would be swarming around her while he was left behind. If only her mother hadn't come along on the drive, he knew he could've gotten some kind of a commitment out of her. Hadn't he promised his father as much in order to get the two weeks off?

Damn, maybe he should've gone on with them, left the auto behind.

His lungs tightening with frustration, Jack swiped his watch from off the gearshift and stuffed it into the fob pocket of his tan waistcoat, then hopped down. He didn't have time to wait around here.

"Young fellow."

Turning, Jack saw an elderly man coming toward him with long easy strides, gripping a wooden tool carrier. A smile formed friendly creases on either side of his mouth as he approached with an outstretched hand. "Name's Fair-child, Oran Fairchild. Hear you're having a spot of trouble."

Jack noticed the girl lagging behind as he took Mr. Fairchild's thin callused hand. "Thanks for coming. I'm Jack Stuart from Richmond. I'm on my way up to Old White Sulpher Springs."

"Figured as much." Mr. Fairchild's deepset blue eyes gravitated to the automobile and his smile widened. He stepped closer and ran his fingers along the front fender. "Beautiful," he breathed. "Just beautiful. I haven't been out of these hills for sometime now. How many of these horseless carriages are there down in Richmond or, say, Baltimore?"

"Twenty or thirty at least. They're the coming thing."

"Who made this one?"

"A couple of Frenchmen, De Dion and Bouton."

"Oh, yes. I read something about their new engine."

The man had read about them? Jack perked up. "Then maybe you know they've perfected a high-speed one, and it has a foolproof constant-mesh box, and a three-way hand pump for lubrication, and—"

"Whoa. Slow down, lad. Let me savor one thing at a time before going on to the next."

"Sorry for the outburst. You're not the only one who thinks I'm obsessed with things mechanical."

"Nothing wrong with that, son. Making something useful out of some worthless scraps is very satisfying. Let's have a look at this new marvel. How fast will it go?"

Jack lifted one side of the hood and propped it. "It has no problem cruising at twenty-five miles an hour on a good flat road."

"You don't say." The older man set down his toolbox and leaned closer. Then looked back over his shoulder. "Music, come take a look. It's a pure sight."

The girl slipped out from behind a tree trunk and tiptoed up to the far side of her grandfather without so much as a glance in Jack's direction. And hadn't Mr. Fairchild called her Music? The name seemed as fanciful as the girl.

Her grandfather draped an arm over her shoulder. "A lot more complex than the one I'm building, isn't it?"

Jack's attention riveted onto the older man. "You're building you're own automobile engine?"

"I'm still working on it. I'd take it as a real kindness if you'd let me study this one for a couple of days."

"I'd love to. And have a look at your progress, too. But I'm sorry, I can't. I'm expected up at Old White. But I'll tell you what. If you can help me get the gasoline tank off and soldered, on my way back I'll give you twenty-four hours with it. I won't have the ladies with me then. Deal?"

The fellow enthusiast's spare features crinkled with a happy grin. "Be looking forward to it." Tripping its prop, Mr. Fairchild lowered the hood. "If we don't have too much trouble removing the tank, we should have it back on and you on your way again by seven or eight in the morning."

Jack's relief was immeasurable. "You don't know how I appreciate this."

"Imagine I do. Music said you had some mighty anxious females with you. By the way, where are they?"

"A Mr. and Mrs. Barker from Richmond were headed up to take the waters and were kind enough to give the ladies a ride."

"Thomas Barker?"

"Yes."

"Did that old miser cut loose of enough cash to buy his own automobile?"

"No," Jack replied evenly, though Fairchild's accurate appraisal of the tobacco buyer caught him off guard. "He was in the same landau he's had ever since I can remember."

Mr. Fairchild nodded with a knowing chuckle—he must've had dealings with the old skinflint, Jack thought. Then, taking hold of his tool carrier, the thin man walked to the rear of the auto and knelt down.

While he did, the girl edged back among the trees.

Jack tried not to watch as a breeze picked up and flattened her shapeless dress against her legs and thighs again, displaying her slender lines, her smooth curves . . . the strength in her stride . . . the intoxicating rhythm. . . .

"Stuart. Can you give me a hand?" came her grandfather's easy voice from beneath the vehicle, jerking Jack back to reality. "Fetch me the hammer."

Wrenching his eyes from the girl, Jack thankfully sought out the tool carrier. He needed something to get his philandering thoughts off her . . . off the whispery music that floated on the breeze.

# Four

Grateful for anything that would divert his attention, Jack handed Mr. Fairchild a small hammer. Then he removed his shirt and waistcoat, preparing to crawl under the car to assist the older man.

While laying his garments over the back of the passenger seat, he felt the girl's eyes on him. He shot a glance toward the thicket and, sure enough, he caught her staring at his bare chest.

Her eyes flared, and she quickly turned away.

A smile tugged at the corners of his mouth over her embarrassment, not to mention the fact he rather enjoyed the idea that she'd been watching him with enough interest to cause her to become uncomfortable. He wished Sophie would take that much notice, because, all bragging aside, he had a very athletic build—one that had often been envied by the other students at college.

"Stuart," Mr. Fairchild called through the wheel spokes. "Crawl down here. I need a hand."

With Jack's extra strength, Mr. Fairchild had little problem removing the gasoline tank, although he made several remarks questioning the probability of it rupturing in the first place. Within fifteen minutes the two of them pulled the weighty iron canister from beneath the auto.

"Now, all we have to do," the older man said, helping Jack hoist it up on a muscle-padded shoulder, "is go back to my place to solder it."

"What about my auto and luggage? Do you think they'll be safe?"

"I'm sure of it," Mr. Fairchild said while wiping his hands on a rag from his pocket. "We're the only ones who live within miles of here. And late as it's getting, there won't be any more folks passing through to Old White."

Jack glanced down the lonely road and back at his mechanical treasure. If he wanted to be on his way, he'd have to chance it. Balancing the heavy can with an upraised arm, he grabbed his shirt and waistcoat. As he tossed them over his other shoulder, he remembered the girl and swung around. Again he found her watching—or, maybe, still.

This time she ducked behind the furry head of that strangely familiar animal she'd had before.

Jack felt a twinge of disappointment. Just once he'd like to have her look at him long enough, close enough, for him to discern if her eyes truly were that light a hazel, that translucent, that all-seeing.

"Music." Mr. Fairchild walked toward her, his tool carrier in hand. "Where on earth did you come up with that new pet?"

No less interested, Jack followed close behind.

The girl backed up, nervously looking both ways. One would think she had something to hide.

Jack advanced. "Yes, I'd like to know about that animal, too."

Clutching the ball of fur to her bosom, the girl hesitated but a fraction of a second. Then whirling, she ran away.

Within seconds Jack lost sight of her. She seemed to actually melt into the dark woods.

Mr. Fairchild wagged his head and started walking toward the same thicket. "Don't know what could've gotten into her, running off like that. Maybe it's seeing a strapping young fellow like yourself. I guess we've been a bit too isolated since we came here to live. We hardly ever see anyone except for old Ethan McPhee. He delivers our supplies and mail every month."

"How long have you been living here?" Jack asked, grasping more tightly to the canister he held while stepping over a fallen tree. It must have been years from the look of the girl. The phrase "wood sprite" came to mind.

Mr. Fairchild slowed and looked at Jack, a small frown creasing his brow. "The turn of the century came and went a year or so ago, didn't it?"

Obviously the man wasn't kidding when he said he'd lost touch with the outside world. "It's July, sir. July second, Nineteen oh four."

"Hmm." The elderly man pursed his lips, then picked up the pace again. "Time does have a way of getting away from one, doesn't it? I brought my little Music here back in Ninety-one."

"The two of you have been living up in these hills for thirteen years?"

"I suppose so. Music was four when we found our little haven. But you'd be surprised how much of the world a man can have brought right to his doorstep no matter where he lives."

Jack had heard about people living deep in the Appalachians, some never stepping down in the lowlands. But for a girl as enchanting as Music? What a waste. But, then, he reminded himself, it was none of his business—his was to get the tank soldered, this "ten-ton" iron can that was digging deeper into his shoulder with every step. "How much farther to your place?"

"Oh, as postman McPhee would say, just a short stretch of the legs." Chuckling, Fairchild glanced Jack's way as if he'd said something very amusing. He pushed aside some low branches and stepped back for Jack to pass through.

Reaching the other side of a dense stand of pines, Jack almost bumped into a steep ridge. Ten tons now became twenty.

Music's secret glen drew her with the surety of a butterfly to a flower. This was her private hideaway, her own kingdom. Reaching it, she dropped down on a blanket of tender grass beside the pool at the bottom of a sheeting cascade. The gentle water sounds called to her. The breeze stilled, wrapping her in the songs of the birds and the gentle roar of the falls. She was safe at last.

Her newest friend sprang out of her arms and raced to the gently lapping edge and drank its fill.

More overheated than she could ever remember, Music did the same, cupping some of the frigid wetness in her hands and bringing it to her mouth. Drops slid down her throat, others trailed up her raised arms. The coolness felt so good she scooped more and splashed her face. Then, lying back onto the fragrant grass, she let the rumble of the cascade lull her into the dreamy state it always did.

The little animal ran to her and jumped, landing in the middle of her belly.

Giggling, she pulled it up higher, "My, but you're a sociable fellow. I take it, my other forest friends have already told you what a tender spot I have for furry little snookums." She reached up and traced his head. "Especially if they have big round ears."

The creature squeaked softly and stretched out until its long front paws rested on her shoulders.

"And such warm, loving eyes." Sighing, she closed her own.

Within seconds a picture of the two fancy ladies flashed before her, their expressions wrought with distaste and, yes, disgust. Dressed so elegantly, sitting in the horseless carriage, they'd looked like bouquets of town flowers in a green and gold vase. But they'd stared at her as if she were something that needed to be scraped off their shoes.

The young gentleman hadn't, though. His eyes had seemed so welcoming, eyes as blue as the top of the sky. And his hair, sunny as August, and his voice . . . oh, the sound of his voice had poured over her like warm bath water on a snowy night. At first. . . .

She drew her pet closer until their noses almost touched. "Until you decided to jump into the ladies' laps. Don't you know lawn material is too delicate for those needle nails of yours?"

The creature flicked out its tongue and wet her nose.

Music sat up and wiped the wetness. "Don't think that's

going to make up for the havoc you caused. Surely you could see Mr. Stuart's companions were the delicate sort, like that princess who could feel one tiny pea beneath a hundred mattresses. And you frightened them so badly, they ran away. Left Mr. Stuart all alone. He'll never forgive us for that."

The cute little animal slid its gaze away mournfully as if it actually understood.

Feeling a bit remorseful, Music cuddled it closer. "I'm sorry for taking it out on you. It's not your fault I looked so ragtag. Nothing could've made this shapeless shift any prettier or put shoes on my feet." She wiggled her bare toes. "As beautifully dressed as the young lady was, it would take no less than Cinderella's glass slippers *and* her ball gown to entice a prince as dashing as Mr. Stuart into give me a second glance. But, my friend, did you ever see such a noble chin or more magnificent shoulders? No dragon would ever be safe around him."

She drank in every remembered plane and angle of his manly build, the bulging of his muscles as he'd hoisted the gasoline tank to his shoulder, his golden skin, so smooth . . . until a strange tingling sensation coursed her body. Recalling the sureness of his strides, more chills of excitement ran up her spine.

Then, knowing all was for naught, pangs of regret seized her. Sighing, she pulled from her pocket the reed flute her gramps had carved for her. She began to play a simple tune that always let her escape into its beauty.

But this time the melody didn't work its magic. The yearning only grew more intense—much like she'd felt for her parents who were long lost to her. But now it was for someone who wasn't even hers to lose.

Through a blur of tears, she saw a squirrel poke its head out of a tree hole to listen to the haunting tune. Then a bunny popped over a gnarly root. Closer they came, her little forest family, always here to comfort her, to take away any sorrow.

The creature in her lap shut its button eyes and swayed dreamily to the music until she could almost hear it purr.

Lowering the flute to her lap, Music nuzzled the top of its head with her chin and sighed. "Too bad you didn't bring my fairy godmother with you."

"You called, milady?"

*"What?"* Music sprang to her feet, clutching her new pet to her.

An older man with wildly flaring hair stepped into the small clearing—hardly a fairy godmother.

She started to run, then realized that as long as he didn't get too close she had nothing to fear. She could easily outdistance an aging man toting such an unwieldy bag— bright red leather, no less.

He sauntered a few steps closer, greeting her with a smile equally as comfortable as her grandfather's.

Her apprehension eased . . . especially since his lively eyes and bushy brows were almost as funny and flamboyant as his satchel.

"I said, you caught my baby." His voice rang as clear and strong as any play actor's.

After a confused moment, Music realized how easily one's mind could play tricks. He hadn't actually said *"You called, milady"* as she'd thought.

With a broad wave of his arm, the gaunt man brought up a long bony finger and pointed it to the warm fluff in her arms. "Naughty boy."

She looked down. "The animal. It's yours?"

"Yes. Pompeii can be a mischievous little scamp at times. I never know what to make of him. But my lonely life just wouldn't be the same without him. And speaking of lonely . . . " His Shakespearean tones softened, and he paused. "I can't help but notice a sad little tear sparkling on your cheek."

Feeling foolish, she wiped away the evidence. "No, really, it's nothing."

"Don't you know all the gods on Mount Olympus weep when they see their Diana so sad?"

My, but he did say strange things. "You're mistaken. I'm Jane Irene Fairchild, and I'm late. I must be going." She placed the odd animal on the ground, not trusting the man enough to actually put the creature into his hands.

The animal took a backward glance at Music, then scampered to its master.

"Oh, by the way," she asked, "what kind of animal is it? I've never seen anything quite like it."

"He's a koala, my young goddess. From Australia."

She ignored his flattery. "Australia! I've read about that place. Does it have a pocket to keep its babies in, like the kangaroo?"

The man chuckled as he gathered up his pet. "Not this time."

"I see." But she didn't. Tentatively, she reached out and touched the koala's black nose. "Goodbye, Pompeii. I have to go now."

"*Wait.* You can't leave until you're sufficiently rewarded. If it wasn't for you, the poor little scamp might've been lost in the dark woods forever or eaten by a wolf."

"We don't have wolves in these parts. And besides—"

The man put up his hand, halting her words, then bent over and snapped open the big bag. "I have the perfect reward. Something that will help dry your every tear."

A knowing smile played across Music's mouth. A peddler. That explained the showy satchel. No telling what kinds of baubles and trinkets he'd have in there.

"Ah, success," he said, his arm buried deep inside. He brought forth the prettiest bottle Music had ever seen. It sparkled with all the colors of her treasured abalone shell. Even more wondrous, it seemed to glow from an inner fire.

The peddler started to hand it to her, then quickly withdrew it. "Sorry, wrong bottle." Frowning, he held it up toward a shaft of late afternoon sunlight and pulled out the gem-like stopper. "Genie. Are you still in there?"

To Music's astonishment, it answered. "Yes." The well-deep voice sounded like it came from a distant hollow. "And I'm very weary of—"

The peddler shoved the stopper into the bottle's neck. "I know that must seem cruel, but if I don't shut him up, he'd talk all night."

Suddenly, Music remembered reading about someone called a ventriloquist, who could "throw" his voice, make it come out of dolls, rocks, whatever. She burst into laughter. "That was very good, Mr.—uh—"

"Harper, Cherubim V. Harper, at your service," he said with a grand bow before replacing the bottle. Again he rummaged inside the bag. This time he fished out a plain white one with a red-print label. "Ah, yes, here it is. I want to make a gift of this to you for keeping my little Pompeii safe. My Cupid's Delight. It's really quite powerful. A few drops in a cup of tea, and the young man of your dreams won't be able to see anyone but you. Your smile, the lilt of your laughter, the melodies you play on that little flute in your pocket. All will be the only music he'll ever want to see or hear. But take care. One sip is forever. It's powerful stuff!"

# Five

Music clasped her hands behind her back and looked from the bottle to Mr. Harper. "I'm much obliged, but I can't. My gramps doesn't hold with medicine show concoctions. I'm sorry." She stepped back. "I have to go now."

"But you can't!" His voice rang with panic. "I mean," he continued more calmly, "I'm sure I have something else you could take as payment. Some other little token." He dove into the red valise, this time with both hands.

Music took another deft step backward, then another. She really did need to go home. She had to get a chicken in the pot and. . . . Her heart tripped over itself. They'd be having Mr. Stuart for supper. She'd get out the china. . . .

"Yes!" Mr. Harper cried, breaking into her thoughts. "This will be perfect!"

Music gasped. The man held out the shiniest, most elaborately etched flute she'd ever seen. She wanted it desperately. *Desperately.* "I couldn't," she managed. "It's much too expensive."

"Nonsense. Pompeii is worth far, far more." He shoved it into her hands. "Play something. Let's see if it's worthy of you."

The silver flute warmed almost immediately to her hands, and when she held it up, her fingers rested over each hole as if the instrument had been made expressly for her. Hesitantly, she blew across the mouthpiece, and the purest note emerged, then another, until her fingers, of their own volition, brought forth the lightest, airiest tune.

Music became so caught up in the melody, she almost forgot the peddler until the motion of his head rocking with the rhythm drew her attention. His eyes were half-closed and a smile curled the corners of his mouth. Cuddled in his arms, the koala seemed equally entranced.

When the tune drifted to an end, Mr. Harper's eyes popped wide. "Beautiful. A song truly worthy of the gods. And, sweet ambrosia, I almost forgot." Stooping, he shifted Pompeii up to his shoulder, then dipped into the satchel again. "There's a pocket made specifically for that flute. Now, where is it . . . ? I really must get better organized."

Music caressed the lovely instrument one last time, then held it out to him. "Mr. Harper, I can't accept it."

He looked up with an impatient glower. "You must. I won't have it any other way."

"Well . . ." Just how many times was she expected to refuse, for goodness sakes. "All right, if you insist."

"I do."

That settled, Music couldn't suppress her smile. She tightened her grip on this gift she knew she would keep always.

"Ah, here it is." Mr. Harper stood up, and as he did, he shook free a gown.

At first glance, it seemed to be made of layer upon layer of the sheerest white material. But as it stirred in the breeze hints of various pastels appeared, as if a subtle rainbow had been woven into the purest white. Music ached to touch it.

Mr. Harper draped it over his arm as if it were no more elegant than gingham or calico and began searching the folds. Abruptly he stopped. "Yes, I knew this was the one."

"The one what?"

"Pocket, of course."

"The pocket you were looking for is *sewed into that gown?*"

"My child, surely you know pockets don't just float through the air waiting to be plucked at will. They must be attached to something. Here, take the flute's pocket." He tossed the gown at her.

Music had no choice but to catch the yards and yards flying at her, dropping over her.

"And now I must really be off. It's getting quite late, you know."

By the time she managed to unbury herself enough to protest this additional extravagant gift, Mr. Harper had gone . . . vanished from the glen along with the koala and that fascinating satchel. She was alone. Even the nosy squirrel slipped back into its hole high in a stretching elm.

Then, from out of nowhere, something small and pink sailed toward her. It landed at her feet—a piece of paper folded for flight.

Careful not to drag any of the gorgeous dress on the ground, Music retrieved it as she searched the dark woods surrounding her for the sender. She saw no one, heard nothing save the happy chirping of birds and the murmur of the waterfall.

That peddler was a tricky one, indeed.

Returning her attention to the pink missile, she spread the stiff paper open to writing penned in the most elaborate flourish. It read:

Of this dress it is written—
She who dons the gown becomes music
And from that day forth
Music, alone, will play in his heart
Forever.

"Oh, my." Unable to believe her eyes, she scanned the note again. She hadn't mentioned her nickname to Mr. Harper. Perhaps the dress was as magical as it looked. For certain, the prophesy could be meant for no other. She hugged the mound of silk to her bosom. "Oh, my."

Jack followed Mr. Fairchild, straining under the weight of cast iron. They walked through trees and spiny brush until they reached a large clearing where Jack halted. Forgetting the biting ache in his shoulder and sweat streaming down his temples, he stared in disbelief. An acre of lawn shaded

mostly by fruit and nut trees surrounded a delightful home
like none he'd ever seen. Not large by Richmond standards,
it was irregular in shape and sported turrets of glass at each
corner. Constructed of stone and wood and roofed with
slate, it looked like a castle—a cozy castle. Certainly not
the simple cabin he'd expected.

"Not much farther, son," Mr. Fairchild called over his
shoulder. "My shop is the big building to the right of the
house."

Hurrying to catch up, Jack shifted his attention to a large,
more ordinary fieldstone structure. He then realized they
were walking onto the Fairchild place from the back. Other
sturdy outbuildings edged a wide gravel drive, and beyond,
a flourishing garden edged the road. The entire place looked
as pretty as a painting, right down to the swing hanging
from a large oak near the front of the house—a swing put
there, no doubt, for Music's enjoyment.

As Jack neared the shop, a very strange three-wheeled
contraption came into view alongside the garden. At its rear
a plow was attached. "Mr. Fairchild," he called, and pointed.
"What's that?"

"Oh, yes." A smug grin accompanied the older man's
shrug. "My mechanical mule. I think I have most of the
bugs worked out. It didn't break down once this spring. I
also use it to mow the lawn. But I'm having problems
coming up with a hoe attachment, though, that'll keep this
old back from aching. But I think I have some darn good
ideas for harvesting implements."

Jack couldn't believe his ears as he rounded the corner to
the front of the shop. He'd actually stumbled upon a
bonafide inventor. "I'll bet you designed that unique-
looking house, too."

Mr. Fairchild's intelligent eyes sparked as he looked
back. "If you think the outside is unusual, wait till I show
you the inside. But first we need to take care of your little
problem." He grabbed the handle to one of a pair of wide
doors and slid it open.

Stepping inside, the coolness of the high-ceilinged room
washed over Jack's sweat-dampened torso, a wonderful

welcome. As his eyes adjusted to the light, he began to identify all manner of shop equipment and tools—far more than he'd ever seen at college. Jack's excited gaze leaped from one item to the next. Some hung from the walls or rested on long work benches and larger pieces stood on the floor. From the rafters hung chains and pulleys that held aloft a large combustion engine. And at the far end of the room waited a half-finished automobile.

Jack laughed outloud. "I can't believe it. Here, hidden deep in the mountains. You have a better equipped shop than the one at the university. Can you imagine what an incredible coincidence it was for me to break down where I did? And all your granddaughter said was, my gramps likes to tinker."

With a soft chuckle, Mr. Fairchild motioned Jack to place the gasoline tank on a stone slab, then helped him ease it down. Once securely in place, he nodded to a metal tub attached to the back wall. "There's a sink over there. Turn the handles above it for water."

"Of course you would have running water even in your shop."

"Cold *and* hot."

Shaking his head, Jack laughed. "Naturally. Gramps tinkers."

While Jack washed and dried his upper body, Mr. Fairchild fired up a brick furnace and began yanking on a rope leading to a metal box attached to the furnace.

"What are you doing?"

"My version of a bellows."

Jack wagged his head again. "I can't believe someone with your genius is living away from life like this.

"That's where you're wrong. I moved here so I wouldn't miss out on any more life. When I was a young man I was so wrapped up in my business, I missed watching my son grow up. Oh, we may have slept in the same house, but I was rarely home before he was in bed."

Jack understood that only too well. Until this past year when he went to work for his father, they'd rarely exchanged more than two sentences at a time.

"Then one day," the older man continued in a weary voice that betrayed his age, "they were all dead, my wife, my son, his pretty young wife. Everyone except the little one, little Jane Irene. A train crash. By some miracle she'd escaped without a scratch . . . not to her body anyway. I got there as quick as I could, and when she saw me. . . ." Mr. Fairchild's hands slowed pulling on the rope. "I'll never forget the pain or the need in those transparent eyes as she ran to me. I vowed at that moment, I'd always be there for her. And, well, neither of us wanted to stay in our house in Baltimore any longer. So, we just packed up and started exploring. We happened upon this meadow about sundown one spring evening and saw ten or twelve deer grazing—my Jane loves animals as much as her music. We've been here ever since." A gentle smile lightened his expression. "And, I swear, she's made pets of every creature for miles around."

"Let me." Jack took the rope from the older man's hand. He already felt more at ease with this stranger than he ever had with his own father. "But, what about your granddaughter? Doesn't she get lonely for young folks her own age? In Baltimore, she'd have a string of beaus lined up by now."

Absently, he rubbed his chin. "You're probably right. Guess I haven't wanted to see she's growing up. She and I, well, we've created such a happy, peaceful life for ourselves." Abruptly, he slapped Jack on the back and chuckled. "Maybe that's why providence sent you to us."

Grinning, Jack warded off the older man with his hands. "I've already got more courting problems than I can handle."

Music caught a whiff of smoke just as she broke out of the pine-scented forest. It roiled fiercely upward from the shop chimney, a sure sign Gramps and the handsome Mr. Stuart were in there. She veered in their direction, hungry for another look at the blonde Adonis.

As she crossed the lawn, afternoon rays slanted across the bundle of silk in her arms, turning it into a thousand prisms—an incredible sight. . . .

*Too beautiful for an unsophisticated girl like her.* What had she been thinking?

Any cultured person from the city would see past the dress. And besides, this gentleman already had the most elegant of ladies.

"Ouch!" she cried, stepping on a sharp stone. Lifting her foot to check it, she was even more dismayed by her tough, dirty sole. Shooting a shamefaced glance at the shop building, any remaining shred of confidence vanished. No snake oil peddler's fancy-sounding compliments or very clever note could erase the gawky picture she'd made today.

In a sudden hurry, she ran for the back door of the house. She'd just die if Jack Stuart saw her again without shoes on or a proper dress.

# Six

Jack was still reeling with amazement after he and Mr. Fairchild finished soldering the gasoline tank and stepped outside to a balmy evening. Looking back, he took a last peek at several inventions in various stages of development as his host shut off electric lights—lights that had been installed several years ago. And, to think, his own family had only recently had their home wired for them.

Jack helped Mr. Fairchild close the big doors, then turned toward the house. The abundance of glass panes of the circular turrets sparkled like fiery diamonds in the last rays of the setting sun—a glorious sight. "Sir, you're a modern-day Leonardo da Vinci. And your home is your Mona Lisa."

"No, Jane Irene is that," he said, his expression softening with the love he surely felt for his granddaughter.

At the mention of the girl, Jack pictured her as he'd first seen her, the breeze whipping strands of dark hair across her face, her thin shift plastered to her shapely thighs. His heart began to pump harder.

". . . that dishwasher I'm working on," Mr. Fairchild was saying, "is giving me a dickens of a time. But I think I've just about figured out a way to make a vacuum small enough for the ordinary housewife to use right in her home. No more taking up the rugs to beat outside."

Jack forced himself to concentrate on the man's words. "All these inventions you have going—you really have made an exciting life right here."

"And of course there's Music. She's my joy."

As they rounded the turret they reached a stone pathway that meandered across the grass to a thick oak door. And just beyond was another glass enclosure, this one surrounded by a bower of petunias. Charming, undeniably charming.

"When Music was little," Mr. Fairchild said, pointing to the flower-bedecked turret, "she always wanted to eat outside, so I designed a dining room that would give her that feeling."

Jack refused. It would surely break his concentration. "With nothing but glass surrounding you, doesn't it get awfully cold in the winter?"

"Double panes with a little space in between. You'd be surprised what a difference it makes. And," he said opening the front door, "I pipe hot air from the fireplace to all the rooms."

"No kidding?"

"Yep." Stepping inside, Mr. Fairchild pushed a button on the wall, and the large open-beamed room filled with light. Wait till you see the kitchen." A smug grin accompanied his raised brows.

But Music was nowhere to be seen.

"Everything's electric. The stove, the icebox. Even the water heater. Got the idea from the Exposition in Chicago back in Ninety-three. Come on, follow me."

Passing through the main room, Jack spotted a chess board set up on a low table before the hearth with two cozy chintz-covered chairs flanking it. A game was obviously in progress, considering the placement of the pieces. Beyond the fireplace Jack saw a library filled with books. They virtually lined two walls. Looking back at the inquisitive Mr. Fairchild, Jack would expect no less.

Passing by the dining alcove, the older man led the way to another circular room at the far end. And from the aromas wafting from it, Jack knew it was the kitchen before he entered. But where was the cook? Where was Music?

Just as Mr. Fairchild had said, pots simmered on electric coils. And across the room hummed a refrigerator. Jack opened the metal box and touched a pitcher of milk. It was as cold as snow water.

While he inspected the icy rods near the top, Mr. Fairchild grabbed a potholder and opened the oven door. "Biscuits are done," he said, removing a panful. He placed them on the counter, then turned toward the living area. "Where *is* my— There you are. My, don't you look pretty this evening."

Jack swung around with far more interest than he had a right to.

Music walked toward them across the polished hardwood floor, a lace-trimmed white blouse demurely covering her from just below her chin to her wrists and a prim navy bow tied neatly at her throat. As she came closer, Jack noticed that her dark blue skirt hid all but the tips of patent leather shoes. Except for her face and hands that were browned from the sun, she looked as crisply proper as any young lady just returned from a day at finishing school.

And, thank God, Jack added to himself, all that silky hair had been harnessed at the nape of her neck with another, wider navy bow. Although she was remarkably attractive, she no longer had the other-worldly look of a woodland sprite. She was a mere mortal after all. He exhaled his relief. His thoughts—no—his boundless lust, could again be centered on the one he planned to marry. He smiled politely and stepped aside.

Avoiding his eyes, Music moved stiffly to the stove, her earlier fluid grace all but gone—further proof he'd allowed his imagination to run as wild as the girl did.

"Gramps, why don't you seat our guest for supper," she said in a wispy voice, her back to them as she stirred one of the pots. "Everything's ready."

Vastly relieved that he'd regained his reason, Jack accompanied Mr. Fairchild through the wide opening to the dining room in the soft glow of dusk. The table settings took on a special elegance, while an artful bouquet at the center displayed the same pinks and purples as the petunias bordering the low windows.

Mr. Fairchild had, indeed, created the illusion of eating in a garden surrounded by a wooded park.

And Jack suddenly knew that when he built his own house, he'd want a room just like it. He pictured Sophie sitting across from him at breakfast. Sophie . . . squinting and complaining about the sun.

At that unsettling thought, he took a seat across from his host just as Music entered carrying a large tureen. With lowered eyes, she set it on the white linen tablecloth. And not once did she glance in his direction as she removed the lid.

The strong aroma of chicken and dumplings wafted up to Jack, and he realized how hungry he was, and was glad for it, too. He had no intention of spending the entire mealtime following her every move. He picked up his crystal goblet. As he drank deeply of a refreshingly icy tea, his recalcitrant gaze wandered to the girl's gently swinging hips.

She turned to leave, disappointing him. At the entrance, she turned a knob, lighting the chandelier above the table before moving out of the alcove. Her strides then lengthened, became surer, and Jack saw the grace and, yes, the strength he'd seen earlier—a strength young ladies were taught to deny, a strength that was usually stifled by tightly strung corsets and a half-dozen petticoats.

Jack noticed too late that he was craning his neck to keep the departing girl in view, and he now felt as if he were the one on stage, with her grandfather watching. *He absolutely had to rein in his thoughts.* He took another swallow of the tea.

Seconds later she returned with a serving bowl of peas and carrots in one hand, a platter heaped with biscuits in the other, and Jack found himself desperate to know if she was trussed up in whalebone or not. When she leaned over the table, the material stretched tight across her back and not a single bump or ridge marred the smoothness of her slender form. *She was not wearing a corset.*

The knowledge sent a stirring to Jack's loins as he followed her every move while she placed the food on either side of the flowers. He couldn't stop his mind from wondering what, if anything, lay between her thrusting breasts and the weave of her white blouse.

She stepped back, giving him a better view as she wrapped her fingers over the back of her chair and pulled it out.

Jack sprang to his feet. "Let me help you." He nearly tripped over himself in unaccustomed awkwardness as he rushed around the oval table.

Lowering lashes over those illusive reflections of autumn, she turned shy as he held her chair.

As he pushed it beneath her, he breathed the musky freshness of the forest in her hair and watched the rapid rise and fall of her pouty breasts. His heart kicked again, and he began to feel a cramping in his trousers.

"Mr. Stuart," her grandfather's voice interrupted. "If you'll return to your seat, I'll say grace."

Jack uncurled his fingers from the sides of Music's chair. How long had he been staring her? Worse, had Mr. Fairchild read the raw lust in his eyes?

Hurrying back to his chair, Jack caught himself raking fingers through his hair, a nervous habit that surely confirmed his guilt in her grandfather's eyes. When he sat down he also noticed his collar chaffed more than usual. But under no condition would he try to loosen it. Instead, he took another drink.

"Father in heaven," Mr. Fairchild began with what seemed an undisturbed voice, "bless this food you've provided from your gracious bounty. And thank you, Lord, for the pleasure of this enthusiastic young man's company. We ask for a safe and speedy trip for him tomorrow so that he may quickly rejoin his companions on holiday. Amen."

Although his host could not be faulted for his words, Jack feared a double meaning. Yet, when he looked up, he could read nothing in the fine lines of Mr. Fairchild's face as the older man placidly spooned chicken and dumplings onto his plate.

"Do you plan to go to the fair in St. Louis?" Jack asked, introducing a popular topic in the hope of erasing any doubts Mr. Fairchild might have as well as his own baser desires.

"Music and I talked about it." Her grandfather turned her way and smiled warmly.

Jack didn't dare allow himself the same privilege. Instead he began filling his plate.

"Perhaps," Mr. Fairchild continued, "we'll go in the fall after we've harvested the last of our garden."

"Maybe by then the Wright brothers will agree to bring their flying machine to demonstrate," Jack ventured, knowing he'd mentioned the hottest topic of the year. "The whole country is clamoring to see it. To see proof that it actually does fly."

"I doubt they'll come," Mr. Fairchild replied, spreading butter on his biscuit. "From what I've read, they're not going to let anyone get a close look until they've been granted a patent." He pointed his knife at Jack's plate. "Eat up, son, before your supper gets cold."

"Perhaps, Mr. Stuart," Music murmured softly, "you would prefer something else."

Jack couldn't avoid looking across the table at her—she'd spoken directly to him. Her eyes mirrored the lights glittering from the chandelier, luring him into their intriguing depths. "I—uh—the food looks delicious." He took another hasty gulp of tea.

During the meal, Mr. Fairchild's dissertation on the latest wonders and inventions that would be displayed at the fair challenged Jack's imagination almost enough to cool his hunger for the sumptuous young woman. Almost. If it hadn't been that she breathed constantly, he would've faired much better. Every time his gaze deserted his host for her bosom and he saw those tell-tale nubbins poking at her blouse, his trousers became tighter. More than once he'd been obliged to shift his weight.

It didn't help that Jack caught her stealing glances at him, too. And her high lace collar seemed as binding to her as his clothing did him. Watching her run her fingers beneath the ruffled edge, Jack knew she was aching to take it off. *And he was aching to help her.*

When Jack suddenly realized the talkative Mr. Fairchild had grown silent and probably awaited a reply, he groped for a likely response. Stalling, Jack picked up his ever-handy glass and took a sip as he searched for a diversive topic. His gaze settled upon the chess set. "Who's ahead in the game over there."

It did the trick—a chuckle rumbled out of Mr. Fairchild. "Miss Jane Irene thinks she has me trapped." He turned to his granddaughter. "But the game's not over yet."

Her shy demeanor disappeared as she met his challenge head on. "And it never will be if you don't make your move. Or concede."

Breaking away from the good-natured stare-off, she tilted her face toward Jack and smiled openly. "Gramps is so stubborn he won't make another move until he figures a way out of his predicament. *Which he won't,*" she added, swinging back to her grandfather.

"Don't count on it, young lady." Jutting out his chin, Mr. Fairchild stood up and headed toward the game table.

"Oh, but I do," she answered on a light laugh as she, too, rose.

The girl was bloody marvelous. Not only was she the most provocative woman he'd ever seen, she quite obviously played chess with unabashed gusto. Not a speck of that tiresome poor-little-mindless-me act surfaced as she strolled with unhurried confidence after her grandfather.

Jack followed her into the living room, his palms damp from his desire to place them on the hips that swayed her navy skirt, to pull her back against him, against an ache that grew more intense by the second.

He inhaled deeply and shoved his tingling hands into his pockets.

"Jane Irene," her grandfather called while taking something long and silver from off the mantle. "Where did this come from?"

Abruptly Music stopped.

Jack halted within a hair's breadth of ending up exactly where he wanted to be. Again he smelled the wilds in her hair.

"That?" Her voice pitched high, tight, and, Jack noticed, her back stiffened. "It's a reward. I found something very valuable in the woods today. And a nice gentleman gave me the flute for returning it."

Mr. Fairchild examined a musical instrument so elaborate it looked more like a work of art. He glanced back at her, his graying brows scrunching above suspicious eyes. "Where is this generous benefactor, and just exactly what did you find, a pot of gold?"

"Of course not," Music said, stepping toward her grandfather . . . *and taking her seductive self away from Jack.* She lowered her voice and said something he couldn't quite hear.

Apparently neither had Mr. Fairchild. "What was that? Speak up."

She hesitated.

Curious, Jack stepped closer.

Her grandfather held up the flute pointedly. "Yes?"

Music exhaled. "It was the little animal I found today. It's a koala, from Australia. Very valuable it seems." She swung around . . . coming face to face with Jack, her full lower lip a mere nibble away. She blinked and took a backward step. "So you see, Mr. Stuart, I didn't set the koala on your friends. It came to me just before it jumped on them."

"But, still, child," her grandfather said, drawing her away again, "this is far too expensive a reward."

"I know. That's what I thought. But, Gramps, the peddler was so persistent. And after I'd already refused his first gift, it seemed impolite to turn him down again."

Jack noticed the back of her neck flushed with color. There was more to this story than she was telling. Perhaps that traveling salesman tempted her with a lot more than a flute. *A whole lot more.*

Her grandfather must have come to the same conclusion. He cupped her chin. "What exactly did this man offer you? Tell me."

"Just a bottle of . . . something. You know, like snake oil salesmen like to peddle."

"A bottle of what, Jane," he persisted.

She darted a guilty glance at Jack and lowered her tone. "A love potion. Something he called Cupid's Delight."

*Cupid's Delight?* Jack could hardly believe her words. Instantly, an image crystallized, one of a furry little head popping out of the flimflammer's coat. *A koala's.* It couldn't be. Yet it was.

"And he gave you this expensive flute instead?" Mr. Fairchild shook his head. "He must really believe in that love potion of his. He's probably some ignorant backwoodsman. Got it more likely from one of their healing women." He turned toward Jack. "Those old crones can mix together some mighty strange concoctions."

"No," she said. "He wasn't a mountaineer. He was dressed in city clothes, bowler hat and all. And except for his hair—it seemed to have a mind of its own—he was as stylish as—" Her words stopped abruptly and she diverted her gaze.

"Stylish as what, Jane?" Mr. Fairchild had no intention of letting her hide anything else.

She wiped her hands on her skirt and shot Jack a glance before mumbling, "As Mr. Stuart."

*My God.* The truth hit Jack in the stomach with the punch of a prize fighter's fist. The girl was guilty as sin, and not simply for thinking him stylish. She *had* accepted the love potion, *had* given it to him. Drugged him into lusting after her. She'd probably put it in that icy tea he'd found so almighty delicious.

"We'll talk about this later," her grandfather said as he shifted his attention to Jack and forced a smile. "Do you play chess, Mr. Stuart?"

"Yes," Jack returned with the smoothness of one determined to regain control of his drugged senses. "But your granddaughter's fine meal has gotten the best of me." Slanting a glowering glance in her direction, he added, "I'm afraid I'm going to have to say good night. If you'll be kind enough to show me where to sleep. I must be off early. No doubt," he added with emphasis, "my *fiancée* will be concerned."

Mr. Fairchild gave his granddaughter a teasing smile. "Too bad. I could use some *real* competition for a change."

Jack wasn't surprised that the deceitful girl wasn't up to returning her grandfather's jibe.

But Jack had no trouble speaking. "Maybe we can play a game when I return next week, sir." And, he added to himself, he'd be checking into Music's little game, as well.

# Seven

Jack watched Mr. Fairchild amble to the front door. "The guest rooms are over the carriage house. Jane, dear, show Mr. Stuart the way. Oh, and be sure to put clean linens on his bed. It's been a long time since we had an overnight guest. Now, if you two don't mind, I think I'll go out to the shop and work a while longer."

*The man was walking out? Leaving him, a passion-drugged victim to the mercy of a conniving temptress?*

"Follow me, Mr. Stuart." Avoiding his gaze, Music brushed past and walked outside to a star-filled night. As she crossed a shaft of window light, Jack saw the capricious breeze play at the hem of her skirt.

Somewhere in the distance, an owl hooted.

She answered its call as if it were the most natural thing in the world . . . this enchantress of the forest, this mistress of the night.

But she would be no mistress of his! Jamming his hands into his pockets, Jack strode after her. He had no intention of being seduced by anyone who'd schemed his downfall with some ne'er-do-well, no matter how much his body begged to betray him.

Yet, how had the peddler known he'd become stranded along this road. Unless . . . *Of course!* His De Dion had been sabotaged. And since the peddler couldn't be in two places at once, a conspiracy was afoot—a conspiracy intended to keep him from Sophie.

But who would go to such lengths? A jealous beau?

177

Sophie's mother? And what better place to have his De Dion break down? His avid interest in the latest mechanical innovations was no secret. And—the frosting on the cake— the brilliant inventor also came with a granddaughter of such untamed sexuality, she could tempt the pope to sin.

As proof, the wind whipped Music's trapped hair, freeing one feathery wisp that teased the tender skin behind a beautifully sculpted ear . . . a spot aching to be kissed.

Music reached the stairs at the side of the carriage house and started up.

In the woods beyond, a twig snapped.

That flimflammer was probably skulking around out there, right now, Jack thought. Checking to see if the girl was sufficiently enticing him "down the garden path" or, more precisely, up to the bedroom. Well, not this time.

Jack chased up the stairs after Music and caught her hand. "Miss Fairchild," he said loud enough for any other interested parties to hear. "In no way can I allow you to accompany me into my sleeping quarters. It would be most improper."

"But," she argued with an unabashed look of innocence, "the sheets need changing."

"That's no problem. I became quite proficient at that task while I was away at school. I learned to make my bed so taut I could bounce a quarter on it."

"Oh, really?" Her eyes widened. "I'd like to see that."

He let his mouth drop into a slack smile. You would, would you? Two could play at that game. "Then, just for you, I'll leave it that way in the morning. Even with a quarter for the bouncing." Watching for her reaction, he wondered if she'd ever heard the defaming phrase, two-bit whore.

Either she hadn't or she was a better actress than he'd thought. Nothing save indecision flickered across her face. Then coyly lowering her lashes, Music squeezed past him. "Very well, then. Good night, Mr. Stuart. Sleep well."

*Not bloody likely*, Jack gritted out soundlessly as he watched her fly down the stairs and across the wide driveway with the grace of her young deer. The ache to be tangled up in all those arms and legs was becoming unbearable. "But," he vowed out loud, "I will bear it. I will quench the fierce fire that damnable drug set in me. I will."

Music ran for the house. She'd never felt so ashamed, so unwanted and hurt and. . . . True, he had caught her looking at him during supper, but hadn't he been watching her, too? With those intense, utterly blue eyes?

She slammed through the front door and ran to her room. Closing the door behind her, she moved into the enveloping darkness, grateful to hide from the evidence of her disgrace—from her reflection in the mirror over her dressing table. She brought her hands to her hot cheeks, hoping to cool them.

What a fool she'd been. She knew he wanted to return to his lady . . . the beautiful one in yellow. And still she'd asked to come into his room—even after he told her he didn't want her there. Yes, once the subject of the koala had come up again, he couldn't bear to be anywhere near her.

Tears fell unchecked as Music moved on trembling legs through an inky blur toward her bed.

Or was it because she'd said he was handsome? Unquestionably, she'd been too bold. And ladies were supposed to always keep their beaus guessing. That was undisputed in every tale she'd ever read.

But no story had ever prepared her for the pain she now felt. Allowing a sob to escape, she flung herself across the counterpane . . . and landed in a billowing cloud of silk.

The gown! The beautiful gown.

Sitting up, she scooped it to her breast, clutching it close. She took a ragged breath and brushed it across her tear-streaked cheek. "I guess I should've worn you tonight. If Mr. Harper was right, then Mr. Stuart wouldn't have been able to see anything but me."

"Oh, but I couldn't." Sagging against her pillow-backed headboard, she let the dress slip down to her lap. "I wouldn't want anyone I had to trick into loving me. And besides, I couldn't very well wear you twenty-four hours a day for the rest of my life."

Casting the gown aside, she grabbed a feather pillow and hugged it to her until her arms ached from the strain and she couldn't feel the pain in her chest quite so much. "I've got to stop thinking," she said on a sigh, "that the first dashing young man to come along is my one true love, no matter what his eyes told me when we first saw each other. Love at first sight is a fairy tale, just like fairy godmothers and this stupid dress. And, besides, there are probably hundreds, *thousands* of gentlemen more handsome than he." When she and Gramps went to the fair in St. Louis she'd see them by the peck . . . by the bushel.

But would any of them make her heart sing when they looked at her? Would they have that same sparkling smile when they talked to Gramps about the turning of wheels and of wires and bolts and all the wonders they want to create with them? No other visitor ever caused Gramp's eyes to twinkle with excitement or made him want to share his latest discoveries. Postman McPhee never did, and neither had the grown son Mr. McPhee brought along last month. But Jack Stuart did.

And, she had no doubt, Mr. Stuart also had a kind soul. Even in his anger with Pompeii, he'd raised neither hand nor voice to the little imp. He was the perfect match for her. Or could have been, if she hadn't been too proud to wear the magic gown.

Music tossed the pillow aside and gathered up the bountiful garment again. As she did, she felt something hard and long deep within the folds. Burrowing into them, she discovered the flute sticking out of a deep, narrow pocket.

How could that be? It had been on the mantel only a few minutes ago. How odd. With a puzzled shrug, she withdrew the instrument and raised it to her mouth. Then hesitated. Every window in her sitting alcove was open. Mr. Stuart would hear her.

But, oh, how she was dying to create a song so sweet even those gods of Mr. Harper would cry. Unable to resist, she pressed the satiny metal beneath her lips, then blew across the hole ever so lightly until the softest note emerged.

The low trill pierced her heart, then spiralled down to her womb in a sharp tickle that craved more.

She swung her legs off the bed. She needed to play it out loud. She needed to put on the enchanted dress and go someplace where she'd be free to play and dance until all her sadness floated away on the echoes of her sweet song. Oh, how she longed to do that and more . . . so very much more.

Jack couldn't imagine why he'd insisted on locking himself away in his room so early. He hadn't been the least bit sleepy. And now, after what seemed like half the night, he'd tossed and turned until he'd kicked all his covers onto the floor. He should have stayed and confronted the minx. Found out how much she knew of the plot to keep him from Sophie.

No, he'd been wise not to chance it. That damnable love potion made his desire for her too strong. But he could go out and help Mr. Fairchild. Get his mind onto something constructive.

He lunged out of bed and crossed to the window. The moon, a full one, had risen above the trees and now silhouetted the house across the drive. It somehow made the darkness deeper, the silence more lonely, drawing him to the turret windows opposite the main rooms. He could almost see Music sleeping there. The cool breeze brushing across her sultry nakedness, naughty locks of midnight brown tickling her silken shoulders, her ripening breasts. He saw her eyes flutter open, her soft lips part in a welcoming smile, her arms reach out to him, her—

*Damn. Would that love potion never wear off?*

He deliberately shifted his attention to the shop building. But, damn, no light glowed from its high windows either. Mr. Fairchild had also retired for the night. His glance stole back to her window before he could stop it.

"Damn."

Jack raked his fingers through his hair. He needed to be away from his place. Everything he'd ever strived for was in jeopardy—a solid footing in his father's law office, Sophie.

She was a catch even his brother would envy. And this morning nothing had mattered more. Yet tonight, his every goal seemed as distant and cold as the moon. His only warmth came from thoughts of Music. Music. . . .

*"Music?"* Jack listened for the repeat of a faint melody he thought he'd just heard.

But only the croak of a bullfrog broke the silence.

Leaning out farther, Jack again caught the haunting refrain of sweetest purity. It seemed to come from someplace deep in the woods.

Instinctively he knew only one person in this wilderness would play with such heavenly perfection. He searched the forested shadows, straining to see into the darkness.

The music faded to an occasional gift from the wind. Then nothing. The night became silence again, a silence too painful to bear.

Jack wheeled around and grabbed his trousers off a chair and yanked them on, then his shoes. Within seconds he was out the door and down the stairs while thrusting his arms into the sleeves of his shirt.

Reaching the bottom, he stopped, unsure of which way to go.

The whispery waltz called to him again . . . called him into the shadowy arms of the woods. The enchantress was luring him to her. Even knowing it, he couldn't stop himself.

The moon, too, seemed a part of the bewitching as it lighted his way along a narrow winding path. He ran on feet that missed no step, stumbled over no root as he rushed unerringly toward the lyrical call.

It grew louder, swifter.

His pulse drummed harder, keeping pace.

Then, suddenly, it stopped . . . then slid into a fragile aria that seemed to say, *Not too fast. Softly, gently, or you'll frighten me. I'm but a tender kiss away.*

Biding the music's request, Jack slowed to a quiet walk. As he did, a peace washed over him—a peace as ethereal as the melody filling the fragrant night air. Then the purest of notes began to swell and so did his heart until he thought it would burst if he didn't find her soon.

The moonbeam abandoned him to pour its silvery mist over a small clearing only a few yards farther.

As he felt his way through the last of the trees, he caught shimmering streaks of something swiftly circling. Reaching the last line of trees, the flashes of light converged with Music, Music aswirl in a moon-kissed prism of color.

Fireflies circled in rapt attendance.

Jack's heart stopped, then lurched into hard aching beats. Never had he seen anything so beautiful, so celestial.

Eyes closed, she waltzed to the dreamy nocturne coming from her flute, her face glowing with the aura of an angel. Nimble fingers flitted across the flute, while her bare feet brushed earth with the lightness of morning dew. Her gown's voluminous skirt swept after her, always a step behind, the bodice molding itself to her back, her waist, tugging at the lower walls of her breasts.

He didn't move, didn't breath, bound by her spell. Then slowly, gradually, he became aware of several pairs of shining eyes on the other side of the tiny clearing. From low in the shadows, they reflected her glory.

More eyes watched from tree branches above. They'd come, all her forest creatures. Come in love and awe to worship the purity of her grace and beauty.

And in that instant Jack knew there could be nothing false in her. She was incapable of any kind of deception. He also knew he'd been given the rare privilege of being the man to discover this precious gem.

He inhaled deeply and felt new purpose flow through him. He could go to her now. Take her into his arms, tell her of the miracle he'd just come to understand.

He moved to the edge of the glen.

Beneath his shoe a twig broke.

A screeching owl dove into the clearing, wildly flapping its great wings.

Music came to an abrupt halt, and the animals bolted into the undergrowth.

Feeling like an intruder, Jack stepped beneath a low-hanging branch as Music lowered her flute and swept the enclosing forest with a searching gaze. "What is it, owl?"

The large bird circled her one last time, then flew into the night.

The moon, too, went into hiding behind a cloud, dropping a veil of darkness over the girl as she fled into the trees.

Wheeling around to follow, Jack found himself trapped in a tangle of vines. Spiny thorns pierced his trousers, pricked his legs. He reached down and ripped himself free. Then, circling to avoid them, he listened for Music's footsteps. But he heard nothing. No crunch, no rustle. Nothing save the lament of his own sigh.

# Eight

"Wake up, son," came a gruff voice that must've been attached to the hand jiggling Jack's shoulder. "Rise and shine."

Groaning, he rolled toward the sound and managed to lift one eyelid.

Twinkling blue eyes and a jaunty grin greeted him. "Your breakfast is waiting, sleepyhead. I've already had mine. Come on out to the shop when you're finished."

Jack rose up on one elbow and attempted an alert nod. "Be right with you."

"Good boy," Mr. Fairchild said, giving him a final pat.

A chuckle tumbled out of Jack as he watched the lean older man walk out of the cramped guest room. How many times had he himself said, "Good boy," to his pet collie while ruffling its coat?

Swinging his feet to the floor, he stretched his back and arms. He felt as if he hadn't slept more than a dozen minutes all night—which he probably hadn't. That love potion Music had given him had taken hours and innumerable splashings with cold water to cool his hot blood enough to allow him to drift off.

Jack shook his cotton-stuffed head. How could someone with eyes so utterly innocent, so open that they drew one to her very soul, have known what she unleashed in him? If she'd given that drug to a baser fellow, there was no telling what might have befallen her. *And to tempt him yet further with that haunting music, that gown.* He had no idea any

fabric could cling so sensuously and still swirl away into
yards and yards of flirting skirts.

"And," he said, springing to his feet, "the reason I've
never seen anything like it before is because it doesn't exist.
I never left this room last night. It was a drug-induced
hallucination." And worse, he groused as he clamped his
mouth shut, the girl even had him talking out loud to
himself.

Jack reached for his trousers that, he noted, now lay
haphazardly across the arm of the chair beside his bed.
Hadn't he folded them and placed them neatly across the
chair back last night?

"No!" Ignoring his doubts, he thrust a foot into his pant
leg. Today he would allow nothing but thoughts of his
purpose. Breakfast, return the gasoline tank to his auto, and
be gone from this place for good.

His other foot midair, he paused. He *had* promised Mr.
Fairchild he'd come back. A most unwise offer considering
everything. Instead, perhaps he could allow the helpful man
a few extra minutes to examine the De Dion this morning.
Then he really needed to get back where he belonged.

Belonged? His second leg halfway in his trousers, he
paused again. Did he really belong in a stuffy law office,
spending hour after dreary hour searching dry volumes for
some boring precedents? And worse, did he belong with the
rest of the pack who were vying for Sophie Monroe's
favors? Small wonder she was so incredibly vain, so
callously cavalier with other people's feelings.

Vain? Callous? Was that how he truly felt about Sophie?
Did he even like her? Had it just been the chase? The
competition? Or his endless quest for his father's accep-
tance?

Jack expelled a harsh breath. He simply had to desist with
these destructive thoughts.

A loud scraping drew his attention to the small window
overlooking the grounds. He spotted Mr. Fairchild just
before the older man disappeared through the portal of the
amazing workshop. Warmth infused him. What a wonderful
old character. And hadn't Mr. Fairchild called him "son"

earlier? And for once, the word held no inflection of disappointment or disapproval. If anything, it seemed very close to an endearment.

Music was fortunate, indeed, to have her gramps who just "tinkered."

Music. . . .

Jack caught himself as he started to envision her loveliness, this tempting bait of the flimflammer. "Not today, thank you."

He whipped his shirt off the bedpost and put it on. Buttoning it, his attention wandered to the chenille bedspread heaped on the floor, and he remembered his promise of the night before. With a triumphant smile, he reached into his pocket for a quarter. Not only had he *not succumbed* to the flimflammer's trickery, he *would* win Sophie's promise of marriage before the end of the week and beat whoever masterminded his downfall.

Looking out the dining room window, Music spotted Mr. Stuart and her heart picked up pace. He strode across the driveway with the assurance of a young prince. The morning sun added to the picture by turning his thick blond hair into a crown of the lightest gold.

Her hands flew to her own hair to make sure not a strand had escaped the coil she'd so painstakingly fashioned. She was sure it and the cocoa-brown voile she'd donned made her appear much more grown up, for certainly he was twenty-two or three, at the very least. And today, if nothing else, she refused to shame herself in front of him. He may never think of her as desirable, but this time he would see someone as sophisticated as any lady in the magazine stories. Gay, too. Like the French belles. And she *refused* to let her "telltale" eyes give away her true feelings.

Music scanned the table once more to make sure everything was pleasingly displayed. Fresh flowers again took center stage to complement the rose-trimmed china. Circling it were platters of precisely lined bacon, golden-browned potatoes, and biscuits. And placed on each plate, bowls of freshly picked and sliced peaches swam in sweetened cream, giving a mouth-watering glow to the picture. To each she'd added a sprig of mint, just as the June issue of *Ladies Home Journal* had suggested "for that extra touch of glamour."

His loud knock at the door echoed through the rooms. Yet it banged no louder than Music's heart as she rushed to the entrance. After one last smoothing of her skirt, she reached for the handle with trembling fingers.

"Good morning, Mr. Stuart." The confident greeting she'd practiced for the past hour came out as a bare whisper, yet his eyes flared as if she'd yelled.

"Good morning, Miss Fairchild," he said, then swept his fingers through his hair, though to Music, there wasn't the slightest need. It brushed away from his tanned forehead with perfect fullness.

Realizing time had passed while they continued to stare, Music lost her confidence. She lowered her lashes. "Breakfast is ready except for the eggs. How would you like yours?"

"Over easy." He, too, murmured his words quietly, as if to say them any louder might have caused the yokes to break. Could he be shy, too?

No, impossible. Not the worldly Mr. Stuart. Whirling away, Music fled to the kitchen.

With hands shaking so much she barely managed to crack the eggs into the skillet, she placed them over the electric coils, then hesitantly eyed the coffeepot. She knew she should take it into the dining room and serve him, but she feared more coffee would end up on the tablecloth than in his cup.

Yet he was just sitting out there waiting. And probably listening to her every move. She grabbed a potholder.

Walking into the dining room, a small measure of confidence returned when she noticed his attention was trained on two half-grown bunnies cavorting outside on the lawn. She, too, paused and watched.

Their overgrown ears flicked back and forth almost as fast as their tiny tails as they hopped around each other in play. The dew-sprinkled grass beneath their paws sparkled in the young sun as did the weeping willow just beyond, reminding Music that this was her favorite time of day.

She felt her tension drain away and confidence return to her hands. She stepped up beside Mr. Stuart and smoothly tipped the blue-speckled pot over his cup.

At the first splash, Mr. Stuart swung toward her. "*No.*" He flung his hand over the cup's rim—too late for Music to stop the hot brew's flow. It spilled over him. "Ow!" he cried and jerked away.

"You're burned!" Swiftly she set aside the pot and dipped her fingers into a dollop of butter. She swept up his hand and began to slather it with gentle strokes.

Grimacing at first, his expression changed as his eyes followed her ministrations, then trailed slowly up to her face.

She could actually feel the heat from his gaze sear her cheeks. It took all her willpower not to wilt into a quivering mess again as she also realized that she lovingly stroked the back of his hand.

Abruptly he pulled away. "I don't know why I stuck my fool hand out like that." He picked up his linen napkin and dabbed at the overflowed coffee. "I simply should've said I didn't want any."

Music retrieved the pot. "Would you prefer tea?"

"*No.*" Eyeing her, he arched a brow. "I'm not the least interested in *anything* you could give me to drink."

His sudden hostile tone unnerved her. She couldn't imagine what she'd done this time to offend him. He couldn't possibly blame her for his scalded hand, could he? Feeling helpless, she turned away. "I'd better get back to the eggs."

Later, after she'd returned and served them both, she did her best to eat while sitting on her side of a gaping chasm of silence.

But he seemed to have no trouble at all. He virtually wolfed down his food . . . everything, that is, except the peaches and cream—which he never touched. Finished before she'd hardly begun, he pushed back his chair and came to his feet. "Excellent," he said, his gaze holding hers in its force. "Your biscuits were light as air, and everything else was cooked to perfection. Now, if you'll excuse me, your grandfather is waiting." Then without giving her the slightest chance to respond, he strode out of the alcove.

When the slam of the front door announced his departure, Music allowed the hot tears banked at the back of her eyes to escape. Something about her must be terribly wrong. Had Gramps been lying to her all these years? Instead of the pretty young lady he said she was becoming, was she in truth some kind of a backwoods freak?

Numb, Music rose and began stacking the dishes. Perhaps that was why Gramps had kept her in this remote hollow all these years. She wasn't fit for polite society. No handsome young prince for her. Her chest grew unbearably tight, and she sighed.

Just then, the two bunnies hopped from beneath the petunias. One pressed its nose to the window and looked up at her with big moist eyes.

Wiping her own, Music attempted a smile. "Oh, my sweet little ones. I'll always have you, won't I? And all my other forest friends." She knelt down to where they waited and touched the window glass.


Panting for air, Cupid chased after the chugging sounds of the Fairchild tractor . . . *as he'd been doing for the last ten minutes*. On aging legs he staggered to a stop and slumped against an accommodating pine.

Pompeii, following close behind, flopped at his feet in an exhausted heap.

"I should've . . . taken the chance . . . and flown," Cupid sputtered between breaths. "This old body isn't what it used to be."

Echoing up the wooded ridge, he heard the tractor's engine backfire, then die.

"Young Jack and Mr. Fairchild must have reached the De Dion with the gas tank." He pushed himself away from the trunk. "Too bad I didn't realize a full tank would be too heavy to carry." He nudged Pompeii with his toe. "Come on. We've got to get close enough to hear them talking.

Maybe I'll find out why Jack's being so stubborn. Why he insists on denying his heart."

Pompeii scampered up his leg and into his arms.

Cupid eyed him with a stern expression that dissolved into a chuckle. "You lazy imp." He settled his pet on the crook of his arm and started through a patch of ferns.

After a few steps, his puzzlement over Jack's attitude this morning resurfaced. "I just don't understand," he muttered. "Our young man was so close to reaching out to our Music last night. His desire for her couldn't have been more evident than when he watched her dance. But, blast the luck, the lad stepped on the world's noisiest twig. Then this morning he wasn't merely distant, he was downright rude. *Why?*" Cupid heaved a sigh and carefully made his way over the last steep hill.

Reaching the bottom he stepped as lightly as possible across an inch-thick carpet of crunchy pine needles as he edged from tree to tree until the dark green of the auto came into view. He spotted two pairs of legs sticking out from beneath the back bumper. Hearing voices, he put a finger to his mouth and gave Pompeii a stern look of warning, then tiptoed closer.


While Mr. Fairchild tightened a half-inch thick bolt, Jack strained to hold the gasoline tank in place, wishing he had nothing more on his mind than a timely completion of their task. But he couldn't forget Music and her stunning appearance this morning. Never again would he consider brown boring. . . . The blend of her hair, skin, her eyes, with that sheer chocolate day gown . . . clinging to her every curve till it reached the satin tie at her waist. Even the draped skirt had teased him, leaving him aching to see as much of her legs as he had yesterday.

Again she'd acted as shy as a day-old filly. *And after what she'd done to him?*

"Scoot to the side a little, son," Mr. Fairchild said. "I can't quite reach that hole."

Jack obliged, glancing at the older man's grease-smudged face . . . a face as wise as it was honest. And even though

Jack knew he should just drive away, let sleeping dogs lie, he couldn't leave without asking one last question. "Doesn't it disturb you to have a strange man wandering around your property, trying to pawn off some potentially dangerous drug on your granddaughter?"

Mr. Fairchild pulled a bolt from his shirt pocket and began threading it. "It did. But I questioned Music about it this morning, and I'm satisfied."

"Satisfied?"

The old fellow picked up the wrench and fitted it around the bolt. "As innocent of the outside world as she is, I had to be far more blunt than I would've liked. But at least," he said while twisting down on his tool, "I don't have to worry about yesterday. She was very adamant about the fact that he never touched so much as her fingertips when he gave her the flute."

"Are you sure?" Jack shifted the canister's weight from one upraised arm to the other. "Maybe she's afraid to tell you everything. About the love potion, for instance."

"Never in all the years we've been together has she lied to me. But then I haven't kept anything from her either." He chuckled. "We even made a pact after I read her *The Three Musketeers*. You know, all for one, one for all.

Jack warmed to the thought of a nut-brown tyke curled up in her gramps' lap while he read to her. Jack hoped he, too, would be that kind of father someday, one who would take the time to read an entire novel to his own children.

Of course, Jack knew as he pulled himself out of another well of wishful thinking, Music *had* lied to her kind old grandfather. *She had taken the potion, had used it.* How else could he explain his overpowering desire to remove all her clothes and kiss every inch of her windswept body?

"All done." Mr. Fairchild began scooting from beneath the auto.

Jack waited until the older man was on his feet, then followed. After dusting himself, he dug into his pocket for his money clip. From it he removed a five-dollar bill. "You're been a life-saver, sir. Please take this with my heartfelt thanks."

Mr. Fairchild waved it away. "No. I should be thanking you. It's been a rare pleasure, having someone to talk to who follows the latest innovations and their development. I don't know when I've enjoyed anything more."

A flock of game birds took instant flight out of a bed of ferns. Something had flushed them. *Or someone.*

Jack wheeled around.

When nothing else stirred, Jack turned back to Mr. Fairchild and lowered his voice—he had no intention of making lurking sneaks privy to his plans ever again. "I've never had a more stimulating experience, either. My hands are itching to explore some possibilities of my own." His thoughts flashed to Music. He wrenched them back to his benefactor.

Mr. Fairchild took hold of Jack's shoulder and gave it an affectionate squeeze. "Drive carefully, son. And hurry back."

Having made the decision not to return and feeling like a liar for not telling the dear old man, Jack braved nothing more than a nod as he headed for the starter crank.

*"Jumping Jupiter!"* Cupid's outburst was lost in the roar of the two departing vehicles. "The lad's leaving. Going on to that snooty debutante. And if she realizes his affections are starting to stray, she won't be able to stand it. She'll wangle a proposal out of young Jack before the week is out."

Pompeii sprang up on his hind legs and clutched Cupid's lapels, staring into his master's face with beseeching urgency.

"Don't worry, my little friend." Cupid scratched behind Pompeii's furry ears. "I'm not beaten yet."

# Nine

An iridescent wisp of rainbow fluttered from behind a tree.

Jack slammed his foot on the brake pedal, sending the De Dion into a screeching, sliding halt.

"My God," he blurted as the auto rocked back and forth on its axle springs. "I've gone absolutely mad."

Nodding aimlessly, he shifted to the lowest gear, but couldn't bring himself to move his foot onto the accelerator. Instead, he found himself searching for another glimpse of the dress from his dream . . . and Music, especially Music.

After all, he rationalized, he hadn't had the opportunity to bid her farewell. By the time he and Mr. Fairchild had lashed the tank onto the mechanical mule and gone to look for her, she'd disappeared.

"It's for the best," he reproved in a stern tone. "For the best." And, he noted, talking to himself was becoming a habit.

He pressed down on the pedal while easing off the clutch.

To the side, he spotted another flash of the filmy material.

Jack hit the brake again.

This time the auto bucked and died.

"Blast!" He jumped down and strode to the front to crank the starter. "Serves me right," he muttered, "for acting like a lovesick fool. And I know I haven't had any more of that blasted potion."

Another spark of rainbow caught his eye no more than twenty yards away.

As if the fabric were a starting flag, Jack broke into a sprint. Dodging through the trees to the spot where he'd seen it, he found nothing . . . not even Music's footprints. Quickly he scanned the woods around him. The idea of leaving the loveliest of songs without hearing that soft airy voice or watching the grace of her light steps one last time sent another pang of yearning straight to his soul.

A squirrel ran up a tree.

Jack was surprised it wasn't chasing after the Pied Piper of the Alleghenies. Smiling, he pictured Music with a long parade of creatures following behind . . . creatures like the one Sophie and her mother had thrown a tantrum over. Like mother, like daughter.

*Like mother, like daughter.*

The thought of marrying Sophie suddenly lost the last trace of its charm.

Music, on the other hand, was a delight. And what if he was wrong and she truly was the innocent her grandfather claimed she was. What if, in fact, she hadn't given him the love potion and every single feeling, every single desire had come from his own heart?

Jack had to know. He headed for the ridge separating him from the Fairchild farm.

Off to the right, he caught anther glimpse of the shiny fabric and suddenly had the strongest inkling that fate or some kind of providence had taken a hand in bringing him to Music. And if that were so, he certainly didn't object. He veered away from the incline and started into a narrow hollow sliced by a wide murmuring stream.

Soon the murmur grew louder as if it were telling him he was getting closer. He pushed through low-hanging willows after his own will-o'-the-wisp . . . and stepped into an emerald glen. Grass and ferns framed a pond fed by a waterfall sheeting down from a high stone shelf. Beside the pool, the white gown with its illusive array of color was draped across a boulder. Next to it lay the shiny new flute.

Irresistibly drawn, he moved to the rock and ran his fingers over the silky fabric, half-expecting it to vanish before his eyes. But it was real. *As real as last night in the woods.*

But where was Music?

He watched the pond for a moment, hoping she would emerge. When she didn't, he turned in a full circle, yet found no other sign of her.

Perhaps she'd seen him first and run away.

Without her dress?

Then his rudeness at breakfast crept into his thoughts, twisted his insides. As brash as he'd been this morning, it had not been the first time. In fact, he bemoaned, he wouldn't blame her if she never spoke to him again.

Something broke through the seamless waterfall.

A hand! Music must be standing *behind* it.

Had she seen him? Jack dismissed the possibility as he watched her slender fingers slice the cascade, curve downward, then return.

Mesmerized, he continued to stare, following the constant rhythm of her moves and gradually became aware that Music's hand was waltzing with the water. He remembered seeing a gramophone in a corner of the Fairchild living room and pictured an awkward little four-year-old being taught to dance by her grandfather. The child emerged into a beautiful young woman whirling gracefully around the floor in Mr. Fairchild's arms.

An instant desire to take her grandfather's place left Jack's own arms feeling unbearably empty. His Music danced with water when she should be dancing with him. *Him.*

Recklessly he tore off his shirt and discarded his shoes, then clambered up to a narrow ledge. It looked slick.

But Jack hesitated no more than a second. Music was waiting.

Cooled by a chill spray, he edged across the slippery surface. Reaching the side of the cascade, he moved between the wall and the water. As he did, the roar of the falls became muffled. Another step and the stone behind Jack cut away to a cave-like room . . . and Music.

Sunlight streamed through a thin cleft in the ceiling,

bathing her every curve in a golden aura. A thin, wet chemise clung to her body . . . her firm breasts . . . their nipples puckered against the cold.

His desire to take them, warm them . . . feel them come alive in his hands was. . . .

She must've sensed his presence. She turned toward him.

Music's lips parted. A dream, a wonderful dream. Hesitantly she stretched out her hand.

He stepped closer, took it. His felt hot against her own cold one, and it warmed almost instantly to his touch as she watched his eyes turn as dark as the cave they stood in.

After a breathless time, this very real apparition spoke. "Forgive me," it whispered.

Not understanding, she searched his face.

"For my abrupt behavior this morning. And last night. I've been a fool. An absolute fool."

He seemed so real. She reached up and touched his cheek.

His breath caught. Then he covered her hand and moved it to his mouth. His lips, pressed into her palm, sent lightning bolts to her heart, her head, to her innermost secrets. Her vision blurred.

Abruptly he released her. "I'm sorry. I shouldn't have been so forward. It's just—I haven't had a clear thought since I first saw you, the wind in your hair." He lifted a wet strand from her shoulder. "You are the most glorious, the most desirable creature I've ever seen."

"I am?"

Taking hold of her, he looked deeply into her eyes. "Yes. —Oh, yes."

Could Jack Stuart truly be here, saying everything she wanted to hear and more? She felt the very real bite of his fingers. But this couldn't be happening. He was so handsome, so sophisticated, and she was just. . . . Music lowered her gaze from his princely face to her simple undergarment . . . *that clung to her body as transparently as wet tissue paper. She was as good as naked!* "Heavens!" Wrenching away, she shot him a horrified glance, then dove through the wall of water, down to the pond below.

She could die of embarrassment, just die.

Emerging from the depths, she saw Jack slice into the pool a couple of feet from her. Frantically she swam toward the bank. Then stopped. She couldn't step out with him watching. Nonplussed, she lowered her feet to the sandy bottom of the chest-deep pool. She had no choice but to face her latest shame head-on. This was no dream—this was a nightmare.

Jack quickly closed the gap and stopped in front of her. He, too, came to his feet as water fell away from his shoulders and chest . . . looking as wondrously powerful as ever.

She desperately wanted to escape. *She desperately wanted to stay.* Catching her lip between her teeth, she looked away.

"I've done it again, haven't I?," he murmured. "I never seem to do anything right when I'm near you."

Fleetingly, she glanced back and saw his hand reaching for her.

He quickly withdrew it. "Please, if you'll just stay long enough to let me explain, I promise I won't touch you or do one more thing to frighten you."

In amazement, Music returned her gaze to him. He thought she'd run away because she was *afraid?* Surely, he must have noticed she was the next thing to naked.

"You'll stay? Thank you," he said, relief ringing in his voice.

And, Music noted, if anyone seemed frightened it was him. His worried expression attested to that.

"I've done you a grave injustice," he continued. "When you mentioned the love potion the peddler offered you, I assumed that you must have accepted it and used it on me. It seemed the only logical explanation for me turning into such a lovesick fool."

His words stung with the sharpness of a face-slap. Did he think only a drugged fool could love her? Tears clogged her throat. She swallowed them down. "I see. Now, if you'll be gentleman enough to turn around, I'd like to leave."

"No!" He clasped her hand. "I mean, please don't go. I'm saying everything wrong. You're so beautiful, your eyes, your voice. I can't seem to look at you and do anything right. I . . . care for you. More than you could ever imagine."

He cared for her! Tears threatened again, but this time from unbelievable joy.

Jack's grip tightened. "I know now that you would never do anything deceitful. You are as good and pure as you are beautiful."

A tear escaped, rolled down her cheek. He made her feel as if she were a princess. Looked at her as if she were his own true love.

Jack brushed her tear away. "Please," he said, his own voice sounding choked. "Say something. Tell me I can stay. Let me show you I'm not the oaf you think I am."

"Impossible."

"Oh, well, I—" He dropped her hand and stepped back.

She moved through the water to him. "No. I meant you could never be an oaf. You're . . . you're wonderful."

Instantly she found herself enfolded in his embrace, her thinly sheathed breasts pressed tightly against his bare chest. She gasped at the electrifying sensation.

Jack released her and stepped back. "Forgive me. I did it again. I'll try harder. I promise. I'll do my utmost to wait until you have the same feelings for me that I have for you."

Did his skin tingle at her touch, too? Did his pulse race with the same wildness? She reached out and placed her palm flat against his chest.

His heart kicked, then thudded hard and fast.

Music looked up to eyes that were still as dark and seeking as they'd been in the cave. "I think, Mr. Stuart, that you and I are already sharing the same feelings. So," she said, removing her hand, "I think maybe I'd better get my clothes on."

His eyes widening slightly. "Of course. Absolutely. I certainly wouldn't want to compromise you. I love you. I want you to come to me as my bride. I want," he finished in a rushed whisper, "to wake up with you in my arms for the rest of our lives."

*He wanted to marry her!* Ecstatic yet a little frightened by his glorious news, she backed through the water's cool caress until she reached the grassy bank. And not once did she take her eyes off him. She drank in every muscled plane of his back, his stout neck, that sunny hair. And wasn't he being the truest, dearest gentleman? Not once did he venture even the quickest peek.

As swiftly as possible, Music wrung out the hem of her chemise, then swept her dress from the rock and dropped it over her head. While fastening the back buttons, she sought Jack again. "You can come out now."

He swung around and stared, a grin slowly growing. When it was full-blown, he strode from the pond. "The peddler gave you that dress, didn't he?"

"Yes. But see?" She retrieved the musical instrument and put it away. "The dress is the flute's pocket."

"The flute's pocket?" He exploded into laughter.

The happy eruption so infected Music, she joined him. And besides, it *was* funny. And he was marvelous.

By the time their laughter had subsided, she found herself in Jack's arms again. But this time all trace of her nervousness was gone.

Dropping his hands to her waist, Jack leaned back enough to peer down at her. "I'm beginning to think I've misjudged the peddler. Drastically. Did you happen to be anywhere near the road this morning?"

"No. I came straight here after I did the breakfast dishes."

"That's what I thought." Jack looked over her head and scanned the dark forest surrounding the glen. After a moment, he returned his deep blue eyes to her. They sparked with mischief. "I know I just promised I wouldn't do anything, but I think there's someone out there who deserves to see that his efforts have succeeded."

"You mean?"

"Yes," he whispered a breath away, "the peddler." His lips claimed hers, spilled across them, caressing . . . tasting . . . demanding until his passion consumed all her strength. She flung her arms around his neck.

As she did, he pulled her tight against him and deepened the kiss, his mouth exploring with increasing swiftness.

She rose up on her toes, seeking more, ever more as one of his hands cupped the back of her head. She heard a sweet moan and vaguely knew it had come from her.

He, too, groaned and pulled away, holding her from him. "I think," he said, his voice as ragged as her breathing, "we've more than shown him."

Maybe it would be enough for his Mr. Harper, *but not for her.* Music pressed forward. "*I think* we should do it again, just to make sure."

His hands dropped from her arms, and she fell against him . . . exactly where she wanted to be.

Threading her hands in his hair, she pulled him closer.

"My God," he groaned as he wrapped himself around her. "You are my undoing."

His lips descended, and Music's eyes fell shut at his touch, so wondrous that even the wind overhead whirred like the wings of an angel.

And on those wings came a new song. "Young love," it sighed, "true love. . . . Sweet ambrosia from above. . . ."

# JUST FRIENDS,
# OF COURSE

*Aileen Humphrey*

# One

"The horses are about to fall asleep in the street. Has he forgotten we're out here?" James Hastings snapped shut the lid of his watch and slumped back into the seat.

"He knows we're waiting," replied Archie, leaning back in the cab in a more relaxed attitude than Hastings had been able to achieve. "It's just that he has some new trousers that are a tighter fit than humanely reasonable. He can't get into them without help. I don't know how he'll sit down once he gets out here."

That's when an old fashioned carriage turned the corner and pulled up two houses away. It wasn't all that remarkable, but enough to cause Hastings to lose interest in the sleeping habits of carriage horses. His attention shifted to that same neighbor's front door when it swung wide. A footman hurried down the stairs to open the carriage door and let down the steps. A ladies' maid with a cushion in hand followed the footman. She climbed into the coach. A second maidservant appeared with a work basket over her arm, followed by another footman who carried a large, shallow basket with its own cushion. A glistening bowl sat on that cushion like a crown.

The servants stood at attention.

The gentlemen continued to watch as two more footmen appeared at the door with a small, bird-like lady between them. She was all but hidden beneath her billowing skirts, tasseled cloak, and an antiquated bonnet laden with silk flowers and taffeta ribbons. A portrait in matronly black.

The lady was assisted down the stairs, across the sidewalk, and into the waiting carriage. The maid with the work basket carefully eased her mistress's monstrous hooped skirt through the small door, where it went a long way toward filling the carriage. From the way the carriage tilted it could reasonably be supposed that Madame was being settled onto the cushioned seat by the maid inside. Then the work basket was handed in. Finally the basket with the bowl.

If Hastings had been closer he could have seen the name "Snooky" engraved on the side of that bowl. "Sheffield Silver" stamped on the bottom.

At a nod from the man at the carriage, another of the retinue appeared at the door of the house. This was a much younger lady than the last, plainly dressed in gray. She had a disagreeable looking pug dog in her arms. A toast-colored, yelping animal with a dark, pushed-in face that might have been the cause of its bulging eyes. Its drooping ears, however, were unobjectionable. Around its neck was a wide blue ribbon tied in a big bow. Descending the steps unassisted, the young lady approached the carriage at a stately pace. A footman reached for the dog. The dog bit him and got a smart snap on the nose before being handed to the maid inside the carriage.

Kid-gloved hands lifted pale gray skirts just enough for the young woman to enter the carriage without tripping. One of the footman wadded up the last of her skirts and stuffed them inside before he pushed in the steps and closed the door. When the carriage rolled away, all Hastings could see at the windows were mounds of black and gray fabric.

"That was Mrs. Fitzfender," said Archie. "She's a crony of my godmother's. They're both widowed ladies with time on their hands if not on their sides."

"Really? She's rather nice looking."

"Then you're referring to Miss Gladwin. I wouldn't be a bit surprised if they're heading for my godmother's house. This is Wednesday, isn't it?"

Hastings consulted the newspaper beside him on the seat and said that there was trouble in the mines, a sale of gentlemen's high quality leggings, and that it was most certainly Wednesday.

"Well then, Mrs. Fitzfender is off for an afternoon of rejuvenating gossip and exotic teas. They thrive on gossip. Anything about anyone will do. There's nothing too trivial and no one too insignificant for their interest."

"What a help they must be to Scotland Yard."

"Don't laugh. It's through Godmama that I found out about the bum and leg padding Henny Romburg wears under his trousers so he won't look like a marabou. Thought he looked a bit strange when he sat down, like he had a cheese in his drawers. You must have noticed."

"I will admit that I did wonder what the problem was."

"Godmama said she heard it from her maid, who heard it from someone else's maid, who got it from who knows where, but she thinks it was the boy who sweeps up for Henny's tailor. It's shameful the way they gossip with their servants."

Hastings crossed an ankle over the other knee, noticed that his shoes had been resoled since the last time he'd worn them and said, "What else might your aunt have to say?"

"About anything in particular?"

"That young woman in gray."

"Ah yes, Miss Gladwin, ladies companion and dog's nanny. Been there for over a year. Comes from Yorkshire. Or Shropshire." Archie shrugged, and said, "No matter. Her parents follow the horse races or whatever happens to take their fancy at the moment. Last I heard they were on their way to Greece to look for ancient Troy, but I doubt that they'll stay long enough to find it. I don't know if they're even aware of their daughter's altered situation. The young lady's brother and his wife live on the family estate, wherever it is. She has no other siblings."

Hastings had become especially thoughtful. "You did say *Miss* Gladwin, didn't you? She appears as though she might be rather . . . aloof."

"She does give that impression. I suspect it's because she's trying to avoid further scandal. Godmama said the young lady in question was going to be married until she found out that her intended's true love was the money she would inherit when she said I do. Knowing that she broke it off."

"A fortune hunter was he?"

"And badly dipped at that. She had a narrow escape. It really doesn't seem fair. I mean the law. Everything would go directly into her husband's keeping as soon as they tied the knot. As I understand it, she was no longer welcome in the ancestral home after she broke the engagement. The word is that there was a loud, unpleasant row. Something about her brother's wife taking her to task for acting selfishly, with no thought for the embarrassment she caused the family." Archie wagged a finger and said, "Injustice if you ask me. Parliament should recon—"

"Never mind all that. What about Miss Gladwin?"

"Patience, Hastings, patience. We shall come to it presently." Taking his own sweet time he shifted around in his seat to adjust the window next to him. Then he leaned over to adjust the window on the other side of the cab. Gleefully aware of his friend's foot-tapping impatience he compared the windows and made another adjustment. It wasn't until then that he leaned back and said, "Now about Miss Gladwin. Godmama told me—and she ought to know— that after the blow up with her family and the loss of a friendly roof over her head, the lady wasn't inclined to take charity from friends. Neither was she eager to join the endless search for the cuckoo birds of life in the company of her migratory parents. That's why she became a companion to Mrs. Fitzfender and her nasty little dog."

"How can it be that you've left out the lady's height, weight, and birthday? Preferred scent?"

"The merest oversight. But her eyes are hazel, and under that hat her hair is a silky nut brown, not so dark as your beard. Wears it in a bun, as you may have noticed."

"So you've observed her that intently have you?"

"Briefly, on one occasion, while in my godmother's parlor," replied Archie, glancing out the window to see what else might be going on. "She, that is Miss Gladwin, hardly goes out except in the company of Mrs. Fitzfender, so she sees very few people and very few people see her. Furthermore I found out that she doesn't receive callers."

"Then I can assume that she has lost interest in finding her lifelong companion?"

"Whatever her inclinations are, there's no one to introduce you to her, if that's what you've got in mind."

"There's your godmother."

"She won't do it. She isn't at home to anyone else on the days she's having tea and gossip."

"Just be a chum and introduce me to your godmother."

"But she won't—"

"Then again, she might."

"Even if she did, Miss Gladwin won't say any more than good manners require. No drives through the park with that one, though you're welcome to try." Archie was obviously tiring of the subject.

"I only want to get into the Fitzfender house a few times," persisted Hastings. "Miss Gladwin doesn't even have to be there. With or without her, word is sure to get around that I'm calling at a certain residence to see someone. People are bound to jump to the wrong conclusion. In fact I'm depending on it."

"The truth now, what is this sudden interest in a woman you've hardly seen?"

There was a pause before Hastings said, "You might call it a smoke screen."

"You might call it that. I call it damned fishy."

"It is damned fishy. You know that my family is forever suggesting this woman or that as a wife for yours truly because I'm the only son. It's like telling a loved one that they need a toothache or a head cold or a boil that lasts forever. You, being a younger son, have missed such glad tidings. Hasn't your oldest brother complained?"

"No. Father just says that with so many of us sooner or later someone will do something foolish and bring home a wife."

"I applaud your father, while rejoicing in the fact that your godmother is a hopeless gossip. It shouldn't take too long before my family finds out that I have an acquaintance with this Miss Gladwin. If they happen to form the opinion that I have serious intentions in that direction, they'll leave me alone for a while. Perhaps a long while." Hastings looked all too pleased with himself.

"It's much too dangerous," warned Archie.

"No need to sound so gloomy. I don't want any entanglements, and Miss Gladwin is too busy hiding from fortune hunters to want a husband."

"It won't work."

"Look here old chum. I can't very well tell my family that I'm not interested in respectable women, can I? You can see that I can't."

"What's wrong with respectable women?"

"You never know what you're getting, that's what's wrong. Look what happened to poor Osgood."

"Osgood is a sad case."

"They seemed like such an agreeable pair," sighed Hastings.

"I remember."

"All those evenings at the opera, dinner parties, chaperons to direct what little conversation they had for the two or three months they courted."

"I know, I know," groaned Archie.

"Then they were married, had a week alone together, and found out that they couldn't stand one another."

"Regrettable."

"Then there's what happened to Gilly. He hasn't been the same man since."

Archie looked pained. "Bloody awful what happened to Gilly. But they are allowing visitors now if the room is darkened and you don't make any sudden moves or loud noises." Both men observed a moment of silence for their friend. Then he said, "In remembrance of what Gilly used to be, I'll take you to meet my godmother, but don't expect too much."

"Good show!"

Archie shook his head. "It won't work."

"What exactly is it that won't work?"

"For one thing I don't think you can convince your family that you're serious about this. For another—"

"Not convince them? Ha! For tuppence I'd prove it."

"Tuppence it is! I'll give you . . . oh . . . a fortnight. No," he said, waving away that offer. "I'm feeling particularly generous. I'll give you an entire month in which to accomplish your end and come out of it unscathed. Mind you, it must be all business and only business."

"It's as good as done!"

"When it's all over I trust you'll remember that I told you so. I might even remind you of it. I've already begun to think of ways to spend the money. You see *old chum,* you have yet to meet Miss Gladwin."

The two men spent the next day in Hastings' rooms discussing what he would have to say to Archie's godmother to get her to arrange the next introduction he needed. Everything depended upon him being invited into the Fitzfender house.

Hastings began the exercise by saying, "Let's suppose that I'm interested in old carriages, like the one that belongs to Mrs. Fitzfender. Make it sound like vintage carriages and vintage wine."

"And vintage old ladies? I don't think so," said Archie. "Though if Mrs. Fitzfender just happens to have a collection of unidentified tropical sea shells with which you could offer your assistance. . . ."

"Does she have any sea shells?"

"Don't know, but that's the sort of thing we need."

Quiet again.

Hastings said, "Could we find her family tree on file in the library? I could say that I'm interested in one of her ancestors and wanted to ask her if—"

"Won't do. Godmama happened to say that Mrs. Fitzfender's great-great someone got hung for piracy in Scotland near a village where she used to holiday. The story persists there, and it's a sore spot with Mrs. Fitzfender, who insists that her ancestor was unjustly accused, which he may have been, but probably wasn't. Next idea, if you please."

"Old ladies have usually traveled extensively. Perhaps I should ask her about that."

"Egad! I think we need to agree on a signal before we get there. If I whistle . . . no. If I clear my throat it means that you would be better off to change the subject."

It was hours and ideas later, after making an impressive dent in a plate of cold roast beef sandwiches and a pitcher of beer that Hastings' man had produced, that Hastings cried, "I've got it!"

"I should hope so," said Archie, wiping the foam from his mustache. "We've been at it half the day."

"I'll tell her that I've been longing to meet Miss Gladwin and would she please be of assistance. I could even produce a bank statement to prove that I don't need the young lady's money. It's a safe enough thing to do because we already know that Miss Gladwin won't have me or anyone else."

Archie cocked an eyebrow, and said, "What else is sprouting in the compost of your mind?"

It was two days later when Archie took Hastings around to meet his godmother, Mrs. Estonia Chesterfield, widow of the late Emery Chesterfield, though not one of *the* Chesterfields. Even so they were a good family.

The three of them were in the morning room, with its marble bust of Lord Nelson and a battery of extravagantly drooping ferns on tall, decorative stands. They stepped around numerous little footstools for ladies, though one of the more delicate ones got dragged along by Mrs. Chesterfield's immense skirt, to be snagged off when she passed the fireplace fender. They turned at the sound, then ignored it. They finally settled in chairs, among too many embroidered pillows before the rosewood tea table with a dolphin base, to sip hibiscus tea that flowed from a fine china teapot.

After the polite things had been said and the new exhibit at the museum thoroughly discussed, Hastings went on to tell Mrs. Chesterfield how he had persuaded Archie to bring him along to call on her.

Archie listened with great interest to find out what the persuasion had been.

"It's because of the dog," said Hastings. "More precisely a pug dog. You see I'm entertaining the thought of getting such an animal, but I don't know the least thing about taking care of them." He ignored Archie, who was looking at him as though he'd gone mad. On the other hand, Mrs. Chesterfield seemed to be hanging on his every word.

Hastings shifted around and said, "I know about ordinary dogs, but the pug appears to be of a far more complicated nature. For this reason I would be hesitant to use ordinary training methods."

Mrs. Chesterfield smiled encouragingly. Archie took up a magazine to hide the expression on his face and began clearing his throat. His godmother noted the unfortunate sounds along with the fact that the magazine in which he displayed such remarkable interest contained an illustrated article on methods of improving the womanly bosom by artistic enhancement.

"Archie tells me that you are often in the company of such a dog," said Hastings. "For this reason I assume that you've gained considerable knowledge of the animal and might be persuaded to share that information with me."

Archie shook the magazine vigorously and cleared his throat with a roar.

Mrs. Chesterfield just smiled benevolently at Hastings, tapping his hand with her fan. She said, "My dear boy. Though I often see this dog, I assure you that I know next to nothing about its care. You simply must discover these things for yourself by talking with Miss Gladwin. She cares for the dog. Can you call Wednesday next? I'm certain that Mrs. Fitzfender and Miss Gladwin will be delighted to tell you everything you need to know."

Hastings exclaimed, "My goodness! What a very clever idea! I would be most pleased to meet your friend!" He then leaned toward the lady and said, "May I have another cup of that delicious tea?"

The lady beamed and said that he certainly could have more tea and would he like more cake as well? Hastings said yes and added a few more remarks about his interest in the pug dog.

When the subject of dogs was abandoned, Archie emerged from behind the magazine to give a colorful account of their previous evening at the theater. It had been an inept performance of *King Lear,* where people threw things at the actors in recognition of their talent. The well-aimed offerings consisted mostly of overripened fruit.

Hastings said, "I've always wondered if those people carry the stuff around just in case there might be an occasion to use it up or if they planned to fling it no matter what the performance was like."

It hadn't been necessary to explain that the play, a tragedy on many counts, wasn't a product of the better theaters in the city of Birmingham. Mrs. Chesterfield said she had it on good authority that it was a rival theater owner that supplied both the fruit and the incentive to throw it.

When her guests were preparing to leave, the lady was glad to note that her beloved godson didn't give the wrinkled magazine another glance. After all, she knew of a gentleman who secretly—he thought it was secretly—collected women's shoes of all sorts. He rented a room for them in another part of town. She also knew that he visited his shoes several nights a week. His wife thought he was playing billiards. Mrs. Chesterfield thought the visits excessive, especially on those occasions when he spent the night with his shoes. But it seemed harmless enough when one considered that he couldn't contract anything disagreeable from the association.

The following Wednesday at precisely one-thirty in the afternoon, Archie and Hastings returned to the home of Mrs. Chesterfield. The red drawing room this time. Pictures from foreign lands covered the walls, though they didn't crowd the gas light fixtures. It was the fireplace mantel that was crowded with stoneware statues of the royal family and other prominent figures. Napoleon III was there along with George Washington.

Mrs. Fitzfender and Miss Gladwin were having their second cup of oolong in the shade of a large Chinese vase topped with ostrich feathers. Snooky had been served his tea in the silver bowl, in which he showed no interest whatsoever. A folding screen with scenes from eighteenth-century France had been positioned so that Snooky wouldn't get any drafts from the open windows.

Introductions were made, which included Snooky, who displayed as much interest in the gentlemen as he had in his tea. Hastings made a point of giving Miss Gladwin little attention beyond a courteous good afternoon with their introduction. He didn't want to look like another fortune hunter. Still, he did happen to notice that her eyes were more green than he had expected them to be and her hair was darker than he'd thought and she had a complexion that reminded him of rose-tinted cream, though he didn't really look at her that closely. Even so he found it nice to know that her name was Ruth.

Mrs. Chesterfield set her teacup aside, making room for it on a table covered with enameled snuff boxes. She said, "My dear Mr. Hastings. I have apprised my guests of your reason for joining us today. Mrs. Fitzfender," she nodded toward that lady, "has said that she would be delighted to have Miss Gladwin tell you what you wish to know in regard to the care of the much-prized pug dog. Isn't that so Mrs. Fitzfender?"

In a voice as slight and fragile as herself, Mrs. Fitzfender said that it was indeed so.

Having done his homework, Hastings turned to Mrs. Fitzfender and said, "Snooky is a Dutch pug, isn't he? The breed having originated in China?"

Mrs. Fitzfender smiled sweetly and said that he was indeed correct.

Not wanting to be thought a slug in his quest for knowledge of the pug, Hastings gave out with a cheery, "Nice doggy." Ever so slowly he squatted down before that animal in his basket. Taking a small piece of jerked beef from his pocket he held it out. Snooky sniffed it and took it from his hand. Then Snooky bit him. Hastings bit back a rude word and squeezed the affected finger.

Through a strained smile, he said, "My, what a playful

fellow he is," and accepted a lacy white handkerchief from Miss Gladwin to wrap around the injured member.

She said, "Soap and water, Mr. Hastings. That's what I always recommend when Snooky bites someone. Perhaps you should sit where he can simply look at you from a distance and become accustomed to your presence."

Hastings removed himself to just such a chair on the other side of the room.

It was Mrs. Fitzfender who suggested that Miss Gladwin should join Hastings so that she might tell him about the dog, so she did. Hastings expected her to say something, but she didn't. She simply sat quietly, hands folded, and smiled politely. She didn't stare at him, quite, yet there was something about her that dared him to say something stupid. No, it was more like she *expected* him to say something stupid.

After contemplating the very soul of the animal across the room, considering its place in the universe, its doubtful benefit to mankind, its black bulging eyes, its sacred place in the Fitzfender household, Hastings said, "Does he shed much?"

Miss Gladwin said, "No." Then looked at him like she was waiting for the next stupid question.

He said, "How awfully considerate of him. Do you brush him anyway?"

"Yes."

"How often?" Hastings went on, having decided that getting the desired invitation to the Fitzfender house wasn't going to be as simple as he'd thought it would be. It wasn't easy to think up polite questions about a dog he had already begun to dislike. If he said what he'd been thinking when Snooky bit him, the game would have been over before it had ever begun.

"Every day."

"I beg your pardon?"

"The dog," said Miss Gladwin, speaking slowly and clearly. "I brush the dog every day."

"Do you use a special brush?"

"Yes."

"How refreshing."

"Yes."

He could see that this would get him nowhere and stared at a collection of Staffordshire shepherdesses. They were gracefully arranged among a mass of porcelain sheep on a carved mahogany table in front of the velvet and lace-draped window. After this study of the little sheep and their keepers, he lowered his voice to a near whisper and said, "Miss Gladwin, for reasons of my own it's important that I find out as much as I can about the nasty little dog in your care." He saw a faint but encouraging crack in Miss Gladwin's socially correct expression.

"I won't bring any embarrassment to Mrs. Fitzfender, or to you either, unless you mind the world knowing that I've taken an interest in the animal entrusted to you. Furthermore, my designs are wholly and completely on the habits of the nasty little dog, not on you or your fortune." He concluded with, "I trust you will treat this confidence with as much discretion as I would treat your own and lend me your cooperation with this necessary misadventure."

Hastings waited so long for a reply that he began to wonder if Miss Gladwin had paid him any attention at all.

She took a deep breath and said, "Snooky has a bed in Mrs. Fitzfender's bedchamber, where he sometimes naps when she does. He also has a bed in the kitchen, where he spends the night. It's close to a warm stove and a constant source of food, of which he gets far too much. He has other beds in the parlor, the morning room, library, and dining room. Next to each bed is a water bowl and food dish. Most of the sets are of hand-painted china, each done in a different wild flower. His traveling dinnerware is of silver to prevent breakage. Is that what you want to know?"

Hastings' eyes crinkled at the corners when he gave her a grateful smile. "It's a marvelous beginning. Thank you."

Miss Gladwin returned a slow, conspiratorial grin. Hastings couldn't help but notice that it changed her from nice looking to quite pretty. She visibly relaxed and her eyes sparkled. Not that it mattered, except that he needed to get himself invited into the Fitzfender house. To visit Snooky.

Miss Gladwin's sparkling eyes reminded him that he'd heard that a pug's bug eyes could pop out with little trouble. He had no desire to test such a possibility and hoped he'd never have the occasion to find out if it was true.

More talkative now, Miss Gladwin said, "The man who cleans Snooky's teeth comes to the house every two months. At the beginning of the Season he also clips the Fitzfender crest into Snooky's fur, both sides." Noticing the quiver of Hastings' chin, she smiled ever so slightly and nodded. A tribute to his restraint. She was pleased to see his nod of recognition, delighted to have shared this piece of nothing at all with someone who laughed at the same things that amused her. And Hastings was safe enough to visit with, because she knew why he was there and it didn't have anything much to do with her.

Hastings was doing his very best to appear serious about Snooky. "Does the dog always wear a blue ribbon? Does he have any preference as to color?" What he wanted to ask was if the emerald in the ring Miss Gladwin wore was her birthstone and who it was that had given it to her, but asking would have been too forward. It was just that it appeared to be a nice stone and he occasionally admired them, more or less.

"No, though blue is more flattering to Snooky than green or yellow."

"Oh, yes," he said, "The ribbons. Blue ones."

While Miss Gladwin went on to speak of Snooky's cushions and blankets, Hastings could imagine her in green. The rich green of late summer. It would compliment her eyes. As for the prim gray stuff she wore . . . then reminded himself that what she wore wasn't any of his business. All he needed was her assistance concerning the dog. Still he could see no reason why they couldn't be friendly while they were about it. Nothing more than that, of course. Just friendly.

Before the clock struck three, Mrs. Fitzfender had begun to gather up the things from her workbasket, and Hastings began to wonder if all his efforts had been for naught. The invitation he wanted hadn't even been hinted at. The gentlemen stood when Miss Gladwin got up to empty the water from Snooky's silver bowl into the potted begonia. Their hostess sent the tea things away. Then Mrs. Fitzfender stood, looking little taller than she had when she was sitting on the sofa. Her maid, having been in the kitchen for refreshments with the other servants, came into the room and took up the dog basket. Miss Gladwin took up Snooky. Snooky pretended not to notice. Or perhaps he really didn't notice. It was difficult to tell with Snooky.

They all said good-bye and how charming it had been. Mrs. Fitzfender and Miss Gladwin were on their way out when Mrs. Fitzfender turned to Mrs. Chesterfield and said something. Mrs. Chesterfield then turned to Mr. Hastings and said, "If you would care to continue your observations of the pug dog, you may make arrangements with Miss Gladwin whenever you like. Mrs. Fitzfender says that three or four days a week for a while should be sufficient for you to learn what you must know and understand about the delicate sentiments of the animal. Such intimate things cannot be learned in a single afternoon over tea. They must be studied diligently. Is that correct Mrs. Fitzfender?"

In a tiny voice, Mrs. Fitzfender said that it was indeed correct.

Hastings started to say how pleased he was to have such an opportunity, but the ladies simply walked from the room and he completed his halting words of thanks to empty air.

When the men were out of the house, Archie said, "One week down, three to go *old chum*. Just remember that this is business."

"Of course," said Hastings.

He still had Miss Gladwin's handkerchief in his pocket.

# TWO

Early the next morning Hastings arrived at the Fitzfender house to be ushered directly into the library. Since that room had been the private domain of the late Mr. Fitzfender, and Mrs. Fitzfender didn't care for it, Miss Gladwin was given the place to use as her own. The office of doggy affairs. Hastings found her sitting at the table looking at lists of some sort. She had pencils stuck in her hair.

The lady looked up, smiled her polite smile, and said, "Good morning Mr. Hastings. Do sit down, won't you?"

He smiled his own polite smile and wondered where the camaraderie of the day before had gone. It certainly wasn't available from the dozen or so wild animal heads hanging on the walls above the shelves. Especially the one that stared down at him with singular condemnation. He almost checked to see if his fly was buttoned.

Miss Gladwin had been watching Hastings watching the animal head. "It's a warthog, but you mustn't mind it. The thing makes everyone uncomfortable. That one," she indicated the head of a water buffalo, "has a squint. The taxidermist had a peculiar sense of humor."

"Quite so." Hastings took a surreptitious glance at the front of his trousers.

Putting the papers in order, Miss Gladwin went on to say, "You'll get used to it, most people do, except Mrs. Fitzfender, and that's why she doesn't use this room. I've been going over Snooky's menus for next week." She pushed the papers toward Hastings. "I suppose this is as a good a time as any for you to begin your study of puggery. Even with all this careful planning, Snooky might not be inclined to eat any of this no matter how carefully it's been prepared."

Hastings placed a chair across from Miss Gladwin, not beside her. Anything closer would have been too close. At least that's the feeling he got. Granted, she had smiled, but it was that proper smile again, not a *real* smile. Not a smile that said *I'm ever so pleased to see you*. It's as though she had reconsidered her friendliness of the day before and decided not to let it happen again. Not that it mattered to Hastings. He wasn't here to see Miss Gladwin. He was here to see Snooky. Snooky was his ticket to get into the house to create the *impression* that he was here to see Miss Gladwin, which he wasn't. So it didn't matter if she smiled or not.

Having sorted all that out, he tapped the papers against the table to square the edges, then glanced over the menus. The selection began with chopped chicken with gravy and veal poached in cream sauce. It was much the same all the way to coddled eggs with saffron.

"What happens when Snooky won't eat any of this?"

"Mrs. Fitzfender usually manages to tempt him with a bit of something from her own plate. If Snooky still isn't persuaded, she has cook make him a pudding."

"Does he have a little silver spoon with which he is fed?"

She lifted one elegant eyebrow. "Mr. Hastings, are you being facetious?"

"How can you even *think* such a thing?"

The lady hid a smile behind another collection of papers. "It was just a thought." Gesturing toward the menus, she added, "You may copy those if you like."

Hastings was uncommonly glad to see that smile and said, "Thank you," but made no effort to copy anything. "May I ask what you're looking at now?"

"Snooky's health records." She gave him those as well.

After a perusal of the first page, he said, "Good old Snookers seems to be plagued by any number of complaints, including weakness of the legs and shortness of breath.

Does he actually wheeze?" When Miss Gladwin said yes, Hastings said, "It looks as though the old boy could use some exercise and a less fancy diet to unload some doggy fat. Does he get out much?"

"Every day. Mrs. Fitzfender is quite conscientious about the necessity of fresh air for the maintenance of good health. In fact one of the footmen is walking him right now."

"And what about you?" Hastings asked impulsively. "Do you get enough fresh air?"

"On nice days Mrs. Fitzfender and I often take a carriage ride."

He shook his head. "What I'm wondering is if you get out to do things. There must be something you'd like to do if you had the opportunity. Something just for the fun of it."

"I'm really quite content with my life as it is."

Hastings rocked his chair back on two legs. "You don't sound very convincing. Do you ever long to steam up the Amazon? Ride elephants in India? They can make you seasick, I can tell you that."

"Have you ever done that?"

"Been seasick on an elephant? Once and only once, but it isn't something I admit to everyone."

"Then you've been to India?"

"Nothing that exotic, I'm afraid. The elephant I rode was in a Zoological Garden in Germany, though it did have two Indian keepers. Had to actually. The beast couldn't understand anything but one particular dialect of the native tongue."

"Are you teasing me?"

"Absolutely not. And he liked ice cream, this elephant. His name was Fritz. Probably still is."

"Honestly? I mean about the ice cream?"

"Most assuredly. Now tell me, what would you do if you could do anything you wanted to?" His voice was mellow, his tone coaxing.

She looked at him curiously, trying to read the thoughts behind his dark eyes, wondering just how much of the truth he wanted. If he was expecting her to say that it had been her life's dream to become a missionary in a jungle, he was way off the mark.

She finally said, "I'd go to Scotland to hear the pipes played on the moors. Gather an armload of heather. And I'd go to pubs and listen to the songs the people sang. I might even have a glass of ale." Did she sound just a little defiant?

"Shocking," he said, scowling like the warthog. "Simply shocking."

She grinned.

"Even worse than that, I know seventeen versions of 'John Barleycorn' and can sing them all. I promise you I don't admit *that* to everyone."

Hastings' chair came down on all fours with a bump. "Do you happen to know 'Sweet William's Ghost'?"

"The one that goes, 'There came a ghost to Margaret's door, with many a grievous groan'?"

"Yes!"

"With a version where the ghost vanishes into the mist and another where she follows him back to the grave?"

"That's the very one!"

"I've never heard of it."

When he laughed she did too.

They talked of their favorite songs and where they'd heard them. Miss Gladwin's most fruitful source was the laundry maid in the family home in Shrosphire.

In harmony they sang "Lord Randolph," until Hastings interrupted to say, "You sing awfully well."

To which she said, "Good heavens, look at the time! We mustn't dawdle or we'll miss the peddler—he is such a love. Comes by once a week. Mrs. Fitzfender thinks Snooky could do with one of his tonics."

"A peddler of dog medicines?"

"He has wonderful things for animals. Sometimes he has sweets for children, too, and once he had something for cook's sunburn that also got rid of mites on the canary."

When the pair of them came up the area stairs from the kitchen, it was to the swish-swishing of a soapy scrub brush on the front steps. A footman in a white apron opened the

front door and said something to the maid doing the
scrubbing. She giggled; he winked and shut the door.

The knife sharpener with his grinding wheel was still a
block away, calling out his trade in a singsong chant that
echoed off the solid row of houses.

It was only a minute or two before the peddler and his
pushcart came rattling around the corner. He was a white-
haired, jolly looking fellow, who pulled a string that jingled
a set of bells attached to the front of his place of business.
He smiled angelically, tipped his hat, and stopped at the
curb in front of the Fitzfender house.

Miss Gladwin said, "Good morning," and stepped up to
examine everything on display. Something smelled faintly
of camphor.

The cart was a heavenly shade of blue with painted signs
held up by painted cupids. Anyone who could read could
see that the peddler was the one and only Professor Harper,
world traveler and friend to things that could walk, jump,
creep, slither, swim, fly, or sit there. For those who couldn't
read there were drawings of creatures that did those things.

The peddler noticed Hastings giving his cart a close
inspection, and proudly announced, "I decorated the thing
myself, though the blue was devilish hard to mix. Is there
anything in particular you're looking for?"

It was Miss Gladwin who said, "Have you a tonic for a
bored dog who is a fussy eater?"

"I've seen the condition before," said the peddler gravely.
"Have you tried giving him a little beef tea? Better than that,
you could get a cat. A quick one. The sort of cat that likes
to sneak up and pounce on whoever or whatever happens to
be lounging about. A cat with good reflexes. A champion
among pouncing cats. That will pep things up."

"Well. . . ."

"And you might put a looking glass behind the dog's dish.
It's for Snooky, isn't it?" He rubbed the marks on his finger
and muttered, "Nasty little beast." Then he said, "Seeing
another animal looking at his food might make him less
fussy about what he eats." The peddler peeked into his coat

pocket, gave it a friendly pat, and said, "I know just the cat for you. It loves to play."

"That's nice," said Miss Gladwin. "What do you have for a sore lip on a horse?"

"Carriage horse or riding horse?"

"Is there a difference?"

"The horses think so."

"It's for the milkman's horse."

He handed her a tin of salve and she paid him.

While watching the peddler rattle and jingle down the street, Hastings saw something else. "Look there," he said, "with the blue ribbon. Isn't that Snooky?" He took Miss Gladwin by the arm and turned her around as though they were old friends. "There," he repeated. "That dog being carried, it isn't wearing a collar and lead. Did I misunderstand? I thought you said Snooky had gone for a walk."

"Snooky gets his fresh air while someone else does the walking. You see, he can't really go for a walk. He can only go for a waddle and not very far at that."

"I see."

"Mrs. Fitzfender insists that—"

"Perhaps we should take Snooky for a walk."

"But Snooky won't like—"

"Who's he going to tell?" said Hastings, imitating the squinting water buffalo on the library wall.

When they were back in the house there was nothing left to do but visit Snooky. Hastings wasn't eager to do so, but it was that or leave. He had to remind himself that the reason for being in the house in the first place was to become better acquainted with the little dog. So he couldn't very well not see the little dog. He couldn't just hang about talking to Miss Gladwin—not that he had planned to. It was just a figure of speech.

They found Snooky in the morning room with Mrs. Fitzfender. Here his dishes were decorated with purple violets. His cushion was in shades of purple. In a soft little voice Mrs. Fitzfender asked Hastings what he had learned thus far about caring for pug dogs.

Hastings recited the menus, then said, "I understand that Snooky is also given ample fresh air and I must agree that it's good for him. The thing that concerns me is that he doesn't seem to have much time for cultural pursuits."

Miss Gladwin looked at him the same strange way Archie had looked at him on another day when he was talking about the same dog. Mrs. Fitzfender, however, didn't seem to find anything strange in what he'd said.

"There seems to be an unfortunate blank in Snooky's life," continued Hastings. "A gap that could be filled gradually, beginning with simple things. Things like . . . other animals. Yes. He can get to know other animals so that he may gain confidence among his own kind."

Mrs. Fitzfender said that indeed she had never thought of it quite that way and asked what he would suggest.

"Well, there is the traveling zoo with animals from North America," said Hastings. "It's much like a collection of circus wagons, except the creatures don't come out to perform. There's no better place to find new animals for Snooky, for he might have seen the old ones." When he saw the horrified look on Mrs. Fitzfender's face, he was quick to say, "Snooky can see them from a distance, of course. There's really no need for him to socialize with them."

Mrs. Fitzfender relaxed then, agreeing that seeing the creatures without being too close would be acceptable indeed.

Miss Gladwin found it necessary to bring out a handkerchief to dab at her nose. Or it might have been that she was covering up the lower part of her face. The part that was grinning. Mrs. Fitzfender wanted to know just when Hastings proposed to make this expedition to the traveling zoo.

"This very day, if you have no objection, though you must have noticed that today's weather is of the sort that Snooky would most certainly enjoy."

Ever so softly Mrs. Fitzfender said she had noticed and that Snooky would surely like it and that today would be fine indeed.

It was soon arranged that the Fitzfender carriage would

take Miss Gladwin, Mr. Hastings, and Snooky to the park that had the visiting zoo, then wait for them just in case Snooky should tire and want to leave earlier than planned. Hastings agreed that such a thing might happen. He neglected to say what he would do about it.

After they were on their way, Miss Gladwin fitted the rotund dog with a harness of fine Morocco leather. He had last worn it a few years before and the thing was now a tight fit. When they reached the entrance, she took the dog from the carriage and placed him on the ground. Hastings took hold of the lead. With a gentle tug and words of encouragement, he indicated to Snooky that they were about to begin his waddle.

Snooky indicated his sentiments by lying down.

Miss Gladwin indicated her sentiments by laughing out loud, unseemly as it was. Tilting her sunshade over her face did nothing to hide it.

That she was laughing not only at the dog but at his own efforts to get the animal up again was irrelevant to Hastings. He liked to hear her laugh. If it took a battle of wills with a spoiled dog it was worth it. Just as a matter of principle, of course.

What finally inspired Snooky to move was another dog. A mastiff with impressive teeth. Snooky became instantly animated. He got up on his chubby, stubby legs, saw the direction Hastings wanted to go, and went ahead of him. A clever ploy that placed the large man between himself and the mastiff with the large teeth.

Once Snooky developed a rhythm to his waddle, Hastings offered his free arm to Miss Gladwin. With the traveling zoo ticket stubs in his pocket, they went along like an ordinary couple with an ordinary dog for an ordinary day in the park. That's when Hastings decided that there was something rather special about being ordinary.

As for Miss Gladwin, she felt anything but ordinary. Strolling along like this, she couldn't remember when the grass looked greener or the sun brighter. Or the company more pleasant. Without being too terribly trite she thought it was a perfectly wonderful day. Even Snooky was behaving surprisingly well.

"Snooky is behaving surprisingly well," said Hastings.

Smiling broadly, she said, "Yes, he is."

He looked at her curiously, wondering what was so amusing.

She noted his expression but decided not to explain that he'd just said what she'd been thinking.

It had been a long time since Miss Gladwin had felt comfortable enough with anyone to indulge in playful teasing. The sorry events that ended with a broken engagement had left her feeling like a chicken that escaped the butcher. Today she felt like a rare bird with beautiful feathers. And it comforted her to know that at the end of the day her feathers would still be her own. She lifted her face to the sun, breathed deeply, and gave Hastings' arm a squeeze.

He said, "Look at those feathers!"

"Feathers?"

"Feathers," he repeated in a low rumbly voice. "Birds make them."

"Oh, *those* feathers. How terribly clever birds are."

Sunshine danced on the iridescent green plumage of several mallard ducks. The males, actually. The females were drab brown so that they might sit unnoticed on the nest. They were established park residents that went waddling across the walk to get from one pond to another. Everyone stepped aside to let the birds pass. Snooky, having had an unpleasant experience with an aggressive pigeon, hid behind Hastings' legs. He took it as a sign of submission and carefully picked up the dog. Snooky, his brow wrinkled in perpetual, though vague, thought, decided that he was too tired to bite him.

Continuing their leisurely perambulations, they eventually came to the animals they were looking for: the assortment of curiosities from North America. First there were raccoons, gray animals with fluffy ringed tails and black masks like highwaymen. About the same size as

Snooky, they had grown fat from the treats people threw into their cage and quickly learned to beg for more.

And there were the opossums. The one that was awake looked like a ball of light gray fur with a toothy snout on one end and the tail of a rat on the other. According to the sign it was a shy, nocturnal marsupial with a prehensile tail.

Hastings held Snooky up to see. Snooky shut his eyes and refused to look.

Suddenly a gentleman went over the rope that kept the public away from those cages and banged his walking stick against the bars. When he had everyone's attention, he said, "Ladies and gentlemen, what you see before you are all fakes! There are no such things as raccoons or opossums! These are merely mongrel dogs with painted faces and shaved tails!" He stabbed his stick toward the pen of prairie dogs and said that he knew for a fact that they weren't really dogs at all and that he would demand his money back!

Miss Gladwin thought it prudent to move on before Snooky decided to bite the noisy fellow.

Hastings thought about telling Snooky what a good dog he was, then decided he'd better not push his luck. And he thought about telling Miss Gladwin that she had a glorious smile, then decided that he'd better not do that either. It might be too intimate a remark for the kind of friendship they had. They were chums, not lovers. He'd never tell Archie he had a glorious smile. And if he wouldn't say such a thing to Archie, he probably shouldn't say it to Miss Gladwin either, though there were things he'd tell Archie that he wouldn't be caught dead saying to Miss Gladwin. Necessity was the mother of discretion, or something like that.

They were side by side at the stout enclosure where two great shaggy bison were munching hay, when Hastings said, "Would you care to stop for lemonade?"

Suspecting that his arm must be cramped from holding on to the dog for so long, she said, "Yes, I'd like that."

So they found a shaded table where they were served tepid, watery lemonade. Even so, neither of them were particularly eager to leave. Nor was Snooky, who collapsed on a shockingly common piece of ground.

Hastings looked at the dog, then at Miss Gladwin. He said, "Snooky's bow has slid around under his chin," but he was more interested in Miss Gladwin's eyes. They were still green, though not quite as green as they had looked before. Now they were more golden brown, with eyelashes that shone copper in the sun. Her perfume reminded him of something. Lilacs? Yes. And he wanted to know what books she read, what other music she liked, but didn't want to dash through it now. He wanted time to talk about those books. Listen to the music.

He said, "Have you had an opportunity to see much of Birmingham?"

"Mrs. Fitzfender and I have gone to the theater on occasion, and we attend musical evenings at the homes of her friends, though late hours don't agree with her." With Hastings' urging she went on to tell him more about those musical evenings.

When Snooky rolled over and groaned, he said, "Do you think we might plan another outings? I mean for Snooky, of course."

"What would you like to do?"

With those few words and her gentle smile, Hastings' brain turned to mush. Wisely, he didn't tell her what he'd like to do. It had nothing to do with Snooky.

She wondered at his change of expressions and said, "Was it the lemonade?"

Hastings studied her anxious face. "No. It's bad, but not *that* bad."

For no sensible reason he desperately wanted to say something impressive, something intelligent to the woman on the other side of a table so small that their knees would bump if they weren't careful. He had to be careful where Miss Gladwin was concerned. Her knees had already been bumped by a man who had lied about loving her, but Hastings wasn't thinking about that sort of thing. He was thinking about trust. And friendship. He knew that she might have difficulty trusting him enough to be friends because of another man's lies. Besides, she hadn't even invited him to use her first name. Ruth. It felt soft and nice on his tongue.

In a scramble for brilliant remarks, he said, "Do you think Snooky would like to go to lunch one day?"

"Luncheon out with *Snooky?*"

While Miss Gladwin wondered where they might take a dog with Snooky's disposition, Hastings began to ramble on about a dog his mother had. "He pinched things," said Hastings. "Nothing predictable, like always taking someone's slippers. This dog just carried off whatever happened to be lying about when he took it into his head to add something to his collection."

She said, "How very annoying that must have been," and thought about what Hastings had said when they first met. He had assured her that he wasn't interested in her or her money. An unflattering statement in one way, yet reassuring in another, because she didn't feel preyed upon. She wasn't really surprised that he had known about the broken engagement. She wouldn't have been surprised if the whole of England knew of it. It had just been a surprise to hear him mention it. It was the kind of thing that was whispered about at dinner parties. Snickered at behind lace fans.

". . . and when Lady Forbes finally came out to the stable, she was missing one glove and her scarf. There was nothing to do but tell her that Arthur, did I say that the dog's name was Arthur? Well, my mother had to tell her that Arthur was a kleptomaniac. Fortunately my parents never extended invitations for a week in the country to stuffy people."

Invitations. That word certainly rang a bell with Miss Gladwin, and she gave Hastings a melancholy smile. For a long time after *it* had happened, after the scandal she'd caused, the usual invitations to social events came to an abrupt halt. Then a few were extended by the curious. She refused them. Now, what time she spent away from Mrs. Fitzfender was in the company of trusted friends of long standing. Never anyone else.

Yet here she was in the solitary company of Mr. James

Hastings, a gentleman whose family was quite comfortably supported by the manufacture of hooks and eyes. A stranger with whom she was spending the day because he wasn't interested in her and she wasn't interested in him either. At least not *seriously* interested. Nothing like that, though she found him a charming fellow. But charming wasn't enough for serious thoughts. She knew that he had other reasons for coming to the Fitzfender house. An odd arrangement, she admitted that, but it suited them both.

"It was my youngest sister who could always find Arthur's cache," continued Hastings. "In addition to the missing glove and scarf, she discovered my father's braces, shaving soap, two candle sticks—one still had a candle— the housekeeper's hairbrush, a soup bone, and a child's dress that none of us had ever seen before. We suspect he'd taken it from a neighbor's clothesline."

"Clotheslines are so vulnerable," said Miss Gladwin, who wished she'd worn a different dress. Perhaps the blue one with the bishop sleeves and pleated skirt. There were dark blue kid shoes that almost matched the braid trim. She felt pretty when she wore that dress. Summer silk. Then a breeze from the direction of the mountain lion's cage drifted by and reminded her that this might not be quite the place for any such frock. What she wore today was much plainer, though it had the fashionable lifted hem that showed a bit of red petticoat, and that was better than nothing.

Hastings reluctantly pointed out that it was time to return to the carriage. Miss Gladwin reluctantly agreed. Yet neither one of them was the first to move. It was Snooky, who had spied a small piece of cake on the ground and waddled over to get it, beating a flock of sparrows to the prize.

Miss Gladwin's theatrical sigh faded into, "Mrs. Fitzfender would go into a decline if she saw that."

It was an act of bravery when Hastings went over and picked up Snooky. Snooky just hung there in his hands. Hastings thought he'd conquered the animal. Actually Snooky had thought about biting him, then considered that the chunk of meat in the lion's cage was about as big as he was himself. This wasn't his home territory. He went quietly.

They had a quiet walk back to the carriage. Snooky was soon asleep, drooling on Hastings' sleeve.

Miss Gladwin wanted to ask Hastings when he'd be back to see them, but didn't feel she could. After all he wasn't calling to see her. She didn't want to sound like she was snooping into his private life. Didn't want to appear as though she was flirting with him. Flirting would imply that she was interested in him and hoped that he returned her sentiments. So it was just as well that she didn't find his eyes too merry or his mouth too nicely shaped, but his mouth didn't matter. All men had mouths. Perfectly nice mouths. And hands.

She glanced at his hands.

They were ordinary hands that had slid over hers like warm bath water when she'd handed him Snooky's health records. Nothing of importance. He'd hardly touched her. The heat of the day undoubtedly accounted for the warmth she'd felt. Yet it wouldn't do to wonder about how warm the rest of him might be on a cold night cuddled up by the fire.

They reached the carriage and got in. What little conversation there was came with friendly smiles. He said, "Let me hold the door," while she said, "Let me take the dog." Each supposed that the other one's modest supply of words was the result of fatigue. That the other's effort to please was an apology for that quiet.

They were both a little bit right.

After going on about Arthur, the thieving dog, Hastings was doing his best to keep from saying anything else that would make him sound empty-headed. What he wanted to do was ask Miss Gladwin how soon he might return to the Fitzfender house. But he didn't ask because he didn't want her to think he was a fortune hunter disguised as a dog fancier. Didn't want her to think he was a man who sought her time and attention for reasons other than what he had professed them to be, even though that's what he had done. Except he hadn't done it because he was after her money, but now he was afraid it would look like he was. So he looked quietly out the window.

Miss Gladwin supposed Hastings was trying to think of a way to ask for a favor where Snooky was concerned. To make it easier for him, she said, "Would you like to come back on Monday?"

After a pause, he said, "Yes, I suppose I would . . . now that you mention it."

She smiled and he smiled and they were quiet again. The Fitzfender coachman dropped him off at his home.

Following a quiet supper, the only thing Hastings wanted to do was stretch out in his favorite chair and read the newspaper. He leaned back, propped up his feet, and recalled the last time he'd relaxed in that chair. It was when he and Archie had been trying to figure out how to get invited into the Fitzfender house. It turned out to be much easier than he'd thought, though he'd had a few anxious moments. Archie's worry over the plan had proved to be nothing at all.

Hastings congratulated himself for not only getting invited into the house, but for having managed to get so much cooperation from Mrs. Fitzfender. He was going to get all the time he wanted with Snooky. All the time he needed to get the rumor started that he was interested in someone, just to keep his family out of his personal life for a while. And when he next went to the Fitzfender house, he thought he might ask Miss Gladwin if she'd like to go out again. Perhaps to the museum. A perfectly respectable place to take a young lady. They might even attend a concert in the park, though not on the same day. Later in the week would be better. If it rained they would go someplace else.

Humming "Sweet William's Ghost," Hastings snapped the newspaper into shape, opened it to the business page, and became quite still. He remembered that Archie had said it had to be all business and only business where Miss Gladwin was concerned. But that's not quite how it had been. Hastings didn't even know how it happened. He'd only known the lady for two days and he'd already lost that bet to Archie.

# Three

It wasn't as though she didn't have anything else to occupy her thoughts. Neither was she obliged to think of him out of boredom. There were always more cookery books and magazines to go through in search of the receipts Mrs. Fitzfender wanted for Snooky's carefully prepared meals. And the treats in between. His bedtime yummies. A little something in his bowl in case he might wake up hungry during the night. With a lid on the bowl so whatever was inside wouldn't dry out. A loose fitting lid that he could push aside with his nose.

She smiled when she thought about how James Hastings would laugh at it all.

Yesterday, when Miss Gladwin returned from the zoo, there hadn't been an opportunity for her thoughts to wander. She had changed for dinner, then after dinner she and Mrs. Fitzfender went to a poetry reading. Snooky had been too tired to attend.

Snooky was still tired today and lay quietly under the library sofa where he couldn't see the animal heads and they couldn't see him. Occasionally he'd open one eye to see if Miss Gladwin was still at the table. Wheezing audibly, he waddled over to lay down on one of her feet so he'd know when she got up.

When the lady would have left the table, she didn't because she would have disturbed the little dog. Besides, she thought she really should thank Mr. Hastings for taking them to the zoo and this was a good time to do it. Just a polite note.

She wrote a polite note.

Upon reading it over, she wondered if it might sound too polite. Too stiff. Yet she didn't want to sound too friendly either, not that she wouldn't like to be more friendly. It was simply prudent to remember why the man was coming to call and it had little to do with her.

So Miss Gladwin wrote another note, then wiggled her foot under the dog, and said, "Snooky, listen to this." Snooky snuffled and sneezed.

She sat taller in her chair and began, "My dear Mr. Hastings." Snooky groaned. She thought about it, said, "Perhaps you're right," and started over.

This time, she said, "Dear Mr. Hastings." Snooky made no comment, so she went on. "Our day at the zoo was positively grand. Thank you ever so much for taking us. I'm looking forward to another outing to expand Snooky's knowledge of the world, especially as he didn't bite any-one . . ."

And her thoughts wandered off to what a day with James Hastings might be like if only he had something of a romantic nature, then stopped before she thought of anything else even more foolish. There were other reasons why he wanted to spend so much time in Mrs. Fitzfender's house. He had never tried to pretend otherwise.

With a sigh she crumpled the page and said, "Never mind, Snooky. You can go back to sleep."

It was the polite note that went out in the post.

After luncheon Miss Gladwin read to Mrs. Fitzfender until the lady nodded off. If she'd had a guest, the reading material would most likely have been an inspiring work by a compassionate doctor of divinity about some far-off place with disagreeable insects that one might read about but never want to see. If guests weren't in attendance they read novels.

Mrs. Fitzfender thought it was quite daring.

Mrs. Chesterfield had said it was about time.

Miss Gladwin closed the book without a sound to watch

the misty rain bead up and run down the window pane, wondering if Mr. Hastings had read about Darwin's voyage on the *Beagle,* reasonably certain that he had. She longed to know where his travels had taken him. What he'd seen, what he'd done besides take an unfortunate ride on an elephant. She hadn't really traveled a great deal, but she could tell him about the cat she'd had. A black one with a white paw. It had a passion for marzipan. And she knew he'd want to hear more about the laundry maid who sang the old songs . . .

She really had to stop thinking like this.

By Saturday she'd managed to resign herself to the fact that Mr. Hastings had certain ends in mind and when he achieved those ends he'd go and he wouldn't be back. It was no use thinking about him.

After dinner she wondered if he liked apple pie.

Sunday was much better. She had almost entirely forgotten about his rumbly laugh. And how shivery nice she felt inside when she'd heard him sing, his voice so in tune with her own. So when she was up bright and early on Monday morning, it wasn't because she wanted to be dressed and downstairs before the man arrived. Not at all. She just wanted to make certain that Snooky was ready for company.

Hastings hadn't adjusted quite as well. He'd spent the evening after the zoo in a curious state of suspended reason. He simply couldn't figure out how he'd got to where he was with Miss Gladwin.

By the next morning he'd come to realize that he wasn't anywhere with Miss Gladwin. He hadn't pursued her, hadn't promised her anything, hadn't even implied anything. It's the dog he had taken to the zoo and she happened to come along. He was as unencumbered now as he had ever been and he liked it that way. There wasn't a problem. He and Miss Gladwin were simply friends. Not even old friends. More like ships-that-pass-in-the-night friends.

Except that he'd never seen her at night. He'd only seen her in the daytime, with the sun glinting off her hair and lighting her eyes. Eyes that never seemed to be quite the

**Aileen Humphrey**

same color as the last time he'd seen them. A golden-brown-greenish something, like dark, iridescent amber.

When Archie called that afternoon, the first thing he asked was, "How are things going with the nasty little dog?" and Hastings said, "What dog?"

*"What dog*? All that trouble to get yourself into the Fitzfender house to see the dog, play with the dog, study the dog, and now you say, *what dog*?"

Hastings didn't reply. Archie helped himself to an orange from a bowl on the table and said, "You've obviously got something else on your mind. What did this remarkable creature do?"

"Nothing actually, though she knows the words to 'Sweet William's Ghost,' and we—"

"You're doomed!" cried Archie, tossing a peel back into the bowl. "Certainly didn't take long."

"Dash it! We only sang part of one song and then went to the zoo. A small zoo at that. One is not doomed by a song or a zoo!"

"My goodness, defensive aren't we? What else did the two of you do?"

"The two of us? Must I assume that you mean myself and Miss Gladwin?"

"No, I meant you and Snooky! Who in hell do you think I mean? If you're trying to put me off the scent, you can't do it. All you had to do was go a month—three weeks actually—without being affected by the lady. How long did you last?"

"Two days, but it's nothing serious. We're just friends."

"Of course you are," said Archie. "That will be tuppence, old chum. I should have made it a shilling." Smirking, he held out his hand for the coin.

Over his next breakfast, Hastings contemplated a holiday in Spain or, perhaps, the South Seas. Other than overseeing the accounting procedures at The Hastings' Never-fail Indispensable Ready-grip All Purpose Steel Hook and Eye Company—established 1838—he could come and go as he pleased. And it pleased him to plan a trip without Snooky. He'd write to Miss Gladwin, of course. She was a friend. A good friend . . . as women go. When he returned, he might take her somewhere and he'd tell her all about wherever he had been.

Except that he couldn't very well take her out and tell her anything if she acquired a husband while he was away. Husbands usually didn't go for that sort of thing. He certainly wouldn't. But he wasn't anyone's husband, for which he thanked God, and helped himself to more sausage and another cup of coffee.

It then occurred to Hastings of Hastings' Hooks and Eyes, that someone else might take Snooky out for a day in the park while he himself was traveling. In that event he supposed Miss Gladwin might go along. She'd probably smile at the fellow, but she surely wouldn't smile at someone else the way she smiled at him, would she? He felt distinctly uncomfortable and blamed it on the sausage. By then his coffee had grown cold, but that hardly mattered because he couldn't eat any more anyway.

It became obvious that he'd have to explain a few things to Miss Gladwin before he began his travels. He doubted that she knew enough about the dangers that men—some men—could present a young woman, though she'd already had a near miss with that fortune hunter.

He pushed his plate aside, frowned, and considered what he would say to the lady. His voice was barely above a whisper when he said, "Miss Gladwin, as a friend I hope you will allow me to advise you as to your intercourse with men." With a disgusted snort he slapped his napkin on the table.

Standing in the middle of the room, where he could take a deep breath, he gripped his lapels, stared at ivy on the wallpaper, and said, "Miss Gladwin, as I will be away for some time, I feel that I must warn you of the possible dangers presented by unscrupulous men to an unprotected young woman such as yourself." But that wouldn't do either.

Turning to the draperies, he said, "As I hold you in high

regard, I must warn you about men. Not all men, of course, only the kind that aren't completely honest."

That brought Hastings up short because he suspected that *he* might be one of *those*: a man who hasn't been completely honest, at least not about why he'd got himself invited into the Fitzfender house in the first place. He'd told Miss Gladwin that he had his own reasons for wanting to be with that miserable little dog and it was the truth. He just hadn't said that his reasons for seeing Snooky were to fool his family into supposing he was interested in an eligible female at that address. He had no intention of making any overtures toward her. In fact, he liked to think of himself as someone to watch over her and give sound advice.

He cleared his throat, faced the mirror, smoothed his beard, polished his halo, and said, "My dear Miss Gladwin. Because we are friends, there are a few important, very important, things I feel compelled to tell you for your own good."

Then he quit the mirror because he didn't think that speech sounded very convincing either, and it troubled him because he would worry about Miss Gladwin while he was away. Another villain might come along, one more skilled than the last, who would break her heart. Hastings couldn't stand the thought of Miss Gladwin with a broken heart. It disturbed his sleep that night.

After checking the morning paper to make certain that it really was Monday, Hastings made his way to the Fitzfender house again. He intended to apprise Miss Gladwin of his concerns for her welfare as plainly as he could.

He might even warn her of the possible dangers that might result from indiscriminate smiling. A lesser man than himself could suffer apoplexy from one of those smiles. Or a black eye if Hastings was obliged to strike someone for taking liberties due to any misunderstanding concerning Miss Gladwin's smile. That, he told himself, could never be tolerated. He had taken the lady under his wing. He would have that little talk with her this very day, then get on with other things.

When Hastings arrived at his destination to save Miss

Gladwin from the wickedness in the world, he was taken to the kitchen. The entire staff might have been gathered there in the circle. When he would have said good morning, he was waved into silence by Cook, who then laid a finger across her lips. Moving cautiously, he made a place for himself at Miss Gladwin's side. She acknowledged his presence by the lifting of a hand holding a pencil, never taking her eyes from Snooky for a moment, never letting the sheet of paper slip off the pan that served as a hand-held desk.

Lined up on the floor were four saucers of something. He whispered, "Is that gravy?"

She nodded, but remained intent upon the dog. The little fellow was sampling the contents of the blue china saucer, which resulted in certain reactions. To record the findings, check marks were put in the column called "blue," beside "short sniff," "wagged tail," and "cleaned plate."

When the dog had completed the experiment, Miss Gladwin turned to Hastings and said, "You're just in time to go with me to see Mrs. Fitzfender. She's eager to know the results." She smiled brightly and held up the chart with the check marks, determined to keep her mind on the fact that Mr. Hastings was here because of Snooky, not her.

He was trying very hard to keep his mind on the chart, not on her, when he said, "She wants to know about Snooky eating gravy?"

"They were specially prepared health-improving gravies. Mrs. Fitzfender wants to know which one Snooky likes best." She held up the chart again.

Following her out of the kitchen, Hastings said, "Ruth, that is, Miss Gladwin, I really must talk to you."

"I'm listening."

"Alone. Privately. The two of us."

"May I ask why?"

"I'll tell you privately when the two of us are alone."

Looking at him curiously, she said, "I suppose we'll manage to fit it in. At the moment Mrs. Fitzfender is waiting in the morning room."

One would have thought a royal child was being discussed. Mrs. Fitzfender asked Hastings for his opinions on wild game as opposed to farm stock for Snooky's food. Hastings tactfully replied that he would have to give the matter more thought before he could give her an answer. But any thinking he did on that subject was pushed aside by his impatience to talk to Miss Gladwin. He even tried not to look at her lest Mrs. Fitzfender read too much into his expression.

During luncheon the conversation was more general. After luncheon Mrs. Fitzfender showed Hastings all of Snooky's baby pictures, most of them blurry because he couldn't hold still long enough. One by one he admired them, saying things like, "What remarkable ears" and "That tail certainly does curl," which pleased the lady immensely.

Miss Gladwin began to wonder how long he could keep it up without choking.

Hastings began to wonder if he would ever get an opportunity to be alone with Miss Gladwin.

The answer was no, though he wasn't to find that out until Miss Gladwin said, "I'm so sorry to interrupt your visit, but it's time for Mrs. Fitzfender and myself to leave the house. One can't be late for the dressmaker. We need traveling clothes because we're going abroad in a few weeks. She and Mrs. Chesterfield have just decided on it."

There was nothing else Hastings could do other than say the proper things and be on his way. Thinking about Miss Gladwin leaving the country crushed the breath out of him, though no one would have dared call it panic. That night was even worse than he imagined it could be, and insufficient sleep left him more impatient than ever.

By the next day he knew what he had to say when he got back to the Fitzfender house. The maid who answered the door jabbed her thumb over her shoulder and said, "She's doin' her 'broidery in with them beasts," and he found his own way.

He strode through the library door and came directly to the point, saying, "Good morning Miss Gladwin, you're looking well, we need to talk about things."

Looking up from her chair by the window, she appeared rather puzzled. "What things?"

"Is Mrs. Fitzfender waiting for you?"

"What, exactly, are you trying to say?"

Seeing her there in the sunlight, he wondered what her eyes would be like by candlelight. They might look more golden than ever. In addition to the candles there would be soft music. Violins. Perhaps a harp.

He said, "Do you like violins?"

"Mr. Hastings, do—"

"Ruth, that is, Miss Gladwin, have you ever thought of me in a more serious light?"

It took a moment before she said, "How serious and what kind of light?"

"Very serious, in a bright light, as a possible . . . a possible . . . husband," he blurted out.

Shock couldn't begin to describe her expression. She made two false starts before she said, "Are you trying to say that you're in love with me?"

"I believe so, though until a week ago I didn't even know you existed. And you needn't look at me that way. There isn't any madness in my family."

"You may be the first," she said gently. "Have you ever done this before?"

"Never." He looked under the sofa to see if Snooky was there before he sat down.

"Mr. Hastings—"

"Please, call me James."

"Mr. Hastings, this isn't a joking matter. You haven't compromised me by calling here. I do like you, but there's no need for you to feel as though you must do something honorable on my behalf."

"Now that we've determined that I'm not teasing or acting out of guilt, we can get at the problem, which is that we have only these few weeks for you to decide if you can think of me as a husband and lover."

"Mr. Hastings—"

"James, if you please."

"I don't know quite what you've been thinking, but I doubt that they've been the thoughts of a lover."

"You might be surprised."

Exasperation showing through, she said, "Would you call our association the least bit romantic?"

"We can begin today," he offered helpfully. "This moment if you like."

"It isn't that simple! You're making this into a farce."

"No, I'm not."

"It's one thing to fantasize about something. It's something else entirely to consider it a reality."

"Miss Gladwin, have you been fantasizing about me?"

She didn't answer. She didn't have to. She just turned red.

"I see," said Hastings, grinning wickedly.

"No, you don't. There's something missing. A magical something that hasn't been there for us. We haven't even held hands, yet all of a sudden you think we should consider marriage. You've made it quite clear that you're not interested in me but very interested in Snooky."

"I take it all back. How will you feel when we're apart? Be honest."

She sighed, and said, "Lonely sometimes."

That's the only incentive Hastings needed.

In two long strides he was there, bracing his hands on the arms of her chair. Bending over, he brushed his lips against the warm mouth that lifted to meet his. Hesitant at first, it was supposed to be a simple *I'm so glad you're here* sort of kiss. In less than a breath, it became a whisper that roared in his ears and gave him ideas he had no business having in a library with a lady that wasn't his wife. So when she lifted her arms to him, he drew back and turned away, trying not to look as shaken as he felt. Feeling like a bumbling adolescent with sweaty palms, he stared at the warthog until his head cleared and his blatant enthusiasm subsided. With his attention on that animal, he didn't see the confused embarrassment Miss Gladwin suffered when he left her so abruptly.

The lady herself had gone from doubting his intentions to having butterflies inside to a bewildering numbness. It certainly wasn't her first kiss, but it may as well have been. She'd discovered a wonderful something that made her senses whirl. Her heart raced with wanting, and what she wanted was James Hastings. Right here in Mrs. Fitzfender's library, she had behaved positively disgracefully where he was concerned. She knew it, but she hadn't cared. Not then.

She did now.

The butterflies died when he pulled away from her, and now she just felt . . . used. But she had too much pride to let it show.

Hastings felt a bit ridiculous when he turned and said, "I'd like to stay, but I can't. I actually have work to do. Every so often I'm obliged to stack filthy lucre in the family shop. Accounting and all that, you know."

"I see." Her polite smile was back. She could see that he couldn't wait to get away.

"May I come back tomorrow? We can talk about magic."

"I'm afraid not. Tomorrow we have tea at Mrs. Chesterfield's."

"And the day after?"

Miss Gladwin made busy work of sorting through her needlework. She didn't even look up when she said, "Perhaps it wouldn't be a good idea."

He supposed she was more shy than he'd realized, but persevered. "Will the afternoon be convenient?"

She said, "I expect so," remembering that it was Mrs. Fitzfender who had invited him and it was her home. Hastings' departure was blessedly swift.

While fighting the embroidery floss through the eye of the needle, Miss Gladwin couldn't imagine why Hastings wanted to come back. His finger hadn't even healed. She found his behavior difficult to decipher. Couldn't he make up his mind? As improbable as it seemed, she wondered if he just might be shy. It would account for a great deal.

Her musings went on and on, and it wasn't until after she'd embroidered half the leaves on a bouquet of roses that she noticed she'd done it with red thread.

\*     \*     \*

On the morning of the day Hastings was to call at the Fitzfender house, he was riding through the streets east of the place, unaware that he'd left his lady love feeling betrayed and abandoned. He had, however, spent hours wondering what he was going to do about the magical something she expected. Given enough time, he was sure the phenomenon would have invented itself. But they didn't have enough time. She would soon be going abroad if he couldn't come up with a way to keep her here. If he was going to convince her that they were destined to be better acquainted, he had to think of something remarkably clever.

Fortunately he'd done just that.

The cabbie spotted the peddler and stopped nearby. Hastings told the driver to wait, then waited for the peddler's customers to leave. The last one took away a dozen Doggy Delights in a tin box.

When Hastings stepped up to the peddler, he gave the man a cheerful hello and reminded him that they had met before. In a softer voice, he said, "I've come to you with a problem."

The peddler waited expectantly.

"It's extremely important that you make a special sale," explained Hastings. "In fact you're the only one who can possibly do it."

"Good heavens," said the peddler, obviously concerned. "I don't know what's going on, but if you can tell me what the problem is, I can tell you if I've got anything for it."

"What I need is a love potion."

"Sweet Ambrosia! I've sold my last bottle. But tomorrow—"

"Will be too late."

"It might be worth waiting for. Nice labels and all that, but I'm out of it. And I won't be able to . . . a . . . to get hold of any more until later."

Hastings looked through the packets and jars and bottles on the cart. "There must be something there that will do."

"I'll tell you what." The peddler stepped closer and dropped his voice. "You can cast love spells yourself. It's true. Just mix a little dragon's blood with quicksilver, throw it on the fire, and when it goes puff—or boom—you say . . . well, you say something but I've forgotten what it was. No matter. Dragon's blood can be very dangerous, especially when it makes a *big* boom. Let's forget that one.

"Instead, take the left ear of a dried toad and hair from a wolf's tail . . . but that won't do either. Haven't had wolves roaming England for centuries. How time does fly," he said reminiscently. "Well then, you might try a few drops of pansy juice with a little attar of roses and—"

"I'm a desperate man," said Hastings, flashing a coin. "I need that potion *today.*"

The peddler pocketed the coin and said, "Desperate? You should have told me that right off. Let's see what we have here." He sorted through the little green bottles, pushing on labels that read, Hairball Slider and Barkers Cough Syrup. Flea Begone. Claw Lotion. More Claw Lotion. Eventually a label fell away and the peddler triumphantly slapped that bottle into Hastings' hand, and said:

"Love potion!"

Hastings returned the bottle. "I don't want you to sell it to *me*. I want you to sell it to Miss Gladwin."

"I thought you said you were desperate for it."

"I am, so that she can give it to me."

"Then why don't you just take it yourself?"

"It won't work that way."

"Oooh," said the peddler. "Now I see how it is. She buys it, you get it."

"You've got it!

"The thing is, I don't know what it tastes like, so I won't know when I've been slipped the dose."

The peddler twisted the cork out and waved the bottle under Hastings' nose. He winced and his eyes watered. Recorking the bottle, the peddler said, "What sort of results is the young lady expecting?"

Wiping his eyes, Hastings said, "Something romantic would seem reasonable enough."

"Then I'll think of something to tell her. It's part of my job."

"Will you know who she is? It will hardly do any good if you sell it to the wrong woman."

"I believe I remember her. Does she have remarkable eyes? The smile of an angel? A nasty little pug dog?"

"That's her." Hastings clapped him on the shoulder, then tipped his hat in a respectful farewell and sauntered back to his cab.

The peddler wished he felt that confident. He knew very well that Miss Gladwin didn't buy anything she didn't want to buy.

It was quite a while later when he stopped his cart outside the Fitzfender residence. He jingled his bells and munched on a biscuit, dropping the last bit into his pocket.

Miss Gladwin came up the area stairs and said, "Good morning Professor Harper. Lovely day, isn't it? What might you have for a fractious dog?"

"Here's just the thing." He produced a rag doll that looked like a chimney sweep. "See this? Its head pulls off, then snaps back by this elastic strap."

"I don't think so. What else do you have?"

He said, "You might consider this," and held up a shoe. "It's been soaked in chicken soup so the dog will chew on it until his jaws get too tired to bite anything else." Miss Gladwin said she'd give it a try.

"And here's some new merchandise I might add to my selection." He handed her the little green bottle without a label. "The thing is I don't know if people will take to it."

"What is it?"

Softly now, he said, "Some people call it a love potion. It's an ancient formula. This is a free sample. Perhaps you know of someone who would care to try it . . . just as a curiosity, of course."

"Of course," replied Miss Gladwin, staring at the bottle.

"If anyone decides to try it, both parties should have some. That will direct the properties in the potion to the intended partners. Heaven forbid such energy should go astray."

"Heaven forbid. How much is enough? . . . just in case I know anyone who's interested."

"Well, let me think."

He was trying to compare the size of a dog to the size of the chap who wanted him to get this bottle into the hands of Miss Gladwin. "I suppose about two spoons' worth should do it if he's the average size man. More if he's bigger, less if he's smaller, though you'd best mix it with something that tastes awfully good." For a dramatic touch, he added, "There's also the phase of the moon to consider."

"Ah, the moon, yes. I'll remember . . . just in case."

With the transaction completed, she slipped the bottle into her pocket, picked up the shoe between finger and thumb, and went into the house.

The peddler went jingling on his way, certain that neither Miss Gladwin nor her young man would ever be troubled by worms.

# Four

Dropping the shoe beside Snooky's kitchen bed, Miss Gladwin wiped her dainty fingers and complimented Cook on the cake she was decorating. To the girl working quietly over the copper pots, she said, "I don't know when the shine has ever been better." Leaving her an encouraging smile, Miss Gladwin went to her bedchamber at a dignified dash.

Closing the chamber door, she surveyed the place with a critical eye, looking for the safest place in which to hide the bottle she had in her pocket. She decided to put it in the second dresser drawer among her corset covers. Then she decided to use a slipper at the bottom of her wardrobe. Under the mattress. Inside the case of the shelf clock. It came to rest in a pink glove tucked under some other gloves behind a stack of handkerchiefs in the top dresser drawer.

It wasn't as though Miss Gladwin actually intended to use the contents of that bottle. It was just that she didn't want it to be misplaced or broken in case she decided to give it away. Or try the stuff on Snooky. Snooky, after all, was a creature in desperate need of *something*. Snooky would be the ultimate test of a love potion. But if she gave the dog the potion and it didn't work, she wouldn't know if it was a defective mixture or if it was never intended to be used on dogs, never formulated to influence whatever it was that went on inside the head and heart of a disagreeable canine. In that case it would be a sad waste of something of which there was precious little to begin with.

That problem bumped around inside her head for a great

good while until it was replaced by the need to see to Mrs. Fitzfender's correspondence. The good lady's fingers were especially stiff today. Miss Gladwin would write her letters, send regrets and acceptances, order some new black ribbon to replace the old black ribbons on the favorite hat. Someplace between the regrets and the ribbons came a fleeting question as to the integrity of using a love potion on anyone. It might not be quite honest to do such a thing.

Besides, it probably wouldn't work anyway.

But what if it really did?

She propped her chin on her hand and fancied how nice it would be if Snooky never bit anyone again. If the milkman would be more considerate of his horse. If James Hastings would like kissing. Kissing her, that is. The possibility inspired a sigh and a silly grin.

What began as a delightful idle soon developed a few distracting complications. For instance, she began to wonder what one should expect from a potion. Exactly how much of the preparation must one take to insure the proper direction of the larger dose that would be given to the other party—as long as the other party wasn't Snooky. To further complicate things, she didn't know whether the effect would be permanent or temporary. If temporary, how long would it last?

While the ink dried on the nib of her pen, Miss Gladwin began to worry that the little green bottle might be leaking as it lay tucked up inside her glove. Not wanting to take such a chance with the only supply of love potion she had, she returned to her room. There she opened the drawer and stood the bottle up. Packed gloves and handkerchiefs around it so it wouldn't fall over. Covered it all with a scarf. Adjusted the scarf. Shut the drawer. Stood back to see if anything about the drawer looked suspicious.

That's when it occurred to her that the peddler had said that the phase of the moon was important when using the potion. With a knot in her stomach, she realized that she hadn't asked him *which* phase of the moon. After a few agonizing moments she concluded that he must have meant a full moon. It was often associated with all sorts of magical events. If she tried the potion at all, it wouldn't be until then. Rubbing finger marks off the polished surface, she gave the drawer one last glance and went downstairs to finish Mrs. Fitzfender's correspondence.

When James Hastings walked away from the peddler that morning, he was confident that the fellow would soon have the little green bottle securely in the hands of Miss Gladwin. He liked to think they would be eager hands, though he didn't think it would be wise to rush directly to her side. If he was hanging about when the peddler got there she certainly wouldn't buy a love potion. She'd buy something for Snooky. For that reason he'd just have to find something else to occupy his time until the peddler had come and gone.

When Hastings returned to the cab in which he had chased down the peddler, he called out, "Bernard's!" and climbed inside. Bernard was his haberdasher.

The cab had hardly begun to roll before Hastings decided that it wouldn't do to see Miss Gladwin too soon after her dealings with the peddler. Waiting an hour or two would be better. Waiting until afternoon would be better still. That way there wouldn't be any connection between himself and whatever Miss Gladwin happened to acquire. When he finally sought out the young lady, she would surely offer him tea into which she had secretly poured a little something from the green bottle and he'd drink it. He wouldn't let on that he noticed anything odd about the way it tasted. Then he'd wait a moment before he produced a suitable dreamy expression, take her into his arms and kiss her soundly. She wanted magic, he'd give her magic.

When he got to Bernard's, Hastings ordered a tweed hat to wear on those occasions when he went into the country. He then had his midday meal at his club. It wasn't until then that he had himself taken to the home of the widow Fitzfender. He'd had plenty of time to anticipate what would happen when he got there. He only wondered how long it would take Miss Gladwin to offer him tea with that little something extra in it.

Upon reaching his destination, he left the bright outdoors

for the darker hall of the stately residence. When his eyes adjusted to the gloom, it was to see Miss Gladwin coming toward him. She wasn't offering him tea. She had her hat on, ready to go somewhere.

With a charming smile, she said, "Good afternoon Mr. Hastings. Mrs. Fitzfender says that your desire to take Snooky out to see the world is among the finest, most noble of sentiments."

"How kind of her to say so." He found no joy in the fact that beside Miss Gladwin stood Snooky, wearing the too-tight Morocco-leather harness.

"Mrs. Fitzfender," continued Miss Gladwin from beneath her hat, "has suggested that you might like to take Snooky to the art museum today, so that he may learn to appreciate the many works of art in which dogs—especially pug dogs—play an important role."

With a pained smile, Hastings looked at Snooky, then at Miss Gladwin, and said, "Quite so."

The carriage ride to the museum was accomplished without benefit of the cheerful animation that had accompanied their earlier visit to the zoo. Snooky lay defiantly across Miss Gladwin's lap, glaring at his benefactor. On occasion, his benefactor glared back. Miss Gladwin displayed an extraordinary interest in the twisted brown fringe on the window shades, hoping there wasn't anything about her that would shout to the world, and James Hastings, in particular, that she had a bottle of love potion hidden inside a glove, behind her handkerchiefs, beneath a scarf, right-side up, top drawer, no fingerprints.

Between the black looks he exchanged with Snooky, Hastings would say a little something. This time he said, "You're looking exceptionally well, Miss Gladwin. Have you been doing anything to put such roses in your cheeks?"

She said, "Nothing at all," and became even rosier.

He took note of her high color and said, "Just wondered you know. Never can tell about interesting things."

He had said it all without actually saying that he'd like to know whether or not she'd got that bottle of stuff from the peddler. He'd seen her blush, but that could mean anything.

But if she didn't get the bottle this week, would she get it next week? Perhaps the peddler didn't even get to her house today. Or perhaps he did get there and she didn't want the bottle. If she didn't want that bottle, should he provide her with a different potion from someplace else? And if he had to do that, how was he supposed to do it?

Anyone who knew Hastings would have called his silence a spectacular act of patience.

It was obvious from the moment they entered the museum that Snooky failed to appreciate the wonders he was compelled to behold. In fact anyone who knew the dog could safely assume that he didn't like public buildings in general. There was that look about him that suggested he would bite the place if he could just find where to get hold of it. On the occasion that Miss Gladwin noticed him sniffing the marble base of a bronze statue, she picked him up before he could do anything more remarkable than sniff.

Soon the three of them stood quietly before a large oil portrait of Lord Byron's Newfoundland dog named Boatswain. They had stood just so and watched a great shaggy bison not too long ago. Hastings said, "Would a drive in the country have any appeal for you, Miss Gladwin?"

"It sounds positively wonderful. My grandmother always recommended fresh air and sunshine to inspire pure thoughts."

She could have bit her tongue! As soon as the words were out, she wished she hadn't said anything at all. Pure thoughts didn't allow love potions in one's dresser drawer. Giving Hastings an embarrassed grimace, she started walking and didn't stop until she came to a charcoal sketch of a puppy chewing on the rope that held him. She couldn't very well walk past that. It was, after all, an artistic likeness of a dog, the very thing they had come to the museum to see. It would be impossible to explain if she ignored it and went home. Snooky began to wiggle about, so she put him down.

Miss Gladwin made a long, careful study of the sketch, needing to look at something besides James Hastings. She finally said, "That certainly is a nicely drawn rope," and he said, "It certainly is."

While she studied the rope so intently, he became more

convinced that she must have done something to make herself so uneasy. Something with a suggestion of naughtiness about it to have caused such a blush. Something like the purchase of a little green bottle of love potion to inspire a passionate response from someone near and dear. Someone . . . like himself. His smile was as delightfully perverse as Miss Gladwin's had been uncomfortable.

But it was the man himself that looked uncomfortable when he touched her elbow a moment later to say, "That may well be the finest rope I've ever seen, but let's leave now, shall we?"

She almost cried yes! but didn't, because when they left the museum they'd get into the carriage. In the carriage they would sit facing one another. She didn't feel up to facing James Hastings just now.

"I'm not quite ready to leave," she told him airily. "I had hoped to see the needlework cushion attributed to Mary Queen of Scots. You know, the one with the dog on it. The dear little dog that would eventually accompany her to the block when they chopped off her head. We couldn't miss that."

"I'm not so sure," said Hastings.

"Then there are the brasses with dogs at the feet of the figures. Those dogs represent faithfulness. We couldn't miss them."

"I could."

"We can't miss the prehistoric stone carving of a dog. It's only about this big." She curled fingers and thumb to indicate something about the size of a walnut. "It's in a case with some beads and spear points from—"

"I could miss those too."

"Mr. Hastings, why are you in such a hurry to leave?"

He lowered his voice to say, "I'm afraid Snooky hasn't been behaving himself, and I think it prudent to beat a retreat before someone figures out who did it."

Knowing Snooky, Miss Gladwin didn't even look to see what it was. She just grabbed the dog and left.

The dog was smiling.

*    *    *

When the carriage stopped at Hastings' lodgings, she said, "Can you join us tomorrow for tea? I'm sure Mrs. Fitzfender will want to thank you for taking Snooky to the museum."

He said, "Of course." What he thought was much less proper, having to do with love potions.

Hastings spent the evening in the privacy of his bedchamber in front of the mirror, the draperies tightly drawn. He was practicing expressions of flaming passion. Then he decided that he'd better start with smoldering passion and work up to something more volatile. He tried opening his eyes as wide as he could to look surprised, scared himself, and gave up that one.

In search of something more subtle, he tried various lifting and lowerings of the old eyebrow, combined with a flexing of the nostrils to convey pulsing desire, then went to his club for supper before his face stayed like that.

As if the day at the museum hadn't been bad enough for Hastings, the following day proved equally maddening. It wasn't that he worried about Miss Gladwin slipping him any of the potion while they were having tea with Mrs. Fitzfender. He expected it later in the library while reading about pug dogs. That's why he asked for more tea. But when it came, there wasn't anything extra in it. Neither was his lemonade affected. Nor the trifle.

He wanted to get on with it!

By the time he left for home he had decided that it didn't matter if Miss Gladwin had the potion or not because she wasn't going to use it. And if she wasn't going to use it, the reason could only be that she didn't care as much as he thought she did—as much as he'd hoped she did. A crushing blow. That being the case, he wouldn't go back. Wouldn't darken her doorway. Wouldn't inflict his presence upon her ever again.

He was waiting for her in the library the next morning. Being a gentleman, he had decided to give her another chance.

The thing is, Miss Gladwin hadn't expected to find him there. He stood when she entered the room and she gasped in surprise, especially because she'd been thinking of him at the time. It was as though she had voiced her most private thoughts and he'd heard them.

How embarrassing.

So it was Miss Gladwin who stammered, and said, "Excuse me," and Hastings who said, "What for?"

"I didn't know you were here."

"I asked the maid not to announce me, because I didn't want to disturb you. Have I made things inconvenient by arriving so early."

"Not really. I'm just about to have my breakfast. Will you join me?"

He said, "No, thank you, I've eaten," then hastened to add, "I would enjoy a cup of tea, however, if it isn't too much trouble."

"I'm on my way to see what looks good in the kitchen this morning. I'll be right back."

Hastings stayed there staring at the warthog, thinking grumpy thoughts, concerned about his lack of progress in attaching Miss Gladwin's affections. Into this mental gymnasium came a tap on the open library door. Mrs. Fitzfender. She glanced uneasily at the animal heads and remained firmly where she was. In her tiny little voice she explained that she had come to tell Miss Gladwin that she would be gone for most of the day with her niece, the one from London, and would Mr. Hastings please pass the message along.

He said, "Certainly," and asked if there was any other service he might render.

Mrs. Fitzfender asked if he would be so kind as to satisfy her curiosity about something else.

He repeated, "Certainly," then had to listen carefully. She asked whether he had been successful in his search for a pug dog of his own.

"I'm afraid not," replied Hastings. "There isn't another dog like Snooky in the entire world."

Mrs. Fitzfender smiled wistfully and agreed that Snooky

was indeed one of a kind. Yet she knew that her sweetie pie had been terribly bored and unhappy before Hastings arrived to form a more interesting manly friendship with him. She said that was why she was giving him Snooky for his very own, then left.

"Wait!" called Hastings, in a manner unbecoming a gentleman.

He didn't know a little old lady could move that fast. He made it across the room over the sofa to the door in a flash, but he didn't know where she had gone. He couldn't very well go hunting for her. Still, it was important that he tell her that he couldn't possibly tear her precious Snooky from her loving arms. He'd have to get her to change her mind because he couldn't very well say that he didn't want her nasty little dog.

The loud smack was the heel of his hand hitting the frame of the door.

Wheezing and puffing, Snooky came out from under the sofa and waddled over to him. For the first time ever, the dog looked up and wagged his tail. Feeling that this dumb animal somehow understood their mutual plight, Hastings reached down to pet him, but pulled back his hand instead.

Snooky put a hole in his trousers and went back under the sofa.

When Miss Gladwin returned she smiled enchantingly and announced that breakfast would be along in no time at all. Hastings smiled in anticipation and wondered if he should begin his charmed state with the look of affectionate confusion or the expression of dawning passion. But when the tray got there, he soon found out that there hadn't been any of the potion added to his tea, and he was running out of time.

Though he really tried to pay attention when Miss Gladwin was telling him about what had been going on in the kitchen, his mind would wander to something of a more serious nature. He had already decided that she must have the green bottle. Not only that, everything about her said she would use it if she could. And that, he realized, was the answer. Miss Gladwin hadn't used the potion because she hadn't had the opportunity to slip him any of it! Hadn't had the chance to be alone with the food long enough to fix it up. He had to be calm. It wouldn't do to let her know that he knew. He'd just make sure that she had more time alone with whatever it was he might consume.

He said, "Good heavens, just look at the time! I've just remembered that I've got an appointment that I almost forgot." When she looked disappointed, he was quick to say, "I can be back for tea," and she looked relieved.

By the time Hastings reached the sidewalk, Miss Gladwin was on her way upstairs to her bedchamber. The business about the love potion and the phase of the moon had been nagging her. She had assumed it was the full moon that the potion needed to be most effective. This morning she became concerned about what would happen if she had been wrong in this assumption. What if it was the dark of the moon that was the better choice? If so, then using the potion during the full moon would surely produce dismal results.

Under such circumstances it was only reasonable that someplace between the full moon and no moon would be far more satisfactory. Like now, for instance. Even during the daytime, the phase of the moon was the same as it was at night. To compensate for any possible miscalculation concerning the most desirable appearance of the moon, Miss Gladwin decided that she would use an extra spoon of the love potion. How could anything go wrong when she had worked it out so logically?

When Hastings returned to the house, tea was waiting in the library. They sat; he hopefully, she expectantly. There were dainty cucumber sandwiches, tea, milk for tea . . .

The pudding!

He didn't even have to taste it to know it. Miss Gladwin looked at that pudding with more interest than any pudding deserved. She didn't look at her own pudding that way. In fact she didn't look at her own pudding at all. Only his. So he knew it was the pudding and became insufferably smug.

Ever so carefully he picked up his spoon. He was about to plunge it into the pudding when he stopped, looked around, and asked, "Where's Snooky?"

"Resting."

Hastings lifted the spoon again, paused, and asked, "Does he always rest so much?"

More than impatient, she said, "You don't have to eat that if you don't want it. Shall I take it away?"

"No!" he said, grabbing the dish. Then a more composed, "I shall get to it presently."

Taking his own good time, he tried one spoonful. Terribly bitter. Still she watched expectantly, so he forced down another spoonful. Almost impossible. He assumed she was expecting to see the influence of a love potion. Though he'd practiced those passionate, wilting expressions, he was now incapable of producing them. His jaws were clenched tightly, he felt hot and sweaty and his stomach rolled, but he knew the show jolly well better go on.

After a swig of tea he leaned across the table, clasped her hand to his heart, gazed intently into her eyes, and murmured, "I love you."

This declaration was followed by a smacking kiss to the amazed lips. He kissed the rim of the cup from which she had sipped her tea. He danced around the room peeling off his jacket and pulling off his tie, throwing kisses to the warthog and the water buffalo. To Snooky under the sofa. Pausing for only a moment, he jumped up on the library table and glanced around at the animal heads. His attention came to rest on the wildebeest.

"Hark!" he cried, with grand gesticulation. " 'What light through yonder window breaks?' "

Miss Gladwin looked on in wide-eyed horror, and said, "Mr. Hastings, perhaps—"

"Perhaps nothing!" cried Hastings. "I had to learn this whole bloody thing in school and this is the first time I've had a chance to use it! Now, where was I? Oh, yes. 'Tis the east,' " he said, most convincingly, " 'and Juliet,' bless her, 'is the sun . . .' "

Miss Gladwin stared and listened and cringed and wished she hadn't used such a large spoon to measure out the love potion.

*    *    *

At about the same time that Hastings took the first bitter mouthful of pudding, his friend Archie arrived to see his godmother.

She said, "My dear boy, so good of you to call. Sit there in that chair. It's so much more comfortable for a man of your size, if you don't get too close to the fern. It has cannibal tendencies when it catches one by the hair and do mind the china cat."

Archie smiled, minded the fern, the cat, and sat in the proper chair.

"I must tell you that Mrs. Fitzfender and myself are so pleased that you brought Mr. Hastings to call on us. Would you care for coffee? Tea? Something stronger?"

Archie declined all of it.

"Now about your friend," continued his godmother. "Mrs. Fitzfender has observed him and says that he is quite taken with Miss Gladwin. In my day we would have called it besotted. She is equally bereft of reason, though still a bit skittish. Of course, the attraction is precisely what Mrs. Fitzfender and I intended when we learned that Mr. Hastings was trying to convince you to bring him here to meet me, so that he might then have an opportunity to meet Mrs. Fitzfender and gain admittance to her house for reasons you know all too well, you *naughty* boy."

"You know about that?" said Archie, leaning dangerously close to the cannibal fern. How did you ever find out?"

"My dear, we know about everything. In fact we knew the whole of your plans the morning after you made them. The morning after Mr. Hastings had his first glimpse of Miss Gladwin coming out of the house with Snooky. Archie, are you feeling poorly? You look like you're feeling poorly.

"In any case the driver of your cab—the hatch in the roof was open and he heard everything—met the Fitzfender coachman that night at their pub. They have their own sort of gentlemen's club, you see. For coachmen. It's all quite interesting. Early the next morning when the Fitzfender coachman went to the kitchen for his breakfast, he told the story to Mrs. Fitzfender's maid, who repeated it to the lady herself as soon as she awoke. Such efficiency, don't you agree? Well, Mrs. Fitzfender then sent the maid to me and I heard the story with my toast and jam. It was awfully good. Strawberry you know, from Lady Newcomb. Archie, are you listening?"

She stared at him intently and said, "Are you sure you're not ill? You shouldn't have come if you're ill. Well, that afternoon Mrs. Fitzfender and myself discussed the situation through and through. Then we made discreet inquiries into Mr. Hastings' moral character and financial situation to determine whether or not he was worthy of our dear Miss Gladwin. He was, so we allowed you and Mr. Hastings to talk us into anything we wanted. Archie, you really do look under the weather. Would you like a bit of brandy? As you wish."

Then she sighed, adjusted her cap, and said, "It was unfortunate that Miss Gladwin had taken Snooky in to say good morning to Mrs. Fitzfender when the maid was there. She heard everything about the conversation between you and Mr. Hastings before she ever met Mr. Hastings. So she knew he would be there to deceive his family about his romantic attachments." Then she grinned like an imp and said, "We didn't tell Miss Gladwin everything. Not about the part where Mrs. Fitzfender and myself planned to find her a husband or that the man we had picked out for her was Mr. Hastings. She needs something more in her life than two old ladies and Snooky, dear little thing that he is. Don't you agree?"

Archie could only try to smile and nod his head.

"Now," said his godmother. "Tell me what brings you to call."

"My sister," said Archie, with little enthusiasm. "She's getting married in a month. Cora, the one with all the teeth. Thought you'd like to know."

"Good heavens! Are you certain it will be in a month? Oh, dear. It means that Mrs. Fitzfender and I will have to cancel our traveling plans. Dear me. I'll have to tell her."

When Hastings finished the balcony scene from *Romeo and Juliet*, he leaped from the table and caught Miss

Gladwin up in a lively waltz with no music but his own, holding her much too close for decency. Once around the room and he pinned her to the wall beneath the musk ox and smothered her with tickley kisses to which she showed no signs of objection.

When he nibbled the tender place beneath her ear, she squirmed, and said, "Mr. Hastings, are your intentions honorable?"

He said, "You can be absolutely certain that I'm not after your money."

"Is that a proposition or a proposal?"

"That depends upon whether you want a lover or a husband."

A moment later she watched him blink and shake his head, slump against the wall and yawn. He was a bit wobbly when she steered him to the sofa. Leaning back he shut his eyes to keep the room from spinning, and patted the cushion next to him. She sat down, and he drew her across his lap, crossing one ankle over the other knee to prop her up—she was as stiff as a stick.

Then she laughed at the absurdity of it all and relaxed. Petting his beard, she said, "You're much nicer than Snooky," and he modestly agreed that he was.

Half asleep, he said, "Have you ever been ravished on a library sofa, Miss Gladwin?"

She thought about it and said, "Not recently."

"Well, you might consider it after I have a bit of a rest. And do call me James. I shall call you Ruth. Or I might call you Ruthie. Or Rue. It's the least we can do when we're talking about ravishing one of us on the library sofa. Snooky won't like it, but he'll have to get used to it unless we give him a house of his own or keep him in the barn. I'd prefer the barn." Another yawn, and he said, "After you left this hallowed sanctuary of yours, Mrs. Fitzfender arrived and presented me with her wretched dog."

"She gave Snooky to you?"

"In his entirety, I'm afraid. How long do you think we can go on like this without getting into trouble?"

"Oh, six months I should think, just in case . . ."

"Just in case what?"

She couldn't very well say that she wanted to wait six months to see if the love potion would wear off. She said, "Just in case we won't suit after we've know each other for a while longer."

"Do be serious. One of us will lose their virtue if this goes on for six more days."

"We are of age you know. You could just carry me off to Scotland. Mrs. Fitzfender's favorite cousin's daughter, Mary, was carried off to Scotland and married by declaration."

He opened his eyes and struggled to focus on her. "Does anyone still do that? I mean dash off to Scotland?" Another yawn. "I love you madly, but I'll have to ravish you later. Something has left me inexplicably tired. It might have been something I ate . . ."

"Whatever could it have been?"

He didn't offer any suggestions. He just said, "You might use this lull in our fermenting lust to explain to Snooky that he's no longer the supreme object of your affection."

"There's no need to concern yourself with Snooky's moods much longer. This morning the peddler delivered a cat to be his playmate. It's a kitten actually. A curious looking thing with tufts on its ears. I saw it when I was in the kitchen. As soon as they can catch it, someone will bring it up, though when I left there, the creature had already knocked over a stack of dishes, all the flower pots, and perched on top of a cupboard. Its name is Genghis Khan."

"Do you think they'll capture the dear thing very soon?"

"I rather doubt it." Her laugh was soft, her touch was softer. "Who would have guessed that this is how your pursuit of the pug dog would end."

"This isn't how it ends," he murmured. "This is how it begins, or it will when I wake up." He smiled a sleepy smile and rubbed a seductive finger across her lips.

She smiled, too, and bit him.

Too bad he was sound asleep when they brought in the cat.

*If you enjoyed this book, take advantage of this special offer. Subscribe now and get a*

# FREE
## Historical
## Romance

*No Obligation ( a $4.50 value)*

Each month the editors of True Value select the four *very best* novels from America's leading publishers of romantic fiction. Preview them in your home *Free* for 10 days. With the first four books you receive, we'll send you a FREE book as our introductory gift. No Obligation!

If for any reason you decide not to keep them, just return them and owe nothing. If you like them as much as we think you will, you'll pay just $4.00 each and save at *least* $.50 each off the cover price. (Your savings are *guaranteed* to be at least $2.00 each month.) There is NO postage and handling – or other hidden charges. There are no minimum number of books to buy and you may cancel at any time.

*Send in
the Coupon
Below*

To get your FREE historical romance fill out the coupon below and mail it today. As soon as we receive it we'll send you your FREE Book along with your first month's selections.

------------------------------------------------------